This book is an original publication of Waterhouse Press

This is a work of fiction. Names, characters, places, and incidents
either are the product of the author's imagination or are used
fictitiously, and any resemblance to actual persons, living or dead,
business establishments, events, or locales is entirely coincidental.
The publisher does not assume any responsibility for third-party
websites or their content.

Copyright © 2015 Waterhouse Press, LLC
Cover Design by Waterhouse Press, LLC

Cover Photographs: Shutterstock & Sara Eirew

All Rights Reserved
No part of this book may be reproduced, scanned, or distributed
in any printed or electronic format without permission. Please do
not participate in or encourage piracy of copyrighted materials in
violation of the author's rights. Purchase only authorized editions.

Paperback ISBN: 978-0-9897684-2-9
PRINTED IN THE UNITED STATES OF AMERICA

To the one and only, author Jess Dee.

I love you like family, even though we've never met face-to-face. You have touched my heart and my soul with your guidance and mentorship. I am eternally grateful for your kindness. You will forever be a beautiful part of my journey.

Namaste

Angel

FALLING

Angel
FALLING

BOOK ONE
AUDREY CARLAN

WATERHOUSE
PRESS

CHAPTER ONE

New York City sucked. If the work hadn't been good and the pay decent, I'd have hightailed it outta here and headed back home to my ranch.

People here were just drones, lifeless husks that scampered through the concrete jungle. Always afraid to be late or miss something. They ran around with hopeful looks plastered across their plastic faces as if the next big break were right around the corner. It wasn't.

God, I hated the fucking city.

The only thing that made it bearable was the women. New York was full of beautiful women who ached to be taken by a guy like me. They saw me as a simpleton. A hunk of meat. I didn't mind. I wasn't looking for happily ever after. We were all in it for one thing—to get off.

As beautiful women went, the woman who arrived here every morning at seven sharp had my attention. She was a classy one. She usually wore button-up suits with tight skirts slit up to mid-thigh that held snug to legs that went on for days. Her heels were so tall they were like stilts. It must have taken practice to walk on spikes every damn day. She'd be smokin' hot in a pair of cowboy boots and nothin' else.

I could tell she was smart, or liked to put off that she was. She had money, too, lots of it. Every day a town car or shiny black limo dropped her off. Never with a man though. Sometimes, I caught her peeking over her sunglasses, taking in the view of my crew. Hell, maybe she even sized me up a time or two. I would like that. I'd even consider making a move if I didn't think she was out of my league. Women as fancy as she was didn't date men like me. They dated billionaires with flashy cars—men who drove Ferraris, not Ford pickups.

My company, Jensen Construction, was hired to expand a section of the skyscraper where she worked, add a new lobby with another ten stories above it. When all was said and done, the completed project would add a couple hundred new offices to the building. Even though leaving Texas was rough, the money here was too good to pass up.

My crew and I were making five times as much as we would back home. That was the new direction I'd decided to take my company. I bid on jobs outside the state if they were worth it. Somehow, I kept underbidding the locals here in New York and secured the work.

For me, it was a win–win. I had family back home, but no wife or kids. I also had my ranch, a couple of horses, and Butch, my yellow lab. I brought Butch with me because a man doesn't leave his best friend sitting at home for three months. The horses were being taken care of by my brother in exchange for being able to ride 'em whenever he wanted. It was a fair deal. His boys loved it and I got "Best Uncle" status in the process.

After checking that my men were hard at work and that everything was moving along as planned, I headed for my portable office. The sleek black limo appeared at the curb, sun glinting off the chrome bumper, blinding me with its sharp light. I leaned against the metal railing on the steps, ready to watch the show.

She was a damn vision today. Her usual black suit was left behind, replaced with a tailored white number that hugged every curve. She looked like a naughty angel. She turned around and pulled her briefcase out of the car. Her ass was tight; the white fabric accentuated the perfect heart shape.

What I wouldn't give to smack that ass, make her scream out, and beg me to fuck her.

Those long legs of hers took her past me quickly. She wasn't wearing the big ol' round glasses that hid her gorgeous eyes today. The sun broke across the building, and her blue eyes sparkled in the light. Long golden hair flapped in the wind behind her. A red scarf tied around her neck cut across her form, a slash of crimson splitting a perfect blank canvas.

She dug through the oversize brown bag hanging over her delicate shoulder, her cell phone glued to her ear. A noise screeched from up above. I jerked my head up. A stack of large metal pipes held together by chains swung precariously from the crane. My lady in white stopped right under it, and the scene played out in sickening slow motion in my mind's eye. Her phone fell to the concrete; she cursed and bent to retrieve it, unaware of the danger that lurked above her.

"Watch out!" I yelled as I barreled toward her, pointing upward. Her gaze drifted up as I heard metal scraping across metal, then a loud clink, signaling that the pipes had separated from their chassis.

One side of the chains held, sending one-inch metal pipes flying downward like daggers falling from the sky. My inner Superman reacted, and I shot forward, knocking her to the ground, my much larger body covering hers. Without warning, a gut-wrenching, piercing pain ripped through my left shoulder. She was screaming under me, trying to push me off her. Moving wasn't an option. Searing pain blazed through my shoulder as if I were being stabbed with a large butcher knife. Every movement stole my breath.

I only saw red. This time it wasn't her scarf. It was blood, lots and lots of blood, pouring over her white suit, painting it with color.

"Help him!" she screamed. "It's going to be okay." Cool hands and fingers slid along my temples and cupped my face. "Please, please, look at me."

Pain gripped my upper body as if two plates of metal were pressing me flat as a pancake. I lay on my side, unable to move. Briefly casting a glance over the heart of the excruciating ache over my left shoulder, I could see the glint of metal protruding a good couple of feet out of my back.

The swells of nausea churned in my gut, and my mouth watered with that sour taste that comes just when you're about to blow chunks. Closing my eyes, I tried to take a deep breath, but the pain that followed tore through bone, muscle, and skin. The only things that kept me firmly planted to this earth were those gray-blue eyes. They were like crystal pools, refreshing and inviting.

"So pretty," I mumbled through dry lips.

She smiled, and I closed my eyes, knowing that I couldn't look at God's angel any longer or I'd get lost in her beauty and willingly leave this earthly plane. Sirens blared in the background, but my angel held me, saying softly, "It's going to be okay. You saved me. You're going to make it, just hold very still."

I risked opening one eye for a split second and what I saw almost broke me. Those beautiful blue eyes weren't serene. They were choppy, ragged waters that swirled with fear.

It started to rain. Big fat wet droplets landed on my face. Only the droplets weren't rain. They were her tears.

"You saved me," she whispered against my forehead, her lips moist and soft. I wanted to say something to her. Introduce myself in some small way before she was taken away from me. Tell her my name was Hank and that I thought she was beautiful, but the words didn't come. Wouldn't come. Breathing alone took all my effort.

I felt arms all around me, lifting me up and placing me onto something soft. A cloud perhaps. My angel was pulled away. Time seemed to slow and ebb. So much was happening around me, but I couldn't focus on any of it. Pain controlled my attention, and I succumbed to its sickening grip with a guttural howl.

"I'm coming with you!" tore from her throat as bodies moved around and harsh words were exchanged. "This is my building and he, he...he saved my life! I owe him everything!" my angel hollered at the people who tugged and pulled at my face, my chest, pressing me deeper into the cloud. For a brief moment, I felt happy someone cared. No, not someone—her.

I couldn't feel anymore. My eyes were heavy, and I blindly reached out my hand. An icy, feather-soft hand closed around mine, taking away my anxiety.

"I'm here. I'm here. Just let them take care of you." Her voice was smooth and sweet like a melody. Then blackness enveloped me.

★ ★ ★ ★

I couldn't imagine what was taking so long! It had been hours—hours—since the man who risked everything went into surgery. *Please, God, please let him be okay.* He saved my life. A stranger saved my life. I pulled out my phone and called my assistant Oliver.

"Aspen, where are you?" he rattled off quickly without a greeting. "Something happened today at the building. A man was hurt. A crane dropped some pipes." His voice was higher than normal, and rushed as if he couldn't get out what he needed to say fast enough.

I had worked with Oliver for a number of years and was long accustomed to his eccentric nature. I already knew all he was telling me, but he wouldn't let me get a word in edgewise, so I let him continue. "I've already called Legal; someone should show up at the hospital any minute to find out his prognosis."

"Oliver…Oliver, stop."

"What?" The word screeched out tight and restrained. He took a ragged breath.

"I'm here, at the hospital. The man that was hurt, he, uh… He jumped in front of me. Prevented me from being impaled." My voice cracked and hiccupped to a halt. It took everything I could to hold back the tears.

"Oh my God! Oh my God, Aspen, are you okay? Shit! I'm going to cry. I can't lose you. I love you." And there was my drama queen. His effeminate voice strained, he started to cry.

"Oliver. Ollie, honey, I know. I'm fine." I took a deep breath. "The man that saved me, I don't even know his name. They're not telling me anything here at the hospital. I need you to get me some information. Find out who he is and his emergency contacts."

"Okay, yes. I got it. Anything else?"

"I need to know who runs the show at the hospital. I need to have access to this man. Whatever the cost." Through the receiver, Oliver's heavy breathing and the rustling of papers drifted through the phone.

"Okay, okay. I'll get it. Give me fifteen minutes max."

"Thank you." I sighed and looked down at my suit in horror. "Oliver, one more thing: I need a change of clothes. Don't send a courier. Bring me a suit from the closet in the office."

"Why?"

I shuddered. "Because this suit is covered in blood." A sob tried to escape my throat, but my hand effectively suppressed the sound. The last thing I needed to lose was my control. After I inhaled a couple of deep, calming breaths, my nerves were back intact. Mostly.

"Oh my God, okay. Soon. I'll be there soon. I love you."

I couldn't help but smile. "I love you, too, Ollie. Now hurry. People are starting to stare." I looked over at the couple across from me, mouths agape and eyes opened wide.

The day couldn't have gotten any worse. Not only was a man fighting for his life on my behalf, but also an accident of this nature would undoubtedly set the project back for weeks. I'd promised the stakeholders for *Bright Magazine* that the building would be ready to start work in the next fiscal year. This kind of delay could cost severely, but not as much as a man's life.

And what if my savior sued? This catastrophe had the potential to demolish the plan altogether. If he died, it would be worse. A fucking media frenzy. I rubbed at the headache that started to creep into my temples.

Jesus Christ! When did I become so cold? A man's life hung in the balance, and I was worried about the magazine.

Because all you have is work.

Long ago, I made the decision never to let anything or anyone get in the way of being successful. As I was growing up, my parents were beyond rich, the perfect socialites. I was groomed to be the epitome of high society. After my Ivy League education, I used my trust fund for the start-up costs to build AIR Bright Enterprises from the ground up. Seven years later, I'm worth billions and have my own spot on the *Forbes* Top Ten Most Successful Women list—a huge feat for a woman only twenty-eight years old.

A half hour went by and the stale air surrounding me changed. Oliver must have arrived. His presence hit me before I even heard his wing tips clacking against the linoleum floor. His gait was rushed. A frown marred his familiar pointed face. The frosted tips of his hair gave the appearance he had been in the sun for hours on end, but I knew his secret—a visit to New York's finest hair salon twice a month. It was one of my gifts to him for Administrative Professionals Day. A garment bag hung loosely over one arm, man purse over the other, and he clutched a pair of black heels in one hand. His eyes were the size of saucers. He stopped dead in his tracks when he saw my blood-crusted suit.

"Oliver!" I hugged him fiercely. He was warm and solid as we stood holding one another.

He pulled back, still holding onto my shoulder. His lip trembled as he looked me over. "Princess... I... You look awful. Are you sure you're okay?" Tears filled his eyes, and I wiped them away with my thumbs and smiled for his benefit.

"That bad, huh?"

He nodded. "Here, please go change. I'm burning that suit."

My smile didn't quite reach my eyes, but I took the clothes and changed in the ladies room. Once situated in the black suit and heels Oliver brought me, I exited and handed him the bag of soiled garments. He rolled up the bag, walked over to the nearest trash can, and tossed the whole lot of it in it without a second thought. He just pitched a three-thousand-dollar suit as if it were a wad of chewing gum that had lost its flavor. I couldn't care less. I'd never wear it again. Even if the dry cleaners removed the bloodstains, my memories of the experience would never fade. Oliver knew me well.

"I feel better. You?" He rubbed his hands together and straightened his suit jacket.

I swiped my hair off my face and neck. Oliver walked over and caught it in his capable hands. He pulled a black elastic hair tie and bobby pin out of his suit pocket and adeptly streaked his hands through my hair. The calming motion of his fingers combing along my scalp soothed me, reminded me that I was here. Still alive.

Oliver was not only my assistant, but also my best friend. Technically, aside from my sister, my only true friend. Most people in my world were there because of what I could do for them. Money brought out the leeches in droves. I paid

Oliver more than I paid my high-powered executives, but he was worth every cent. Oliver never complained and was always there when I needed him, day or night. He was the perfect man.

"Have I told you lately that I love you?" I tipped my head back and smiled.

He leaned over and kissed my temple. "No, I don't think you have." His grin was playful.

"Tell me about the man."

Oliver fastened the severe ponytail low on the nape of my neck. He spun a piece of the hair he left out around the elastic tie, hiding it from sight, then slid the pin through the hair along my scalp, securing it in place. I'm sure it looked flawless. He was incredible at styling me, buying my suits, fixing my hair. The best I could do on my own was a blow-dry and a few rounded curls when my hair was down. Growing up, I spent too much time hitting the books and not enough time socializing with women to learn simple things, such as styling one's hair.

The only source I had for things that one would consider "girlie" was my sister, London. She was everything I wasn't. She had honey-colored skin and black hair, like our father, while I had pale skin and blond hair, shared by our mother. We both had our father's gray-blue eyes. London wasn't as big in business, but she was a very sought-after interior designer who did very well for herself. Not as well as I had done; my financial worth far exceeded that of my family's, but it had never been a problem in our relationship. London cared nothing for money, whereas the more money I had, the more secure I felt.

"… and he owns the firm we contracted." Oliver's

voice brought me back from my thoughts.

"I'm sorry, what did you say?"

He rolled his eyes. "I said his name is Hank Jensen. He owns Jensen Construction."

"Hank?" The name rolled off my tongue and ended with a sharp click. It suited him.

"Yeah, Hank the Hunk," Oliver laughed. "Look at the picture from his badge entry photo." He handed me the image. Though he looked handsome in the photo, my memory of him was better, only tarnished by the pain I saw in his eyes.

Oliver was right. The man was attractive, in a rugged manly man way. His hair was dark, full, and thick. Even white teeth stretched into a forced smile. Subtle green eyes complemented his tanned skin. Made me curious as to what color the skin was under the T-shirt he wore for the picture. Would he have a hokey farmer's tan? I wondered if I would ever know the answer to that question. Probably not.

"Where did you say Mr. Jensen was from?"

"Texas. It says here on his background check that he owns several acres of land. According to Google Earth, it looks like a ranch. Oh, color me pretty —he's a cowboy. I love cowboys!" Oliver fiddled with his phone and flipped it over to show me a large green expanse of land.

"You love *men*." I snaked the phone from his hands to get a better look and was surprised by the beauty of the lush landscapes. Ranches always seemed like they'd be full of dirt and cows, like in a western movie featuring John Wayne, not something right out of *The Sound of Music*. The land highlighted rolling green hills with more trees than could be counted and a creek that ran alongside the property line.

"No. Correction, my dear, I love *beautiful* men. Cowboys make me tingle, though." He fanned his hands in front of his face as if he were having a hot flash.

"Did you get me the information I need to gain access to Mr. Jensen? I have to know that he will be okay. Also, what did Legal say?"

"I can get you access, but it's going to cost you."

"Oliver, everyone has a price." I grinned and looked at him sideways. "What's the price?"

"Well, on the way over I called the Dean of Medicine and told her the situation, expressed your concern and your interest in the patient's well-being."

"Get to the point, Ollie."

"All right, all right. You're going to have to make a hefty charitable donation."

"Done. How much?"

"Well, they need some new machines…"

"How much?" My patience was wearing thin, and Oliver could tell.

"One hundred." He looked away and stiffened.

"Fine. Have my accountant cut the check. This man saved my life…" My eyes started to tear up, but I fended off the waterworks by standing and adjusting my shoulders. "Who do we need to see?"

"Excuse me, Ms. Reynolds?" A redheaded woman in an ugly suit that was too big for her petite frame approached us.

"Yes, I'm Ms. Reynolds. And you are?"

She held her hand out to shake mine. "Jane Maxwell, Dean of Medicine. I'm sorry we're meeting under these circumstances." Her eyes were warm and sincere. Then again, when you were about to be gifted one hundred thousand dollars, a personal visit from the Dean could be expected.

I cut right to the point. "This is my assistant, Oliver. He will be taking care of making a one-hundred-thousand-dollar donation on my behalf." There was no reason to waste time. Time that could be spent making sure Hank Jensen survived.

"Oh, my! We can't thank you enough." Her eyes and smile seemed proportionately large on her round face. "A gift of that size will do wonders for our children's oncology division."

I looked over at Oliver, a questioning eyebrow pointed as high as the sky. He looked away, face beet red. He had lied. The woman never gave an amount to him by phone. Probably never mentioned a donation either. He just wanted me to donate to the children's ward. Oliver had been a leukemia survivor as a child and was always dragging me to events related to cancer and children. Sneaky.

"Happy to help, Ms. Maxwell. Now, if you could help me, I want to know what's going on with Hank Jensen? Can I see him?"

"He's in surgery now, but I'll take you up and ensure you're approved access to him when he's in recovery. We couldn't find any familial contact information, and since your office seems to have more information than we do, it only seems fitting you be granted access." She winked at me and then turned on her heel. "Follow me."

As we followed the Dean of Medicine, I leaned over and whispered into Oliver's ear, "You're going to pay for that one."

"I always do." His smile widened, and I shook my head

in mock indignation.

Once we were settled in the waiting room, I grilled Oliver on Hank's next of kin and tried to call the number on file. The phone rang nonstop, with no answering machine picking up. In this day and age, I'd think everyone on the planet had voice mail. Apparently not. I returned countless e-mails from my smart phone and had Oliver cancel all my meetings for the day.

We spent three hours in the waiting room before the surgeon approached us. He was suited from head to bootie-covered toes in medical scrubs. Ms. Maxwell flanked his side.

"Ms. Reynolds? I'm Dr. Nicholls."

I shook his hand. "How's Mr. Jensen?" Worry racked my tone, making it sound as if my throat was laced with sandpaper.

"He's doing very well. We were able to remove the pipe that went through the connective tissue in his shoulder."

"Oh my God. You mean the pipe went in one side of his body and out the other?"

"To an extent, yes. We removed it. We were able to reattach the tissues of his shoulder and stitch both the entry and exit wounds up nicely. He's been in recovery for the past thirty minutes. Should wake up any time now."

"So he's going to be okay? What happens next?"

"He'll need a good four to six weeks of recovery to let the tissue heal properly, need to wear a sling to limit mobility. Then another six weeks of physical therapy. We'll have to check his stitches weekly for infection. The bandage will need changing twice daily. He's going to need help over the first two weeks after he leaves the hospital."

I closed my eyes, relieved. Oliver supported me as I said

a silent prayer, thanking God he survived. He was hurt, and would spend the next weeks recovering, but he'd recover. That was the important thing. "I'll make sure he has around the-clock care."

Oliver pulled out his phone and stepped off to the side. "Ms. Reynolds is going to need to hire a full-time, highly skilled nurse…" I heard him talking softly as he walked out into the hall. Worth every penny, my Ollie was.

"Can I see him?"

"Of course. He should awaken soon. I'll take you to him."

I waved at Oliver who followed a few paces behind us. The Dean led us through a series of doors where machines beeped like a metronome, keeping the pace of the healing process. The hospital held the sour odor of disinfectant and vapor rub as we made our way through the halls. I pinched the bridge of my nose to combat the stench. Hospitals reminded me of death.

Ms. Maxwell led me to a closed door. "Go on in. We haven't been able to reach any of his family."

"Me either," I confirmed. "If you do, please let me know."

She nodded and then walked away. I entered the room while Oliver took a seat just outside the door, phone still held to his ear.

The room was surprisingly large, but my eyes didn't take in much besides the man lying in the bed. His torso was bare, a thin blanket folded at his waist. A large bandage covered his entire left shoulder.

I walked over to get a better look at my sleeping savior. He was a giant: had to be well over six-feet tall, with thick, muscular arms, broad shoulders, and washboard abs. My heart pounded as I took in every inch of one of the most beautiful bodies I'd ever seen. No farmer's tan. All smooth golden skin.

Hank Jensen was a work of art. A smattering of dark hair trailed down past his belly button, the rest hidden from view by the blanket. In sleep, he looked kind, with chiseled features that could have graced any of the big screens or modeling shoots my company managed. Surrounded by beautiful people day in, day out in my line of work, I'd never met anyone who could take my breath away. Until now.

I sat down in the chair next to his bed. Thoughts swam through my head, replaying the day's events. I reached across the bed and tentatively clasped his hand. It wasn't soft like the hands of a man used to the finer things in life. Hank's hands were those of a worker. A blue-collar man who spent his days out in the sun, building things with his bare hands. I felt the roughness of his calluses against my palm and a rush of adrenaline shot down my spine.

This man saved my life.

CHAPTER TWO

Something tickled. It felt as though a feather glided up my arm, starting at my wrist and ending at the crook of my elbow, then back down. Felt nice. I tried to move. Pain exploded through my chest and forced a jagged burst of air out my clenched teeth. Searing hot prickles licked across my body and I groaned. The tickle stopped and a hand as soft as silk encased mine. *What the hell?*

"It's okay, Hank. I'm here." A woman's voice registered in my ears.

I turned my head toward the voice and opened my eyes. A clouded figure stood at my bedside clutching my hand. The softened halo around the form brightened and crisp edges appeared. My angel. Relief soothed its way through every inch of me, coating the hurt a little. A wide smile split across dry lips as things came into complete focus. Damn, the woman was beautiful. Gray-blue eyes shone bright against the dark of her suit and pearl nature of her pale skin. Her sculpted brows knit together as she studied me.

"Angel, my beautiful angel." My voice came out raspy. Confusion set in and I searched the space. *How did I get here? Why was she at my bedside? Why was I in bed?* It was obvious from the white walls down to the scratchy starched sheets that I was in a hospital room. I tried to adjust my shoulders to relieve the heavy ache that weighed me down, but fiery pokers lanced at even the tiniest movement.

She scampered over to a side table and returned with a pink cup. With a straw held between her fingers, she brought the plastic to my lips, and I drank eagerly. My throat was drier than the bales of hay I fed my horses.

After I drank my fill, I watched as she fiddled with her jacket, straightening wrinkles that didn't exist. Her teeth bit down on the pink of her bottom lip, and I felt my heart thud against my chest.

"What happened?" I remembered very little. My left wrist had something tugging and pulling at the skin. I moved my right hand over to feel it and realized there was an IV. I did a mental check of my body, starting at my toes. They moved easy enough. My legs seemed heavier, and every last twinge or slight movement of my upper body hurt. The pain was bad, but tolerable. It wasn't so bad that I couldn't move. My left shoulder seemed to be the worst. Kind of like a burned out hollow oak tree. It was still there but not in any working order.

With caution, I moved the right one. It functioned without problem, though still heavier than normal. Must be pumping drugs through that IV. When I tried to move the left shoulder again, it was as if all the nerves in my body went on alert and rushed to that area to scream in unison. My teeth clenched, holding back the groan dying to get out.

"Mr. Jensen," she started. "You were in an accident. The crane broke and…"

"I remember that much, darlin'. What I don't remember is how I ended up here with a busted wing."

Her eyes ran over my chest. When I caught her staring, she looked away, her face turning a soft pink. I rather liked the color on her pretty skin. "Um, well, you jumped in front of me. One of the metal pipes pierced your shoulder. You've been in surgery the past few hours." Her eyes came back to mine. "I can't believe you would do that for a…"

"An angel in white?" I gave her my best smile, considering the circumstances. Her lips twitched at the corners.

"I was going to say a perfect stranger." Her gaze searched mine, a frown marring her elegant features. She was struggling with something, but hell if I knew what. My woman decoder was broken on account of whatever shit was in the IV.

I shrugged on instinct, and the pain zipped through my shoulder. My head fell back and I gritted my teeth, trying to not cry out. Wouldn't want the dame to think I was a pussy.

"Oh my God, are you okay?" she gasped, as her soft fingers felt all over my face and chest to assess the damage.

The woman's hands seemed to hold magic because when they flitted over my skin I didn't feel any pain, only a deep sense of content. Her scent drifted over me. Smelled like sweet apple pie on a perfect Sunday morning back home. It soothed me, going a long way to ease the full body ache.

Once I'd recovered my composure, I looked her over good and hard. She was all woman dressed in a man's suit. For the life of me, I couldn't figure why the hell she would hide that perfect body in something so masculine.

I took a deep breath, sucking in all her goodness. "God, you smell nice."

She leaned back and grinned. "Yes, well. Thank you."

Just when I was going to ask her name, a pointy little fella in a suit matching hers entered. They must have had a two-for-one sale on the suits. I looked the man over from head to toe. Couldn't be her husband. This man was a pipsqueak. She was taller by half a foot. She didn't wear a ring, and I'm certain a woman like her dated men that looked like Ken dolls, not like Ken's baby brother who hadn't hit puberty yet.

"Aspen, Legal is here." His voice was low, almost a whisper.

"Aspen? Like the place?" I grabbed her hand and she looked back at me. God, those eyes. I could drown in 'em.

"Yes, like the place. Aspen Reynolds. It's good to meet you, Mr. Jensen." Man, she was pretty.

A tall woman in green scrubs entered. She held a clipboard. "Mr. Jensen. How are you?" My angel, who now had a name, backed up against the wall and out of the way. The pointy one whispered something in her ear. I was having trouble paying attention, my eyelids heavy again.

"Oh, I've been better."

"What's your pain level from 1 to 10?" she asked and scribbled down information on her clipboard while reading the machines next to my bed.

"'Bout a six or seven."

She nodded. "That's really good. The doctor will be in shortly to discuss your surgery."

As she exited, a man entered. He introduced himself as Dr. Nicholls and went over the specifics of my surgery. He said I was very lucky. Had the pipe entered at a different location, I'd be lying on a bed in the morgue right now, not in recovery. Based on my prognosis, he saw me being able to leave in a couple days.

When he finished, my gaze caught the gorgeous woman

standing in the corner. She opened her mouth to speak, but I drifted off, not hearing what she'd said.

I awoke only when the nurse adjusted my bandage, checked my blood pressure, and asked me if I wanted to eat. I was starved, but too tired.

"Where's the woman...Aspen?"

She smiled. "I forced her out, practically kicking and screaming, after visiting hours. She stayed the entire day, though. Fussed over you, demanded things from the Dean of Medicine, who by the way, hopped to it. She must care a lot about you."

"I can't imagine why. She just met me today." I grinned, and her lips twisted into a knowing smile but she chose not to comment.

"Get some rest, Mr. Jensen. I'm certain your friend will be back first thing in the morning."

My mind went blank, and I fell asleep once more.

★ ★ ★ ★

I smelled her before I saw her; a light vanilla scent in the air filled the space surrounding me as I came to. She held my hand with hers, pale and little compared to mine. Her phone was in her right hand and she scrolled through messages.

She hadn't noticed I was awake, so I studied her. Golden hair, shiny and bright against her fair skin, and she sported another dark suit.

Her head turned and her gaze caught mine. A lovely smile broke across her face. "Mr. Jensen, you're awake. How do you feel?" She removed her hand. It was strange how I missed it moments after she pulled it away.

"Better than yesterday." I grabbed for the bed controls, and the mechanism whirred to life, lifting my upper body to a reclined seated position. Again, I did a mental check, starting with my toes, up my legs and upper body. Everything seemed better than yesterday. Aside from the throbbing space and dull ache surrounding my left shoulder, I was happy to be feeling more like myself. The cobwebs of anesthesia from the surgery were all but gone.

The door opened, and Aspen's little friend strolled in alongside a different nurse, this time in blue scrubs. The nurse made quick work of checking my vitals, pain level, adjusted some knobs, pressed buttons, and then she was gone.

"Aspen, Legal is expecting to hear back from you today." The small fella spoke so low I could barely catch what he said.

She nodded at him and then turned to look at me. Her professional demeanor I was used to seeing each morning was back. Shoulders stiff, back ramrod straight, teetering on insanely high heels. I missed the soft-spoken angel who held my hand. "Mr. Jensen," she started.

"Darlin', you can call me Hank. So what's with this legal mumbo jumbo?" I gestured to her little friend.

"Mr. Jensen, my name is Oliver and I'm Ms. Reynolds's assistant at AIR Bright Enterprises." Her assistant. Not her boyfriend or husband. The relief I felt surprised me. "Our attorneys are here to ensure you're on the mend and discuss the legal ramifications of yesterday's accident and your injury. The accident happened on company property, and the crane had worn hinges."

I nodded, following along.

"Your company is not at fault, and neither is the company we rented the crane from. It truly has been deemed a random accident. But since it happened on company property and you were injured, it's our responsibility to ensure your needs are met."

"I'm not following. Accidents happen. A lot in my line of work. Construction is a dirty and sometimes dangerous job. Yesterday, well, looks like it was both. Tell your fancy lawyers I'm good. I'll be outta here and back on the job in two shakes of a lamb's tail."

"Mr. Jensen…" Aspen put her hand on my forearm. Her touch was electric, and the little hairs on my forearm stood at attention just to be near her. "We're going to take care of you. My company will pay all hospital expenses and ensure you're cared for through the healing process."

I was about to set her straight, but she spoke fast.

"I am prepared to pay for your pain and suffering. If you want to contact your lawyers, we'll make sure you are comfortable financially." She licked her lips, and I was more interested in sucking on that lip than listening to any more of her bullshit. This girl needed to be taught a few things about good manners.

"Darlin', let's get a couple things straight. I don't need any lawyers, and my medical bills will be covered by my insurance. I've been taking care of myself for thirty-four years, don't plan on stopping now. You can call your liars— er, lawyers—off. I'm not suing anyone, if that's what you're worried about." Her being so worried about her legal team made me wonder if that's the real reason she was here. Maybe she just wanted to be sure I didn't sue.

She took a deep breath. "Mr. Jensen…"

"Hank."

She sighed and blew a puff of air over the layer of hair falling in her face. Even the little things she did stole my breath.

"Hank, you are entitled to financial assistance through this process. You saved my life. I'll do anything to make sure you get well."

The pure need to help shone deep within her eyes as she stared me down. They were a color you couldn't find in a box of crayons. Those clear blue-and-gray eyes made me believe that I would submit to anything she asked and do whatever she wanted just so that I could continue to look at them. Didn't matter why she was here, just that she was. I planned on taking advantage of it.

"Okay, then I know what I want." I was tired from the surgery and needed to rest, but I'd spent weeks watching this woman in her body-hugging clothes and fuck-me shoes. I didn't know when I'd get the chance to be this close to her again.

"Everyone has a price." Her lips turned into a hard line and her shoulders sagged.

My demand came without hesitation. "I want a date with you."

"A date? You want a date?" Her shock was just as pretty as her smile. Made me wonder what her face would look like screaming my name in pleasure.

"Okay, two dates." I gave her my best sexy look. It was my patented "tell me how you'd like your eggs cooked after a night of knockin' the boots" charm. It never failed.

"You can't be serious. I'm a very wealthy woman and—"

"Aspen," the pip-squeak piped in warning.

She held up a firm hand to cut him off. That was hot. She was a fireball when she wanted to be. I liked it. Too much if I was honest with myself. The ol' dipstick stirred. I clasped my hands over my friend to prevent any public embarrassment.

"Look, darlin', I don't give two shits about your change purse. Now, are you going to give me what I want or not?"

She took a deep breath and blew it out slowly. "Fine. We'll go out. When you've recovered. Where are you staying?"

"I share a place with a few of my guys over in the Bronx." Two horrified expressions, one beautiful, one pinched, stared back at me. "What?"

"You're not staying there," she said with a harsh tone. "Oliver…"

"I'm on it!" He flipped his phone to his ear and started barking out orders. Reminded me of an ankle biter that you just couldn't shake.

"I need Mr. Jensen's belongings packed up and moved to…hold that thought. Aspen, to where? The Four Seasons?"

She shook her head. "My place."

"Aspen?"

"Do what I say, Ollie." Her tone was that of a woman in charge. One who was used to that position. Downright comfortable in it. It was sexy as hell. Though once I got a hold of her in a more private setting, I'd like nothing more than to show her how good I was at taking charge.

My loud laugh stopped the staring match that occurred between the prince and the princess. "Not for nothin', but I go where I want to go. I sleep where I want to sleep. You have no right to demand anything." The entire conversation was ridiculous. People with too much money seemed to think they owned the world and everyone in it.

My angel's eyes turned harsh. "Look, Hank, you want to get well, right? I want to get you well. The best way for me to ensure that you're going to heal and not sue me for damages is to have you close by." Her intent was confirmed. Everything was always about money. "The project was going to run for another eight weeks, right?"

I nodded.

"So, you'll stay at my place for the next eight weeks. I will have a nurse at your beck and call, a physical therapist scheduled to suit your medical needs, and in the interim"— she took a deep breath—"I'll have peace of mind knowing that I've done everything I could. You saved my life. I need to pay back that debt. If you won't accept my money, please accept my offer to help." Okay, maybe she did care about more than her wallet.

The woman drove a hard bargain and was a damn good negotiator.

"All right, angel." A beautiful blush covered her cheeks and crept down her neck. I wondered where else she blushed. I was going to have a damn good time finding out. Before long, this woman was going to be wrapped around my little finger. I'd prefer her wrapped around my dick, but that could take a little time. She was wound tighter than a drum. Always in control.

I wanted to see my pretty angel lose it. "I'll agree to stay with you until I feel well enough to move about and go back to the jobsite."

Her smile was brighter than a shiny new penny, and

it made me happy to have put it there. "Good. Thank you, Hank. You won't regret it."

* * * *

I was emotionally and physically drained. After I said my good-byes to Hank, I spoke with Legal about his prognosis. The firm was not happy with the terms we agreed upon. They were going to draw together something more official tomorrow. They didn't believe it was possible for a human being to be so altruistic. Hell, I wasn't so sure I believed it either.

According to them, Hank was going to come off his drugs and realize how much I was worth and attempt to clean house. The accident occurred on my property, falling under the company's liability insurance. Technically Hank could take me for a pretty penny if he wanted to. And I'd pay for the sole purpose of repaying him for the gift of my life.

Hank. The man was infuriating. If he would have just taken a settlement, we'd all feel better. He could go back home a rich man and I could go back to...back to what? Models? Actors? More pretty faces than I could stomach? Everyone wrapped in plastic.

Don't get me wrong. I loved my job. Building my empire was a dream and I'd accomplished it. I was at the top of my game, with more money than I'd ever need in my lifetime.

Then there was Hank. He had a ranch in Texas, a white Ford pickup truck, and a small construction firm that scored my project by bidding tens of thousands under what my team would have paid. A man that seemed perfectly comfortable in his own skin. Oh, and what scrumptious-looking skin it was.

Seeing all that bare male flesh got my blood thrumming and my knees weak. It had been ages since I'd had such a virile man around. The men I'd dated were always high society. Ivy League, big in business and lousy in bed. My pleasure was of little concern as long as they got off. Hank looked like a man who knew how to please a woman.

I slumped down into the comfort of my puffy couch. The penthouse was quiet; all the staff besides my chef, Gustav, had left for the evening.

Again, my thoughts were brought back to Hank. He wanted to date me. It reeked of a bad after-school special on Lifetime television. The story as old as time. It hadn't changed much since Shakespeare wrote his version in *Romeo and Juliet*. Doomed from the start.

It wasn't possible that we had much in common. I could see our first date now. He'd be in jeans, work boots, and a white T-shirt that stretched across that broad chest, outlining every thick ripple of muscle.

My hand slowly traveled down my abdomen, past my shirt, and over my slacks as I fantasized. Hank's ass would fill his jeans like a second skin. My hand reached its target between my legs, cupping and pressing down against the needy flesh. A gasp escaped as I leaned back on the couch and imagined it was Hank's hand touching me, twirling his large fingers around my clit. He'd whisper in my ear, tell me how much he wanted to fuck me.

I undid the button and zipper of my pants and slipped my hand under the lace panties. Cool fingers slid against the slick folds. I was surprisingly wet. Hank would remove my pants and dip his face down toward my center, licking and kissing my thighs, growling as he shredded my panties between his large hands.

My fingers pressed and swirled around the hard bundle of nerves at the apex of my pleasure as I imagined it. Dream Hank would spread me wide open. He'd hold my ass just where he wanted and lick me with one long swipe of his tongue, dipping into my sex over and over until I was screaming out in ecstasy.

The pressure built at my core, throbbed and tingled as I lifted my hips up and pressed deep inside with two fingers, mimicking what I thought Hank would do. Several deep strokes, hips reaching high, I ended the torture with a few furious circles around my swollen clit.

"Hank!" I cried into the empty room, my orgasm ripping through me fast and furious.

I rubbed out the vestiges of my pleasure as Dream Hank fizzled and disappeared. Jesus, I hadn't come that hard in a long time. Too long. So long that I was using a man who was all wrong for me as fodder for my masturbatory fantasies. Pathetic.

In the kitchen, I washed my hands, still dazed from my orgasm, my mind still focused on Dream Hank.

The door to my penthouse slammed and a jangling ruckus could be heard from the entryway. I made it back into the living room when I heard Oliver yelling.

"Sit! Damn, you mangy mutt, don't you know basic commands!" Oliver's shrill voice pierced and echoed through the walls of my home.

A blur of yellow barreled through the living room,

knocking over a small table. Nails clicked and clacked against the hardwood floors, and then a giant dog jumped, pushing me onto the couch. I shrieked, covering my face and chest as it hopped from couch to my lap to the floor and back. A long pink tongue hung out of its mouth and then slurped at my face, leaving a wet trail of saliva along the surface. I tilted my head against my shoulder, wiping the disgusting slime off.

"Holy Jesus. What the hell, Ollie! Get this dog off me!"

"Oh my God. Shoo, dog, shoo! Get down." He pulled at the dog's collar and slapped a hook onto it, restraining him by his side.

"I'm sorry, Pen. You said to move all of Hank's stuff to your place. This"—he pointed to the yellow lab—"is part of his stuff. According to the gentleman who gave me the dog, his name is Butch."

"Butch." The dog turned around in a circle when he heard his name. Tentatively, I reached out and petted the dog. He happily panted and pushed against my palm. I pulled my hand away and a wad of hair was left in its wake. Dogs. They were dirty, they shed, and they made messes as large as they were. This dog was enormous, just like its master. *What a nightmare.*

"You have got to be kidding me." I closed my eyes and tried to will the dog to disappear. I cracked open one eye. No such luck. He was still there. "Okay, fine. Hire a dog watcher or something. For now, bring him in the kitchen and give him some water. He's probably thirsty. Have Chef Gustav make him a steak." Oliver looked at me like I was a psycho. "Please, just deal with it. I'm going to take a long hot bath. Tomorrow I'm going to stop by the hospital in the morning. Reschedule any conflicting appointments."

"Okay, you rest. You've been through a lot the past couple days. And, Pen…"

I stopped at the head of the stairs, turning to look back at my most trusted friend. "Yes?"

"I'm so thankful you're okay. I owe the cowboy a lot. You're still here because of him." His voice was weak and thick with emotion.

"I'm fine. Please, just take care of his dog." I swung a wave behind me as I trod to the haven that was a huge jetted tub nestled in the master bathroom. "Good night."

★ ★ ★ ★

A hot bath was exactly what the doctor ordered. Candles twinkled along the curved edge of the tub, filling the room with the scent of sugary vanilla. Water sloshed over the side as I settled into the steamy water.

Heaven.

Ten minutes passed when the door creaked open and Oliver walked in. He had a bottle of wine in one hand, two glasses in the other. He set the bottle and glasses down on the tiled edge. He pulled the vanity chair over to the tub, removed his blazer and tie, and then folded up each sleeve of his dress shirt. He slumped into the chair, picked up the wine, and poured hefty glasses of the garnet liquid.

I knew what he was doing. For the past decade, it had always been us against the world. He needed me and couldn't leave. Yesterday he was faced with the fear that he might have lost me.

It was the first real brush with death either of us had

experienced. We'd dealt with jealous and jilted lovers before, and the occasional death threat from companies I'd taken over in the past, but nothing so acute or specifically life-threatening as this. Had Hank not jumped in front me, that metal pipe would have gone straight through my heart.

I traced the circular bruise just above my left breast. The purple-and-black area spread across my chest, covering about a three-to four-inch area. I was lucky the end of the pipe that pierced through Hank only left me with the bruise from a much smaller impact.

"Does it hurt?" He broke the silence first. His eyes scanned my entire body, probably making sure there weren't any other marks marring me. If it were anyone else, I'd have covered up. Ollie had seen me naked more times than my mother had. I stopped caring about modesty with him back in college when he started to dress me, then completely when we lived together until he'd gotten with Dean.

"Yes. Not as much as it could have." I took a healthy sip of wine, the berry and plum flavors rushed over my tongue and warmed my belly.

"God, Aspen. I could have lost you." Tears filled his big brown doe eyes.

"But you didn't. And you won't." I reached out a wet hand and clasped his. "We're best friends. We're in it for the long haul. It's always been you and me, Ollie." I smiled to reassure him.

"It won't always be that way. One day you're going to meet a man, fall in love, and have babies, and I'll be a long-forgotten friend." He was having a pity party for one and there wasn't a lot I could do about it.

"You're right. One day I hope to find a man I can share

my life and *bed* with." My pointed look wasn't lost on him.

Had he not been gay, I still wouldn't have been attracted to him. I liked tall, large men who were sure of themselves. Ollie was more like a female than a male, though I'd never tell him that. There wasn't another man I could hold a platonic conversation with while lying completely exposed in a bathtub. My body wasn't perfect, but I worked hard to stay in shape. I'd been told I had a beautiful body by several men in the past. I spent countless hours in my home gym to ensure a fit form. Overall, my self-image was not one of my insecurities.

"Just because I want to have a man in my life doesn't mean I'm going to get rid of the one I already have. You're my best friend, my only true friend. You know everything about me and love me anyway. No one could take your place." I tipped my head over to force him to look at me. "Besides, who's going to pick out my clothes and do my hair?"

We both laughed and a bright smile broke across his face. "I'm sorry I wasn't there to save you." Ah, so now we get to the real problem. He wanted to be my one and only savior.

"I'm not, because that would mean that I could have lost you. That, I wouldn't have survived." Tears welled up, but I tried not to let them fall. It had been a really emotional couple days. "I love you and all your pieces."

"Me too. All your pieces." He stood up and clinked his glass with mine. Then he downed the wine in a couple gulps. I smiled. Waste not, want not. "I'm going to head home and cuddle up with Dean tonight. You okay?" He leaned down on one knee and brought his forehead to mine. He rubbed our foreheads together.

"I am. Now go. Dean already hates me. Go home to him."

He nodded and headed to the door. "Oh, and Aspen?"

"Yes?" I sighed and leaned my head back, forcing myself to relax and enjoy the water slipping around tense muscles.

His gaze scanned my body from head to toe. "Your body has never looked better. Hank's going to enjoy the hell out of it."

My jaw dropped open, eyes wide.

He chuckled and called over his shoulder, "See you tomorrow, princess!" And he was gone.

Oliver was always full of surprises. As I sank farther into the heated depths, my thoughts ran back to Hank. My daytime hero. He was incredibly attractive. His rugged looks and hard body had me aching to touch him. Even though I'd only seen him naked from the waist up, my eyes took in the hard lines of his thighs under that thin blanket.

Long legs had him well over six feet. Instead of a runner's build like all the men I'd dated in the past, Hank was huge…everywhere. He had the power in his form to take me against a wall, and I'd gladly welcome it.

Of course, this was all fantasy. Hank and I would never have sex. No, we were too different—worlds apart, in fact. Our lifestyles could never commingle harmoniously and having sex would complicate things. I'd never understand why I'd chosen to move him into my home to heal. It would definitely be an interesting experience.

I left the bath to find Hank's dog lying on the floor at the foot of my bed. I stared him down, but he just smacked his chops and rested his head against his paws, eyes closing, readying for sleep. At least he was comfortable with the arrangement. I'd never had a dog, nor understood the need for one. Pulling the covers back, I fell into bed without bothering to put on pajamas or dry my hair. Mind, body, and soul were spent. Butch's soft snoring lulled me to sleep.

CHAPTER THREE

An annoying light flickered on and pulled me from the deep recess of an unmemorable dream. Even with my eyes closed, something pierced through the inky blackness. One eyelid was forced up and the blinding light took out my vision like the flash of a camera lens. The offender proceeded to do the same to its twin.

"Good morning, Mr. Jensen," a gravelly voice greeted.

My eyes adjusted to the room. A man in a white coat stood before me. Glasses perched on the tip of a bulbous nose. His bald head had wisps of hair protruding in different directions. His thick fingers poked and prodded at my wound, the bloody bandage lying on my stomach.

The sight of the dried blood and sticky goo coated my mouth with a sourness that could easily have me puking my guts up. He pressed on a particularly painful spot, and I couldn't hold back the cry that tore from my lungs. At that exact moment, my angel appeared through the door and ran to my side. Her cool hands grasped mine tightly, the vanilla goodness of her perfume swirled in the air as her sweet face screwed into worry lines.

"Hank, I'm here, you're all right." The calm timbre of her voice held a twinge of irritation. I couldn't focus on her as much as I'd like because the doctor before me dug into my wound like he was searching for gold. The pressure on the gaping hole resulted in bursts of stars fluttering through my vision.

"Doctor, what's going on? Why is he in so much pain?" My angel was feisty today. Kicking ass. I liked it.

On autopilot, my hand reached to her side and settled on the swell of her tight ass. I gave it a little pat and her eyes flicked to mine; fire swirled in those smoky depths.

"Angel, I'm fine. Just a tender spot. Ain't nothin' I can't handle. Right, Doc?" It hurt but I wasn't a wuss, and the last thing I wanted was for her to think I was.

The doctor pushed his glasses back up his nose. "Yes, well, he'd take it better if he would stop declining the pain medication."

Her left brow arched into a triangle and her lips turned down. "Hank? Why aren't you taking the medication? You're in pain. You just had major surgery two days ago."

Like I didn't already know that.

"Look, darlin', I'm good. Real good, now that I'm looking at your pretty face." Yup, I was feeling mighty good today and to prove my point, I cupped the underside of her butt cheek and squeezed. Nice and tight. Just as I suspected. She started to moan but then clamped her mouth shut. Just the solid weight of her presence gave me energy.

Her reaction to my touch was more receptive than I expected. Yeah, I couldn't wait to tap that ass. She was ripe, and I looked forward to riding this filly all night long. I'd tip her ass just right so I could see my cock slide in and out of her from behind. Pull her hair just enough so she'd know who was in charge. I just needed to get the hell out of Dodge and on more comfortable turf. I wanted to be alone with her. Aside from pinning her to the nearest bed, of which I wasn't capable with this bum shoulder, I looked forward to getting to know her.

Her hand gripped mine and forcibly pulled it off her ass. Her breath was labored and her face a rosy red, either from excitement or embarrassment since the doctor was right there.

I didn't care. The pain was manageable and nothing was going to stop me from touching her. "Soon, angel," I said.

She gasped, and her eyes closed and opened then locked onto mine. It was obvious that she was reading me, feeling out my intent. I wasn't hiding it. I wanted her and she knew it. As I searched those crystal depths there was no denying she felt it, too. The desire was written across her face as if it were a big red X marking off the days of the week on a calendar. Even though I'd only technically known the woman for a couple days, I'd been dreaming about having her for weeks on end. Now that she was here, so close I could smell and touch her, I planned on making good on it.

"So, Doc. When do I get to break out of this chicken coop?" I clasped my hand with Aspen's and she looked away, a fresh rosy blush spread across her cheeks. She was going to be a challenge, but I liked challenges. She may even be someone I could very easily get used to seeing on a more personal basis.

Christ, this woman had me tied in knots with desire. Now that my mind was clear of the drugs and I was on the mend, all I could think about was bending her over and having my way with her.

The doctor applied some type of salve over the wound, completely oblivious to the tug and pull between Aspen and me. I gritted my teeth at the sting. It smelled like horse manure on a hot day.

"Why the hell does it smell so rank?" I asked. Even the pretty girl standing next me had her nose scrunched up trying to avoid the smell.

"It's the salve. Don't worry. The body is doing its job, ensuring no infection. Everything looks good in front. Lean forward."

Letting go of Aspen's hand, I adjusted and groaned in agony as the doctor worked on the exit wound. Okay, so pressure and quick movements still hurt like hell. I gripped the blankets in a tight fist as the pain shot through my chest in every direction. "Shit!" I growled though clenched teeth.

Aspen's hands smoothed over my other shoulder, caressing my bare skin. It acted like a balm, diminishing the agony considerably. I looked into her eyes. We quietly stared at one another, our faces so close I could feel her breath against my cheeks. She held me while the doctor finished the bandage change on the back of my shoulder. Her eyes were a vision. The blue and gray mingled together to create the most unusual color. This beautiful woman was going to be trouble with a capital T.

The doctor moved to the end of the bed and wrote in my file.

My angel took that opportunity to lean forward and place a baby-soft kiss against my cheek. Adoration forced my eyes to close and enjoy the chaste sensation. Before she could pull away, I grabbed her around the nape with my good arm and pressed my lips to hers. She squeaked in surprise but didn't pull away. Just the slightest pressure of her mouth on mine sent tingles running in all directions making me feel bold and needy for more. She gasped, but I held the kiss for a moment longer, enjoying the feel of just that small bit of flesh melded to mine.

As I pulled away, her mouth chased mine, keeping us connected. I wanted to be connected to her forever.

Everything ceased to exist in that moment. The beeping of machines controlling my meds, the doctor scribbling something on his clipboard, it was just me and my angel. I gripped the back of her neck and rubbed my lips against hers with more pressure than before, cementing her to me. As I opened my eyes, she pulled away and sucked in a deep breath. Her fingers immediately flew to her face, covering the proof of my kiss.

"Thank you. That helped with the pain." I grinned and wiggled my eyebrows to lighten the intensity of the moment.

She blinked a couple times as if she didn't know where she was, reminding me of a horse with blinders on. The feelin' was mutual for sure. She straightened her suit, transitioning business Aspen back into place. Made me wonder if she'd ever truly relaxed.

"Yes, uh, okay. So, you're better then?" I nodded, and she backed away from the bed. "Doctor, when can I take him home?"

She backed into the chair and almost toppled over. Even in those stilt-like shoes, she was able to right herself and still look in charge. She smiled as her cheeks pinked. If a bit more than a peck on the lips caused that reaction, I could only imagine what a full-blown Hank Special kiss would do. She might even lose some of that professional resolve. I was looking forward to finding out.

The doctor wrote a few things on the clipboard he held. "Tomorrow morning, as long as everything looks good. I'll need him to come back Monday morning to make sure there's still no infection. I'm prescribing some lighter pain medications you can take orally, Mr Jensen. They won't make you feel loopy but will take the edge off. You need to allow your body to heal naturally and you can't do that if you're fighting pain the entire time." His voice was stern, unforgiving.

"I understand. Thanks, Doc."

"I'm also going to prescribe a circulating cold therapy system. It will reduce the swelling and pain naturally. You'll take the unit home with you and refill the ice as needed. Do thirty minutes on and a couple hours off, and then repeat the process. It will speed the healing time."

"Sounds good enough."

"I'll make sure he gets one. If you could have a member of your team write down the make and model of the best on the market, I'll have it delivered," Aspen interrupted, phone in hand. "Wait." Her voice was clipped, directed at the caller.

The doctor's eyes went to hers and he smiled. I was about to decline her offer when she jutted out a flat hand in front of my face, stopping me in my tracks. It was surprisingly as effective on me as it had been on her assistant but for entirely different reasons. Her take-charge voice and demeanor had me and my dick paying attention. She was going to be such fun to break.

"Doctor, anything—and I mean anything—that will help speed his recovery will be provided by me. The cost is of no consequence. Whatever you say he needs, we'll take care of it." She handed him her business card and then barked orders into her phone. "Oliver, make sure you order whatever Hank's doctor prescribes." A few seconds ticked by as she waited. "Yes, any expense," she said with finality, then pressed a button, and tossed the phone into her pocket.

"Aspen Reynolds. You own AIR Bright Enterprises?" The doctor's tone held reverence, his face set into a huge grin.

"Yes, I'm the owner and CEO." She moved over to her bag and pulled the long strap over her shoulder. Holy hell, she owned the skyscraper my company was adding onto. Did that mean she was my boss? Technically, I guess it must have. It never dawned on me that she had that kind of money. I had figured she was rich, but in order to own a company of that size, she had to be worth a lot of dough. As in billions. Wow. And she seemed so young, too.

"You're famous!" The doctor continued his adoration.

"Hardly."

I watched the exchange, fascinated as she held her head high, back straight as an arrow. Professional Aspen was sexy, but I was sad to see my sweet angel had all but left the building. She'd be back. Her softer side intrigued me and seemed to pop up whenever she was touching me. I'd bet good money on the fact that not many were privy to that side of her. Made me a king among men knowing she let me in, at least a little. At some point, I'd have her in every way possible. Over the next eight weeks, I planned on familiarizing myself with every facet of Aspen Reynolds.

She headed to the door, bag held firm to her side. The woman was even prettier than a perfect sunset back at my ranch, and I'd been known to let a good hot dinner lose its heat just to see one of those glistening horizons. She was wearing one of her usual black skirts, the ones that hugged every inch of her hips, thighs, and ass. What I wouldn't give to run my hands up and down that skirt, scrunch it up to her waist, and take her right here. Damn, I had to get my mind out of the gutter or get this woman between the sheets. I couldn't think straight when she was around.

She turned and thanked the doctor. Her white blouse pulled at the corner, exposing a healthy view of the upper swell of her breast. A purplish-black shadow appeared against her creamy skin.

"Aspen, come here." I squinted my eyes and tried to see more of the purple stain against her flesh.

She adjusted her shirt self-consciously and walked over to the side of the bed as the doctor exited.

"Put the bag down for a second."

She did. "What's this about?" Her brows drew together.

I pulled her closer and placed my hand around the fragile, softer-than-silk column of her neck.

She took a deep breath but didn't move my hand.

Trailing the back of my knuckles down between the small pearly buttons of her shirt, I could see the edges of the discolored skin that caught my attention moments ago. With my right hand, I skillfully unbuttoned the top button of her shirt.

A deep inhale shook her small form and her body trembled under my fingertips. Her gaze held mine as my fingers traced the lacy edge of her undershirt and pulled the white satin aside to expose a huge, angry-looking bruise. It was about four or five inches in diameter, larger than a softball.

"Jesus Christ, angel. You did get hurt."

"No, Hank. I'm fine. You…you're the one who got hurt. This is nothing. Don't you see…"

I shook my head in frustration. All I could see was a giant ugly purple mark that proved just how close she'd been to getting her heart punctured with lead. I was happy it was me and not her. Having this warm, perfect angel in front of me, as if she were sent by God himself was worth it. Almost as if she was meant for me to save, to protect.

Why I felt so strongly near her was astounding. It didn't make sense, but neither did the energy that buzzed just under the surface. It filled the space around us, bringing us closer to each other. I didn't even know her, but it didn't matter. I wanted her. Wanted her to be safe. Wanted her to be mine.

Leaning forward, I placed gentle kisses along the entire surface of the bruise. It was out of line, but I couldn't help it. Her skin drew me in. I wanted—no, *needed*—to make it better. Her fingers twined through my hair as I worshiped her skin with small kisses.

"Hank…" My eyes met hers, her voice thick with emotion. "That pipe would have pierced through my heart. If you hadn't been there, done what you did…" Her eyes filled with tears, and then large, wet drops ran like a waterfall down her cheeks.

That's all it took. The need to taste her thrummed heavily through my veins, the tension so fierce it sizzled and popped around us. One-handed, I pulled her against my chest and crushed her lips with mine. She opened eagerly, and my tongue, lips, and teeth devoured her like a starving man devoured a steak.

There was no holding back, no room for nice dates and sweet pecks on the cheek. No, this was carnal desire. A man who needed a woman and a woman who needed to be kissed. I had to have her. By the way she kissed me back, her fingers tightening at my scalp and holding me to her, she was just as taken.

My fingers tunneled through her hair, over her back, pressing and keeping her near. My mouth slanted over hers and my tongue delved deeper, taking without request. Her little pink lips nibbled and gave just as much as they were getting. Her hands cupped my head on each side, giving her the control. My mouth ripped away from hers, needing air but still needing her.

I trailed wet licks and kisses down the sweet column of her swanlike neck. She tasted like a warm, juicy peach. My right hand clenched her waist, keeping her close. My wounded shoulder screamed in agony against the brutal way I held her to me, but I didn't care. *Fuck it.* My very own angel was panting and moaning against me. There wasn't anything that could pull me away from her skin at this moment. The building could catch fire, and I'd still be worshiping her with my hands and mouth.

Those plump lips found mine and licked my bottom one before sucking it into her mouth. My dick was rock-hard and tenting the blanket proudly. Her hand brushed against my erection as she leaned deeper into the kiss, mindful of the pressure against my bandaged shoulder. I moaned and she stopped. Our breath mingled as she hovered close. Her fingers traced the ridge of my shaft through the blanket.

My breath hitched. "Darlin', you better not start something you can't finish."

★ ★ ★ ★

His lips were addictive. I couldn't stop tugging and nipping at the sensual tissue. Pulling back, I smiled and watched his face contort as my hand circled his cock, squeezing rhythmically. He groaned, and it sent a wave of heat to my core, desire pooling between my thighs. It made me bold, wanton. Free.

"I can give this to you," I whispered against his open mouth and then licked along the curve of his lip. God, the man was sexy. Everything about him screamed fuck me. And boy did I want to.

Looking behind me, I made sure the door was shut and that the blinds of the window were closed. The doctor had just been here. It was unlikely that Hank would need to be seen again so soon. We had a little time but not much.

"Don't you think we're moving a little fast, angel?" His voice was laced with desire. I could tell suggesting we slow down was hard for him, but so charming and chivalrous. It made me want him more.

I closed my eyes for a moment, weighing the options, but continued to stroke his cock up and down in slow, calculated movements. He groaned and I searched his eyes.

"Do you think I'm a whore for wanting to pleasure you?" I wasn't sure if I'd asked for his benefit or mine. Wanting to please him so quickly after only knowing him a short time was unlike me. It was bold and daring in ways I'd never been before.

His response was immediate and righteous. "Hell, no! You're the most beautiful woman I've ever seen and your kisses taste like fucking candy. I can't get enough of you. You want to touch me, darlin', I'm all yours."

Holding back would be too much. My entire body

thrummed and quaked with lust, with the desire to please him. I needed to feel him in my hand, in my mouth. I kissed him hard, and our tongues tangled as we drank from one another. He tasted of mint tea, refreshing and delicious.

His large hand cupped my breast through my blouse, thumb sliding along the tight peak, making it pebble and ache. He swallowed my moan with his mouth as I arched into his palm. I dug my hand just under the blanket to get closer to his heat. When my hand met bare-naked skin, a fresh rush of desire shot straight to my core. Hank's cock was quite possibly the softest thing I'd ever touched and as smooth as satin. All rational thought was leaving my brain, hell, leaving the building. Right now, all I could think about was getting closer, getting my hands on more of his body.

"Jesus, angel," he groaned and sank his teeth into my lip.

His kisses turned my insides to jelly. With slow strokes of his thick length, we continued to kiss at length, learning what one another liked best. Just as the knobbed crown of his head wept and I'd swirled my thumb around the sensitive tip to drive him crazy, my phone started ringing.

"Fuck!" Hank cursed.

The incessant noise was like a beacon, calling back my sanity. *What the hell was I doing?* The professional in me scoffed at what I was doing, had done, in broad day light with a man I'd known for two seconds.

Dazed, I jumped off the bed and away from Hank's warmth. Distance between us right now was a good thing. With one hand, I righted my clothing while the other fumbled for the phone. Heat suffused the skin of my cheeks, and I knew they would be bright red. Regardless of my embarrassment, I couldn't control the huge grin that split across my face. Giddiness swept through me in waves. It was official; I had lost my ever-loving mind.

"Aspen, are you still at the hospital?"

"Yes." Lying would never work with Ollie. He knew me too well.

"It's almost eleven, and you have a meeting with the stakeholders for *Bright Magazine* to discuss the issue from yesterday. Remember, the possibilities of a setback on the project?"

"There will be no setback. That building will be done as promised. We'll do whatever it takes. I'll discuss it with Hank, determine what our next steps need to be in his absence."

Hank's gaze followed me as I paced the room. "Are you going to make it here on time?" Oliver asked.

I looked down at my watch. It would take fifteen minutes to discuss the concern with Hank and at least another twenty minutes to get to AIR headquarters. "My driver's here at the hospital. I'll have him take me shortly. I'll be there for the meeting. Just make our guests comfortable until I arrive." I rang off with Oliver.

"What's the problem with the project? Saw my guys yesterday. They said the accident was contained." Hank's concern was evident.

"Depends on how confident you are in your crew's ability to continue without you. Do you have any idea who will serve as foreman in your absence?"

He lifted his hand to his chin and scrubbed it across his face. The sound of those calluses connecting with the newly grown stubble was intoxicating. I craved to run my tongue along its rough edge.

"If you keep looking at me like that, angel, you won't be making it to any meetings today, and I'll discharge myself against medical advice."

"You wouldn't dare!" The man was insane!

"Oh, but I would. I've been sweet on you for a lot longer than you know." His grin was dangerous. Made me believe he was serious.

"That won't be necessary. I think we can both behave like civilized human beings."

"Is that what they call it when a sexy woman jacks off a man in a hospital bed…civilized? Well, almost jacked me off. Seems as though we got some unfinished business to attend to." His laugh echoed through the room as he pumped his hips in the air. He was still hard as a rock and oh so tempting.

No! Not going to happen. Not now. I have to go. I rolled my eyes but couldn't help the smirk on my face. He had a point. Instead of rationalizing what we did, I made an agreement with myself to not psychoanalyze it and just go with it. If I thought about it too much, embarrassment and shame would ruin the uninhibited moment we'd shared.

"Hank, seriously, I need an answer." He had to realize that it was my responsibility to assure the stakeholders that the project would continue unchanged, even after the accident. "Do you think your crew can handle the job without you to stay on top of them?"

"I do. I told Mac yesterday to serve as foreman on the project in the interim. In the next week, I'll check on the guys, make sure everything is going as planned. Mac is a good worker and I trust him." His tone was firm and confident.

"Okay, sounds good. Do you think the project will be set back from the break in the crane and the pipes falling?" I shivered visibly at the memory of those metal spikes falling through the sky like acidic rain.

"No, we have backup options for cranes, and I'd ordered plenty of materials. I'll work with Mac to determine any delays and touch base with the architect. My men will work overtime to pick up any slack." I could see the wheels turning in that beautiful head of his. A rush of admiration swept through me as I took in his tired face and bandaged body. He was here because of me. My heart swelled, bringing forth feelings I had no business having about this man.

I grabbed his phone off the side table and programmed in my phone numbers. "Please call or text me when you've heard from your contact. I'm going to meet with the stakeholders for the magazine that's going to be housed in that building when it's finished."

"A magazine, eh? What about?"

"Fashion, movies, television."

"So, a smut mag then?" His face screwed into a grimace.

"No, not like a tabloid rag. This magazine will take readers to a thirty-thousand-foot view of making movies, the actors playing in them, television producers, writers, fashion designers and their newest trends, the up and coming hopefuls in each category. Things like that." He looked bored already. "Probably not your taste."

"You're my taste." He licked his lips seductively. Damned if another rush of heat didn't pulsate through my body, landing right between my thighs. His words did things to me. The sultry grin on his face proved he knew the effect he had.

"You're bad, Mr. Jensen." I grinned and tried to pretend I didn't love every second of his crassness.

"Oh, so we're back to formality, I see. As long as you remember that you just had your pretty little fingers wrapped around my cock but good." His lips twisted into a grin, and he gripped his manhood over the blanket for emphasis. "You think about that while you're meeting with the suits today." He flashed a wicked smile. I inhaled deeply, thinking back to my hand firmly gripping his manhood.

I wanted more. To see, taste, and suck every inch of his thickness. Moisture slicked my sex, and I knew I had to get out of here and off to work before I did something worse than palm his goods. It was impossible to leave without one more taste of him.

His eyes were as green as the finest emeralds as his gaze looked me over. I could imagine we were both thinking the same thing. Sauntering over to him, I covered his mouth in a deep kiss, biting then sucking his tongue. I nipped each lip, tugging on his full bottom one, and then pulled away. It released with an audible plop. He chased my mouth with his as I stood out of reach.

"And *you* think about *that* for the rest of the day, Mr. Jensen."

"Oh, angel, I'll think of nothing else," I heard him say as I sashayed out the door, swinging my hips a little more than usual.

CHAPTER FOUR

"Thank God that's over." For the last five hours, I had survived off Starbucks and the memory of what I'd done with Hank this morning to keep me going. No breaks, no lunch just meeting after meeting. I hated to admit it, but I missed my cowboy.

My cowboy. Shit. Thinking of the man with the word "my" anywhere near it was not good. My mother was going to have a conniption when she found out the man was staying in my home. If she only knew what her perfect little socialite did today, in a public hospital room, she'd be mortified. If she found out the dirty things I planned on doing with Hank, it would be worse. The part of my body governing my actions wasn't my mind right now—it was centered farther south. The emptiness I felt not being in his presence messed with my head. Getting back to the hospital was priority number one.

We made our way back through the cubicle farm to the long row of offices. Mine was at the end and took up a tenth of the entire floor. Oliver's space was also large. He had a huge antique U-shaped desk that cut in front of the double doors to my office like a sentinel. No one got through to me without him knowing it. Ever. I preferred it that way, and he took the role very seriously.

Each member of our team knew Oliver had the second most important position in the company. Even my Chief

Operating Officer knew his place when it came to Oliver. He might have the professional second-in-command title, but Oliver held my loyalty and trust. He just had a way with people. He knew what every department was doing, kept me posted on the inner workings, ensured the relationships internally and externally were on par with my corporate philosophy, and was well respected in his role. "You never cease to amaze me, Pen," Oliver praised.

"How so?" I asked.

"You just own it. All those powerful men in that room, you being the only female. You weren't the slightest bit intimidated. Didn't even faze you." He shook his head and smiled.

"It helps when you have more money in your bank account than all of them combined." I grinned, appreciating my wealth for what it was: a means to get what I wanted in life. Of course, now I wanted something a little more visceral, and tall, with skin the color of brown sugar.

"Yeah, but the way you handled Grant Campbell—that was priceless. I wish I could have taken a picture of him when he cornered you and said he missed you and you nailed him," he chuckled.

"Heard all that, huh?"

"Oh yeah. I also heard you ask him how his skank of the week was doing. I did a mental touchdown dance on your behalf."

"I did no such thing. You're putting words in my mouth." I sighed. This was the longest day in history. Memories of my fingers firmly locked around Hank's cock flashed through my mind like a wicked porno reminding me of where I wanted to be right now.

"Okay, maybe I'm embellishing a bit. You did ask him how the tart was doing."

"That I did." I smiled, remembering Grant's smug look when he told me he missed me, and couldn't get the image of me under him out of his head. That's when I asked him how Cynthia was doing.

"Yeah, but you sold it when you came up and mentioned that Hank's things had been completely moved into my penthouse." I nudged his elbow with mine. Grant looked like he'd been stabbed. The mere thought that I had moved on from him, a self-proclaimed "amazing catch" brutalized his ego. I enjoyed every second of his tortured disgraced face.

"I thought that was a nice touch." He blew on his knuckles and then rubbed them across the lapel of his blazer.

I rushed into my office to grab my things so I could get back to the hospital. The prickling twitches to be near Hank, to see him on the mend, was at the forefront of my mind. If I didn't get to the hospital soon, I would most definitely explode from the tension. Just his text earlier stating that everything was set with the new foreman sent butterflies through my belly.

"Aspen! You're okay!" I heard the words two seconds before the life was being physically crushed out of me. A sheet of dark hair smacked against my face. The smell of cinnamon encompassed the space, leaving no doubt as to who held me in a bone-crushing embrace.

"London, what are you doing here?"

My sister's gray-blue eyes searched mine, tears welling in her beautiful gaze. "You could have died!"

"Who told you?" My eyes darted over to Oliver's.

His answering fake whistle indicated his guilt. He swayed from heel to toe and back again looking everywhere but at me, then suddenly down at his watch. "Looks like that's my cue. See you in the morning, princess."

He scampered out of my office so fast I could almost see the tail tucked between his legs. Right then and there, he earned a solid payback for this and the white lie about the donation to the children's ward the other day. He knew not to share details like yesterday's accident with London. She didn't do well with emergency situations or accidents.

London's fingers slid all over my face, her eyes assessing me rapidly, looking for any nuance, anything out of the norm. They landed on my shirt, and her fingers tugged at the blouse that covered the ugly bruise, the only remnants that I was in an accident at all.

Her hand went to her lips at the sight of the black–and–purplish mark, her mouth opened into a gasp, tears filling her eyes like a water balloon that had been overfilled. "Oh. My. God. Aspen, you were hurt." The tears fell down her face, and she pulled me into a tight hug. I soothed my hands up and down her back, letting her connect with me, giving her time to realize I was here and just fine. Her history with accidents didn't have a happy ending like mine.

"I'm fine. A man jumped in front of me. He saved my life, but not without paying a price. He's in the hospital now and I need to get to him."

"Oh my, yes, of course. Is he okay?" She still held my biceps and smoothed her hands up and down my arms.

"He received the brunt of the damage. A pipe pierced through is shoulder when he tackled me. He saved my life." The enormity of the situation, hearing my voice tell her what happened shot more anxiety through me. I needed to get to Hank. Confirm once more that he was okay.

"What's his prognosis?" she asked, genuinely concerned.

"He's going to be fine. A lot of therapy, weeks of healing time. I'm moving him into the penthouse, so he can receive round-the-clock care. Least I could do considering." I tried to pull away, but she embraced me once more.

"Pen, if I'd lost you too, I don't know what… I couldn't bear it. I just…"

I hugged her tight, enjoying her warmth and love. "I'm here. I'm not going anywhere. But I really do need to get to the hospital. He's waiting for me."

She nodded against my shoulder, then stopped abruptly and pulled back. Her pointed gaze searched mine. She tilted her head, her eyes widened, and her mouth split into a huge smile.

"Holy shit, Pen. You're falling for this guy!"

The comment threw me back as if someone had just socked me. "What the hell are you talking about? I'm not falling in love. Your cuckoo radar is off. You need to adjust the setting again."

God, I was so tired of this thing she had with empathy. This unearthly ability to feel what others were feeling. It really was freaky and generally dead on target. Ability or not, I wasn't falling for Hank. I'd barely just met the man. What she was feeling was not love it was fear. Fear that he wouldn't get better. Guilt that it was my fault he was hurt in the first place.

She shook her head. Her once teary eyes alight with pure joy. "I can feel it. The desire in you. It's thrumming around your body like a soft halo of light. Who is he?"

No, no, no. When London got an idea in her head, she committed to it one hundred percent. She claimed to have this empathic ability and lived her life by it. I'll concede that she was more often right than wrong, but really, besides the fear and guilt, what I felt for Hank was not complicated. She was alluding to the idea that my desire for Hank was something more, something likened to love, perhaps. It wasn't. Unless one mistakes pure unadulterated lust for the hearts and flowers thing of love. If I was being honest with myself I felt things for Hank, deep things, but all of them revolved around us being tangled together naked on the nearest bed.

"London, I'm not in love. Don't even go there. Please, please don't worry about this. I'm fine. Hank's going to be fine..."

"Hank? Is that his name?" She smiled brightly. She was incredibly beautiful and had a way of getting what she wanted. People just spilled their guts to her. It was part of what made her so good at what she did with her clients— moving in with them for weeks, and then deciding exactly what they needed to make their houses into a home. It was more than just interior design or decorating. She had a way of filling a void in her clients lives with whatever it is they needed to be happy and she'd made a very profitable career out of it.

"Okay, okay." She waited patiently for me to answer. "I have a little bit of hero-worship. He's incredibly attractive and we've shared a few kisses. All right? End of story. Now, if you'll excuse me, I have to go."

She nodded. "Yes, you have to get back to Hank. Oh, this is so romantic." She clasped her hands together and looked off into the distance dreamily. "He saves you from death, sweeps you off your feet and…"

"Stop it right there. This is not a romance." I sighed. The woman would piss off a priest in confessional.

"But you want to fuck him; I can feel the lust running through every inch of you. It's coming at me in waves. I might have to go get laid tonight just to get over the vibe you're putting out into the universe."

"Must you be so vulgar?"

"Yes. I must. Admit it and I'll leave." She crossed her arms over her tiny form.

I rolled my eyes and took a deep breath. "Okay, I want to have sex with him! It's been months since Grant and I broke up. Happy now?"

She jumped up and down in her sandals, her flowery dress waving in the air with her. It was times like this that I remembered she was my baby sister. Top of her game in the interior design world with a waiting list a mile long for her skills, but she still bounced around like a little girl. Some things never changed.

"Very happy. So, this man, is he hot?"

"You're killing me. Yes, he's good-looking. He's a cowboy from Texas. But it's not going anywhere. We are from two totally different worlds. He's used to barbeques and baseball, not mergers and acquisitions."

Her mouth pulled together into a pout. "When you find your soul mate, it won't matter what he does for a living, or what he wears, or whether his portfolio is as sound as yours. It only matters that he's meant for you."

A sadness blanketed the moment. London had lost the man who she thought was her soul mate to a terrible accident. I pulled her into a hug and she squeezed me tightly.

"I love you so much. I'm so relieved you're okay," she whispered.

"I love you, too."

"I'm looking forward to thanking this real-life hero in person." She wiped at her wet eyes. Still as pretty as ever. "Oliver told me how Hank jumped in front of you and now that I see where you were hurt, I'm more confident in his place in your world."

"Oh yeah, and what's that?" I asked, pulling my bag over my shoulder headed for the door.

"Isn't it obvious?" She smiled wide and her entire face lit up. "He's meant to protect your heart!"

I rolled my eyes for her benefit only. The thing was she wasn't entirely wrong. There was something about Hank that I couldn't define. It was just a feeling when I was near him. It had to be that I was overly sensitive to him after he saved my life. Superhero syndrome of sorts. There really wasn't another reason. Love wasn't on the table or in the cards no matter what London's empathic ability suggested.

★ ★ ★ ★

All I could think about all damned day was my sweet angel's fingers wrapped around my cock. I could die a happy man with that memory to sustain me through eternity. The woman was talented.

Fantasies of me standing, her sitting on the bed, me slipping my cock past her moist lips pressing deep, my dick ready to burst at the seams, rolled through my thoughts all day. Her sucking me like a fucking Hoover, my hands twining through her golden locks as I pumped my seed into her. *Christ!* It was the stuff right out of my most erotic dreams.

I closed my eyes and tried to will away the images, my heart rate slowly coming back down from my thoughts. The meds were finally giving me some relief without making me feel like I was drugged. A pretty angel in white fluttered across my thoughts relaxing me further...

A clacking noise woke me. I craned my neck and looked over toward the sound, realizing I must have drifted off. Aspen sat in the chair next to my bed, blazer removed, eyes glued to her laptop. Her blond hair was piled on top of her head in a bun-like contraption resembling a donut. She had thin black reading glasses perched on her small nose. Her legs were crossed; her skirt had ridden high on her thigh, giving me a healthy view of her long legs encased in sheer black stockings. My angel looked like a sexy secretary.

Every so often, she nibbled on a sandwich. Watching her work and eat, her mind laser-focused on the task in front of her, was a lovely sight. Everything about her pulled at my being, from the wisps of hair falling along her exposed neck to the ticking of her heel as she typed.

It made me wish my shoulder weren't in such a state, or I'd have already claimed that woman physically, and hopefully emotionally. I didn't want her the way I'd used my recent flings. She wasn't the type of woman I could just use to get off. I wanted to know things about her, connect with her on a different plane. See where it led.

"You know what they say about all work and no play, right, darlin'?"

She grinned, but finished typing whatever she was

working on. "I didn't hear you complaining about my playtime this morning."

The morning's activities flooded my mind. She continued to pound at the keyboard, and bit her lip. I waited until she clicked a few more buttons and closed the screen. Her almond-shaped eyes met mine, glasses still in place.

"Darlin', you could bring a man to his knees wearing those things." I gestured to her specs.

She smiled and crossed her legs, reclining in the chair. She made no move to approach me. "How was your day, stud?"

Stud? Hmm. I liked her pet name. Hadn't had a woman give me one in a while. It felt good. Hell, it felt great.

"Can't complain. You?"

She blew a breath over her forehead. "It was fine." Her lips thinned as if she were making a decision. Then her expression changed, softened. "Not as good as my morning though," she added with a saucy little pout.

"Yeah, well, anytime you want a repeat, angel, I'm all yours." My eyebrow cocked and she answered with her own pointed brow.

"How's the shoulder?"

"On the mend. How were the suits regarding the build?"

"I handled it. They're back to believing everything is right on point. So when you check in with your foreman, let him know I plan to pay a visit to the crew, express our gratitude over their willingness to continue the project to completion and on deadline."

"Good plan. Now, are we done talking about work?"

She smiled. "Yes. We should talk about the plans for

your release tomorrow."

I shook my head. "Come here."

"Hank," she said in warning.

I pointed my finger at her and then down to the space on the bed next to me. "Come. Here. Now." Her eyebrows rose, but I held firm.

She stood and I reached for her hand. Gripping her wrist, I pulled her close enough that I could grab the back of her nape and crush her lips to mine. She moaned and I ate up every sound. Our tongues mingled slow and unhurried. Kissing her was like coming home. The feelings were hard to explain.

Being with her was comfortable, safe, the only place you ever wanted to be, with the added benefit of all encompassing lust and need. I didn't want to think about how it could be like this. So easy, so fast. It just felt right.

After minutes of kissing her into oblivion, her body slack against mine, I leaned my forehead against hers and tried to catch my breath. She was just as winded.

"Now, angel, how was your day? Really? I think you skipped over some parts earlier."

She groaned. "Awful. It took hours to convince the stakeholders that we were going to be fine, and one in particular was ruthless."

"Just a bunch of pricks with dicks." I kissed the side of her face along the hairline. "Now tell me why one of them was worse than the others?"

"Because he's my ex and I'm stuck working with him. He put a large sum of money into the magazine start-up when we were together. Bad idea to mix business with pleasure, I guess." Her eyes met mine. She tried to push off me, her face twisting into a grimace. I held tight, my grip relentless.

"Nuh-uh. You ain't runnin' from me, angel. We have a deal. Two dates."

The tension in her body visibly relaxed, her shoulders sagged. Her body melted against mine once more as she nodded into my neck. Her smell was all around me. Vanilla and honey. I inhaled deeply, contentment filling my pores. "I love the way you smell."

She pulled up and sat her heart-shaped ass on the edge of my bed. In my half-reclined position, I moved over as far as I could to the opposite edge of the bed, making sure not to jostle my shoulder too much. She sat and tentatively leaned against my chest and the good shoulder. "Is this okay?"

"Better than anything," I whispered. This small woman fit so perfectly in the crook of my arm, like she was made for me.

"Tell me about you, Hank. I hardly know anything."

Her face snuggled into my chest, her cheek planted against the bare skin. My good arm cradled her. I yanked on the rubber band holding up her hair, letting the waves of silk fall over her shoulder. It eased my pain to have her so near. Running my fingers through the strands of her hair calmed and soothed me. I had a sneaking suspicion it did the same for her. She took a deep breath and relaxed deeper into my chest. Her small fingers rested over my heart. Once more I thanked God I was able to reach her in time.

"How about we start with the basics?" She nodded. "Okay. Family first. Mom is Julia, and Dad is Henry. They are retired cattle ranchers. My brother, Heath, now runs the family business with his wife, Jess. They have twin boys, Holt and Hunter. They're four and putting my brother through the wringer. I love every minute of it." Thinking of Heath and the boys made me chuckle.

She joined in laughing lightly. "So all of the men in your family are named with an 'H' I see?"

I smiled and rubbed my chin against the top of her head. "Yes, ma'am. Old Man Henry likes it that way. And what Dad wants, Dad gets." She smirked. "What about you, darlin'?"

"Well, my father is William Reynolds. My mother is Vivian Bright-Reynolds."

"Why would she hyphenate her name?"

"Because she comes from a very well-to-do family. It's customary in our circles. My name is hyphenated, too. Technically, I'm Aspen Isabel Bright-Reynolds. My mother insisted on all of her children having her maiden name included on their birth certificates."

"Different strokes for different folks, I guess. Will you change it when you get married or will you have five names?" Seemed ridiculous to have so many names.

"I don't know. Depends on the marriage." She tapped her fingers on my chest. "Then I have my baby sister, London, who's an interior designer and my older brother, Rio, who's huge in real estate."

"Aspen, London, and Rio?"

She smiled and nodded. "My parents named us each after the place they were vacationing at when they found out they were pregnant. It's actually the only sweet story I know about their love. They've never been the happiest couple." She seemed to burrow in closer when she spoke of her family.

I tightened my grip on her small form. "I'm sorry."

"It's okay. I've been very fortunate. Never wanted for anything growing up. Went to the best schools. I used my trust fund to start my company, and now I'm bigger in business than they ever dreamed."

I cupped her shoulder and squeezed her tighter. Being with her like this was comfortable. Easy. It had been a long time since I felt such ease holding a woman. She sighed and nuzzled her nose into my chest. The movement sent tingles rushing through my body, and the deep wall around my heart started to crack and shake, small starbursts of light peeked through the crumbling foundation. "They must be very proud of you."

"Not really."

"Why not? Your company is doing well. You've made a name for yourself. And you're drop-dead gorgeous." I patted then squeezed her fanny for emphasis.

"Hank!" She laughed but didn't remove my hand. "No, it's just—they didn't want me to be as successful as I am. They wanted me to marry someone successful, have perfect little high-society brats, and attend charity functions with Mother."

I cringed and my lips twisted into a snarl.

"Exactly!"

"Our parents always have one idea or another for us, but we rarely go that route. Take me for example. Old Man Henry wanted both his boys to take over the business. Technically, I own fifty percent of it, but instead, I opened up Jensen Construction. I'd rather spend my time building new things than herding and selling cattle."

"So what did your dad say?"

"He was honest, darlin'. Told me he was disappointed, but respected my decision to go after my dream, not his."

"Sounds like a great guy, your dad."

"The best." My dad was the best around. He worked hard for his family and rightly deserved the retirement he now enjoyed. A little old-fashioned but so was any good Southern man at his age and station in life.

"Oh, I don't know about that." She smiled coyly. Her hand rubbed along my bare chest. "There's only one guy sitting on a pedestal for me right now." She planted a kiss against my peck. She flicked her tongue against the nipple and bit down on the tender nub. The pleasure-pain went straight to my shaft. I groaned loud.

"I'm sorry, but I can't help myself. You're so...so... I don't know. I just, I want you." First time I'd ever heard her struggle to speak, and it was music to my ears. Knowing that she was just as affected by my presence as I was with hers, made me ache to have her.

"The feelin' is mutual, angel. There's nothin' I want more than to hear you scream out my name when you come, but this is not the place. Once I have you naked, there'll be no turning back, and I'll need a bed and a full night to do it right." I lifted her chin with one finger and planted a quick kiss on her lips. "Now you need to go home and get some rest. You have a man moving in tomorrow." I winked and her corresponding smile melted my heart.

CHAPTER FIVE

"Wake up, princess." Oliver's singsong voice broke through the haze of sleep. "We have to go save your prince from the evils of public healthcare and bring him back to the castle. I'll be in your closet picking out your clothes. You have ten minutes!"

I groaned and pulled the blanket over my head. Oliver had always been a morning person. I wasn't. On top of that, the combination of lack of sleep and sexual frustration had taken its toll. I'd never been swept away with lust before. Did I like sex? Yes. Who didn't? Did I need it? On occasion, sure. With Hank, my skin was literally leaping off my body to be next to the man. It seemed as if the only thing that would take the edge off was having his big body pressing me into the closest mattress. Preferably soon.

Needing someone for anything was new to me. I'd worked my ass off to make sure the only person I needed was the face in the mirror. Oliver and my sister were the only real human ties I had or cared about. I valued the people I worked with and the individuals I employed but never let them get too close. People who claimed to be my friends came and went. Hell, even my own mother and brother I could do without, most days. Sounded harsh, but my mother saw me as a disappointment, and my brother saw me as a challenge.

Even with all my success, I'd never been able to fit into my parents perfect high-society mold. I played the part well enough. Went to the functions, knew which fork went with what food, dressed appropriately. Yet I still never fit in. The only place I'd ever been comfortable was at the head of a conference room table, planning, organizing and delegating. Being in control of my life and my company was top priority.

And therein lay the problem with Hank. He made me feel things I'd never felt. Want to do things I wouldn't normally do. He brought out a reckless side that was unfamiliar, somewhat dangerous. For the first time in my life, I was nervous, uncertain about my footing. Walking into uncharted territory willingly.

"Up and at 'em!" Oliver cooed. He ripped the blanket off my body and tossed it to the floor leaving me bare-assed naked. Before I had the chance to complain, he had me up and out of bed and into the bathroom. "Now make yourself pretty for our cowboy." His grin was loaded with excitement. He practically hopped from foot to foot.

"Our cowboy? I wonder how Hank would feel about a gay man sizing him up?"

"Don't know, don't care. He's as much mine as he is yours." He grabbed a towel from the linen closet. "What's yours is mine and what's mine is mine, too!" He was in a saucy mood this morning.

Butch, Hank's dog, entered the bathroom and walked over to the toilet. I'd forgotten he was here until he leaned over the bowl and proceeded to take messy slurps. Water sloshed all over the lid. Oliver and I watched the dog with matching horrified expressions. After two days of being around Butch, nothing surprised me about the animal.

He'd already pissed off Gustav by digging in the trash and spreading it through the kitchen. Gustav asked me to board the dog or he'd quit. I gave him a raise and told him to deal with the mutt.

"You know, I read an article somewhere that dogs don't understand why their owners won't let them drink out of the toilet because to them it's like a big margarita bowl!" He tipped his head to the side as he watched the dog drink his cocktail.

"That's just sick. Now get out and tell Gustav that I'd like a cappuccino to go for me and one for Hank. I'd also like half a bagel with cream cheese, please. Oh, and make sure he feeds Butch."

"Yes, princess. Your wish is my command." He headed toward the door as I stepped into the shower.

"No, my wish is your job. One you get paid damn well for!" I yelled over the water cascading down my back. "And take the dog with you!" The hot water soothed my aching muscles. I heard Oliver fighting with Butch just outside the room. He didn't care for Oliver. Though he seemed to be fine with me as long as I gave him a good petting before bed and again when I got home. I'd actually started to take a liking to the mangy animal. He was sweet in a slobbery and hairy way.

I finished my shower and threw on the matching black lace bra, underwear, and stockings Oliver had left on the bed. Glancing in the freestanding mirror, I inspected my form. I worked hard to stay in shape. My legs, arms, and abs were all toned, belly flat. I was proud of the defined indent in my biceps. Nothing too bulky, but strong and feminine at the same time. My breasts were large but perky for their size.

I turned around to view my backside, relishing in the fact that my bum was tight and firm. It was my sexiest feature, and the panties with the scallop-trimmed edge were doing wonders for my confidence. If Hank did end up seeing me in this, I think he'd be pleased.

I slipped on a royal-blue dress that hugged every curve. It was plain in the front with a scoop neck and fitted bodice. The back had an exposed zipper encased in leather running down the entire seam. Oliver called it the "business in the front, party in the back" dress.

As I put my makeup on, Oliver came in and gestured for me to sit in the vanity chair. He twisted my hair into a complex system of knots and swirls, every so often adding a bobby pin to hold a piece in place. The man was a sheer genius at styling me. He knew exactly what looked good, knew my sizes to perfection, and was able to create an updo masterpiece.

He put one last bobby pin in place and handed me a mirror. "There, perfect."

"Looks great, as usual. You constantly amaze me."

His return smile was huge, spreading across crisp flawless skin. Oliver was good-looking in a pretty boy way. "Thank you. Now what are we going to do about the cowboy? I've fixed up the spare room, put away all of his clothes, and set up his toiletries in the bathroom. For a man planning on staying for two more months, he doesn't have a lot with him." His eyes scrunched up thoughtfully, thin lips pinched together in thought.

"Well, he's a man."

"So am I, and I would have traveled with five times as much as he has. It didn't even fill the closet or drawers." His expression was shocked, bordering on horrified. "I think I'm going to have to get him a few things. He has one button-down long-sleeved shirt, one tie, and one blazer. That's it!"

I smiled and thought about how manly Hank was. He didn't worry about clothing or dressing to the nines. Frankly, I couldn't care less. The fewer clothes he wore the better, in my book.

"So buy him more clothing if it makes you feel better. Maybe take him shopping when he's up to it."

Oliver's eyes lit up like the sun peeking through on a cloudy day to spread its rays of light in every direction. He clasped his hands together and spun around on one toe in a perfect circle. "Oh, my very own personal man doll." His shoulders squeezed together in excitement.

"Not something you want to say to Hank. He's liable to punch you in the face for suggesting you want to play Barbies using him as your personal Ken doll." I tried to hide my grin.

His eyes went wide, nostrils flared. "You think he'd punch me in the face? Seriously?"

"Um, no." My laugh sounded loud echoing off the bathroom walls. "Now let's go. I need to get him settled and then head to AIR for a meeting this afternoon."

We made it to the hospital in record time. I tried to ignore the butterflies in my belly and the jackhammering of my heart. The moment I opened the door to Hank's room all the nerves dissipated. He stood at the hospital mirror combing his dark hair, dressed in a pair of low-hanging sweats that accentuated his lean hips and firm muscular thighs.

From the back, his white T-shirt stretched across a set of

shoulders wide enough to be a professional football player's. The bandaged shoulder and left arm were held to his chest in a blue sling. Beautiful honeyed-green eyes caught mine in the reflection in the mirror. His face split into a wide grin showing white, even teeth. He was clean-shaven and his hair damp as he slicked the pieces back.

"Mornin', angel."

"Morning, stud. You ready to break out of here?"

He turned around and smiled. "I reckon' there's just one thing I need before we jet out."

He didn't have much with him. I looked around the room for anything that seemed out of place. In a few strides, he stood in front of me large and looming. He palmed the back of my neck, and dug his fingers into my hairline. In seconds, his lips devoured mine.

My hands went around his form cautiously, mindful of his wounded side. Slick strands wet my fingers as I gripped his hair, bringing his face to mine in the process. A growl emanated from his throat as he nipped and tugged at my lips. Liquid heat boiled at the surface between my thighs.

I heard the door open and close behind us. "Holy shit, down, cowboy!" Oliver chastised.

Hank pulled away and petted my cheek with his thumb. "I like your dress." The comment held a gentleness I hadn't expected from such a hulking man. He seemed more the caveman type. One who would grip a woman by the hair, drag her off to his cave, and have his wicked way with her.

The care with which Hank held me close made me feel cherished, special in a way I wasn't used to. It was obvious in how he looked at me as if I was the only woman in the world. The gentle way he caressed my face proved that he was affected by me. Thank God I wasn't the only one whose world was tipping on its axis.

He kissed my lips briefly once more and looked over at Oliver. He gave Oliver a pointed look. "When a man is kissing his woman, it would be best if you didn't interrupt."

His woman. Oh boy.

★ ★ ★ ★

Along the ride to her house, I chastised myself for being so forward and sticking my foot in my mouth. Calling her my woman could have gone to the shitter. Real quick like. It was as if I'd forgotten to apply a filter. I feared I might have played my hand with her too soon. Never a good idea to go for broke when you're not sure your opponent is ready to fold.

With Aspen, I didn't really know what her thoughts were about this thing between us. It was happening fast with no brakes in sight. When she wasn't near, I wanted her to be. When she was near, I couldn't get close enough. If this busted wing weren't in the way, I'd already have her pinned to the nearest bed.

I'd never lacked the company of a woman, a warm body to lie with on a cold Texas night. But with Aspen, there was something more. The filly made my bones feel weak and my chest tight. An ache hung at the pit of my stomach. A woman had never jumbled up my thoughts more than the blond goddess.

Her home was at the top of a skyscraper. Central Park could be seen from her balcony along with an open view of New York City.

The place was modern but comfortable. Art hung over the stark white walls like a museum. Matching white marble floors gleamed across the large expanse. Area rugs were scattered throughout, breaking up the spaces like mismatched puzzle pieces. She definitely didn't lack any modern conveniences. Top of the line entertainment equipment, media room, plush furniture that looked like it should have been on the cover of a home design magazine. The more I looked around the more I realized how different we were. She lived in the lap of luxury. I lived on a ranch that had tattered old furniture, walls of books, and sports paraphernalia.

"Nice digs." My mouth twisted in a smile I wasn't sure she'd believe. I don't know what I expected, but the woman was rich. As in *beaucoup* bucks. I'd never even been in a place that fancy. It was as if every piece of furniture was perfectly placed and nothing out of order. There was no clutter or much in the way of trinkets. Magazines were displayed like fans on different tables.

Before she could respond, I heard the familiar clicking sound I looked forward to after a hard day's work. Butch ran as fast as his hind legs could carry him. He plowed into me, almost knocking me on my ass. He spun in a circle, so I crouched down to pet him on the head and gave my boy some lovin' while he licked my face.

"Oh, good boy. Missed you, Butch. Were you a good boy for Aspen? Yes, I bet you were. I love you, too, buddy."

His long pink tongue gave me one final lick along the entire side of my face. Aspen cringed and grimaced. Then the craziest thing happened. Butch left my side, ran over to Aspen, and rubbed against her legs.

"All right, boy, but no kisses this time!" She petted Butch, scratching her nails along his neck. He curved into her side. I looked at her in shock. Her gaze caught mine. "What?"

"Butch likes you?" I couldn't believe it.

"Yeah, we've become friends the last couple days. He leaves me be as long as I give him attention in the morning when we wake, and then again each time I come home."

"He sleeps with you?" No fucking way.

"Not with me. That's gross. He sleeps at the foot of my bed. Why so shocked?"

"Because Butch hates women. Except Ma and my sister-in-law, Jess, and that took some time."

"Oh, no, he doesn't. Do you, boy?" She petted him on the head some more and smiled down at the yellow lab. Butch preened up at her. I could relate. She was something to feast your eyes on.

"Well, I'll be damned. You continue to amaze me, darlin'."

The situation was interesting and unexpected. My dog really didn't like the ladies. Every time I brought a woman back to the ranch, he would growl and scare the daylights out of her until they would beg me to put him outside. Usually, I would do my business with the lady and then take her home. Butch was more important than a roll in the hay to get my rocks off. Figured if the women were one-night stand type of ladies then they should be okay with not staying over once the deed was done. Worked most the time. Once in a while, I'd have to deal with a clinger. I'd just cut 'em loose right quick and carry on about my business. They eventually got the hint.

Aspen continued to show me around the mansion masquerading as a penthouse. Why someone who lived alone needed so much space was beyond me. She stopped at the door closest to the master bedroom.

"And this is your room for the next eight weeks."

I entered the room and sat on the bed, bouncing it a few times. It was big, with a blue comforter. The room was decked out in a nautical theme. Not my taste, but it didn't really matter. I planned on hanging my hat in her bedroom, anyway.

"How much time you think I'll be sleeping in this bed?" I wiggled my eyebrows at her seductively.

She cocked her head and grinned. "Where, pray tell, do you think you'll be sleeping?"

"Don't be coy, angel. I'm guessing I'll be in here, what? Two nights tops, before I have you lying out under me, begging for me to make you come again."

"Again?"

"Oh yeah. I'm going to pleasure you in ways you've only imagined."

From my spot on the bed, I could see her eyes dilate, her hands curl into fists. "Pretty sure of yourself. For a man with a wounded shoulder, you sure talk a good game." She was acting coy, but her breath sped up, her hands tightened at her sides, and she nibbled on her pink lips. My guess is she was imagining what I'd do to her and gettin' turned on in the process.

I stood up and towered over her petite form. Gripping her hip, I hauled her against my straining cock. She gasped when I rotated my pelvis against her belly. Tingles of pleasure ripped through me. She moaned and wet her lips again.

"Do you feel what you do to me? Just being near you?" She nodded. "When you're ready to do something about it, you let me know."

Her hands cupped my neck and her lips slanted over mine. The kiss was wild. Deep strokes of her tongue against mine had the steel pipe between my thighs reaching toward her, painfully hard. My right hand gripped her ass, grinding her more fully against my aching need.

The pressure was perfect. I breathed into her mouth. That sexy little body of hers slithered along mine, trying to gain friction where she wanted it most. I pulled her back until I felt the mattress behind me, then I sat.

She leaned down and sucked on my tongue, nipping my lips playfully. The woman had me in a tizzy, ready to fuck her in seconds. My good hand slipped under her dress until I felt bare skin. Fucking thigh highs. She was going to be the end of me.

I had to see them.

With one hand, I did my best and scrunched up the dress. She pulled her knee up to the mattress and then straddled my lap. She was in the perfect position for me to smell and touch her where I wanted most. My lips found the soft skin of her belly just under her navel. I swirled my tongue around the velvet expanse. The smell of her arousal intoxicated my senses and left me weak. Shimmers of excitement soared to my cock, filling the thick stalk with an ache only one thing would cure.

She held up her dress for me as I slipped a hand down to squeeze her tight ass. The lace of her panties was so soft. I scraped a callused thumb across the silky expanse. Dragging my fingers around the lace to the front, I dipped down and cupped her pussy. A moan slipped from her lips, her mouth hovering over mine. She was so wet her panties were soaked.

"Shit, angel!"

She groaned a version of my name or God as I tunneled my fingers between the lace and her baby soft skin to sink one finger deep inside. She was scalding hot, and I wanted to drink that heat. Her hips rotated around in circles as I plunged another finger in. She was so tight her body clasped onto my fingers like a vise. I could only image how it would feel when I pressed my cock into her. She sighed and rode my hand slowly. For this first time, I allowed it. In the future, I'd take control. For now, I enjoyed watching her ride my hand as her greedy pussy gripped my fingers. It was so erotic, and only a prelude of things to come. I swirled my thumb around the hard button nestled between her thighs and was rewarded with a deep moan.

"Oh God, Hank."

"You feel that, angel. You feel me deep inside you?" I pressed up with my two fingers until my palm rested against her wet slit.

"Y-yes," she stuttered, thrusting her hips in time with my fingers.

"That's just a taste of what it's going to feel like when I'm fucking you."

Dirty talk worked for her; her entire body went rigid. "I'm going to come."

One of her hands was braced on my good shoulder and the other on my chest, arching into me. "That's it, darlin'. Give it to me. I want to see you lose it." Her hips moved up and down in tight, strong movements. I sucked and nibbled on her neck while she rode my hand. Hard.

A few more strokes of her clit and she shattered, screaming. Her swollen lips came down over mine. Our tongues stroked as she trembled. I kept plucking at her sweet pussy, drawing out her pleasure. When she calmed, I pulled my hand out of her panties and licked the wet digits clean. She watched in awe, her eyes a deep navy. Her taste was rich and sweet like the finest honey. Her gaze held mine, and in that moment, I believed I could look into those indigo depths for a lifetime.

"God, you taste good. Just like honey."

"Jesus, Hank."

"Well, no, but I'm glad you think I'm godlike." We both laughed, and she stood and righted her dress. I cupped a hand over my aching shaft and squeezed to relieve some of the pressure.

She looked down with hunger in her eyes. "You want me to…"

She was cut off by Oliver rounding the corner. In my haste to touch her, I'd forgotten the little fella was here. Had he walked in a minute before he'd have gotten quite the eyeful.

I casually threw my arm over my lap to cover my desire.

"There you are." He looked us both up and down, his lips twitching. "You have a photo session and a meeting with the photographer for the magazine's first fashion shoot in an hour. You about ready?"

"Um, yeah." Her eyes never left mine. The need I saw in them could bring any man to his knees. She took a deep breath and broke the spell. "Just getting Hank situated. Thanks for reminding me about the shoot."

Oliver looked us over with a grin, and then focused on

Aspen. His lips twitched into a frown when his gaze focused on Aspen's head. He put his hands up and started fiddling with her hair. He pulled something out of his pocket, and swept a piece of her hair back in place.

"Excuse me? What are you doing?" I knew I had no right or claim to her but another man's hands on her, touching her in an intimate way, had me ready to stick my boot up his ass.

"Excuse *me*?" His brows knit together as he kept messin' with her hair.

I got up and was to her side in two strides. My hand curled around his wrist in a tight grip. "Why the fuck are you touching her like that?"

His eyes went wide. Good. Little fucker better keep his hands off my woman.

"Hank?" Aspen looked confused. "He's fixing my hair."

"Yeah, cowboy, looks like some big man paws were riffling through all my hard work." His pointed glare confused me.

None of this made a lick of sense. "You think I'm thick, boy?" My tone came off more as a growl.

"Hank, you're misunderstanding. Oliver does my hair. He picks all my clothes. He makes sure I'm always put together," she said.

Explanation received, still in the dark. She must see that I was having a time with this.

"Oliver's *boyfriend* was a makeup artist and stylist. Ollie picked a few things up from him over the years." She smiled sweetly.

"You're into dicks instead of chicks?" Oliver was gay? That explained a lot. I don't know how I hadn't picked up on that earlier. Must have been all the drugs. I looked the man up and down. All the signs were there. He dressed fancy all the time. His hair was never out of place. He even had a perfectly manicured face. Damn, now I felt like an asshole.

"Well, I guess I'm not needed here anymore, now am I?" Oliver turned around and stomped out of the room.

"Ollie, no. He didn't know," Aspen yelled after him. "God damn it, Hank. Haven't you ever met a gay man before? Jeez. You hurt his feelings."

I shrugged. "Sorry. I saw him putting his hands all over you and I reacted. Not going to apologize for that, darlin', but I didn't mean to offend him."

She blew a breath out long and slow. Watching her pink lips pucker in agitation was like calling my dick to attention with a "here, boy, come out and play, boy." This line of thought was not going to get me anywhere but in the doghouse.

"We'll talk about it later. But you will apologize to him." Apparently, I'd screwed up royally. Looks like the little fella was a big deal to my angel. My over-reactive possessive side was going to be hard to squash down. Gay or not, a man like me didn't want any man touching his girl.

Aspen was worth the trouble, so I conceded to fixin' it. "I'll talk to him. He could use a little toughening up though." It was true. The man freaked out and scampered away like a puppy running away from a rolled-up newspaper.

"He is my best friend and the most important person in my life." Her eyes were harsh. It was the first time I'd seen her truly angry. "You will treat him with respect or this"— she gestured between the two of us—"will be over before it has ever even begun."

The most important person in my life. The phrase stuck but good. I didn't like it one bit. I was fixin' to change that about my girl. One day she'd be saying that about me. God willing.

"I get it. Angel, I'm sorry. I don't give a rat's ass if he's gay or not. I'll fix it. Promise." I tried to touch her hair, but she backed away. That stung more than a bumblebee landing one of its stingers in the soft patch of skin at the arch of your foot.

"I'll be home for dinner. Gustav will take care of your lunch. The in-home nurse will be by in an hour. She'll be visiting three times a day to change your bandages and set up your cold therapy." The warmth of our shared experience a moment ago had been destroyed and replaced with a chill so cold it ran bone deep.

I nodded. "Thanks."

She turned to leave and then stopped at the threshold to the door her back to me, head hung low. "I'm glad you're here, Hank." That simple phrase was a start back on the right track.

"Me too, angel."

CHAPTER SIX

The last thing on earth I wanted to do was spend an entire afternoon consoling Oliver after Hank's outburst. He was worried that Hank had a problem with gay men. That wasn't the issue. It was clear after Ollie left that Hank was possessive and old-fashioned. Something that you didn't often find in a man on this side of the country. Still, I could maim the man myself for treating Oliver poorly.

Hank said he'd fix it, and I had to believe he would. I told Oliver that Hank wanted to talk to him about his behavior and apologize. Of course, my Ollie wanted to pout and hell if he didn't have the right. Instead, my focus should have been on overseeing our very first photo shoot for *Bright Magazine*—not dealing with a pissed-off gay man with the undeniable power to use guilt better than my Holy Roller grandmother.

The photographer was a pill, but well known. He shot for all the top fashion magazines and would skyrocket *Bright* right to the top…as long as he was kept calm. That was my job—CEO and babysitter to needy, overconfident snobs. I should take lessons from Ollie. He'd had to deal with me and my crap for years. At least my upbringing gave me the tools needed to deal with men of his caliber and pedigree.

Without much effort, I had the photographer eating out of my hand and following every task needed to complete the shoot in one day instead of two.

My goal was a bit self-serving. If we completed the shoot, I'd have the next day with Hank. How we would spend the day was open for discussion, but I genuinely wanted to get to know him better. We both needed some time to understand this connection between us. Time to figure out if it was just physical, or something more.

Once we completed the shoot, I practically flew home. My driver gave me a placating smile and sped through the streets of downtown New York, narrowly missing a messenger that jetted out into traffic along the way. With jittery nerves, I finally made it home and set down my briefcase on the side table. That's when I heard a woman's high-pitched giggle from down the hall.

I was eager to see Hank—a truth I would only decipher later—but the sound reminded me of a really bad day eight months ago. I had decided to surprise Grant by canceling a meeting and stopping by his house unexpectedly. I ended up catching Grant with one of his assistants, whom I referred to as whore number two. His hands were wrapped around both sides of her head as he jammed his tiny prick into her mouth.

It still hurt thinking about his deception, mostly because I allowed him to cheat on me not once, but twice. Hank's deep throaty laugh floated down the hall, breaking the fog of my past. The sound sent chills down my spine.

I found Hank sitting on the bed, back against the headboard. His shirt was off, and the golden skin of his chest shone like a Greek god's in the amber lighting. A perky brunette in pink scrubs sat next to him holding a bowl of popcorn. They were focused on the TV nestled in the armoire to the side of the bed. Every so often Hank's long, muscled forearm reached across the space, gripping for some popcorn, his eyes still glued to the screen. He didn't see the look of admiration on the pretty woman's face as his hand grazed her thigh.

I did.

Her breath caught, and her body stilled as her gaze gobbled up Hank's attributes. I cleared my throat. Two sets of eyes met mine. One dark and dangerous, the other startled and uncertain.

"Evening, stud." My voice sounded husky even to my ears.

"Angel," Hank said in that perfect Texan drawl. The one that made me weak in the knees and lust coil deep within my belly.

The nurse jumped up, a few kernels of popcorn spilling over the edge of the bowl. She scrambled to pick them up and toss them into the garbage.

"Um, Miss Reynolds. I was just, uh…"

"Keeping Hank company?" I offered. Her eyes grew wide. She knotted her fingers nervously.

"Come here, darlin'." His voice brooked no argument.

I sauntered over, catlike, toward the cowboy. His good arm gripped my hip possessively. I relished his Neanderthal move. Letting the nurse know he belonged to me was exactly my intent, even if it was only for show. His hand slid up to my waist, and he pulled me into his lap. Our eyes locked. A clattering of items hitting the desk and a shuffling of papers could be heard from behind me, signaling that the nurse was packing up her things for the day.

"How are you?" I licked my lips, anticipating what he would do next.

"Better, now that you're here."

I turned my head and caught the nurse's red face. "You're dismissed," I said.

"For good? I swear, Miss Reynolds, we didn't... Nothing happened."

I turned to Hank, his lips quirked at the edge.

"No, just for the evening. We'll see you bright and early tomorrow to change his bandages and prepare his therapy. That is all for tonight."

"Thank you," she said and exited the room lightning fast.

I turned back to Hank and opened my mouth to say something when his lips covered mine. Hank's kiss was slow, sensual, exactly what I needed after a rough day. My fingers skittered down his chest, feeling the bunching and tightening of muscled pecks and strong abdominal muscles.

I pulled away to catch my breath. Hank's lips went straight to my neck; his teeth grazed the skin sending shocks of lust splintering through me settling deep between my thighs. He swirled his tongue around a particularly tender spot on my clavicle. I shuddered.

"Did the nurse take care of you?" I asked as his nose nuzzled just behind my ear. I craned my neck to give him plenty of access to the sensitive skin.

"Yes, I'm healthy as a horse." His teeth nipped at my collarbone and I closed my eyes. One large palm covered my neck. He made me feel so small and fragile in his arms. His dexterous fingers dug into the tight flesh, massaging the day's knots away.

"Have you eaten dinner?"

He shook his head and nudged his nose into the crevice

between my breasts, as much as the dress would allow. "God, you smell so fucking good. I could just eat you for dinner." His right hand boldly cupped my breast and squeezed. I pushed my aching flesh into his palm, needing more friction.

"*Middag serveras*." Gustav's heavy Swedish accent echoed down the hall.

"Dinner's ready." I tipped Hank's face and sealed my lips over his once more.

Hank gave me a few more wet smacks. No man had ever kissed me the way Hank did. He put everything into each and every pull of his full lips, each swipe of his perfect tongue. He made kissing feel like a new experience, something to savor and relish.

"Pen! Pen, where are you?" *Oh, Jesus, no.* Why is everyone and everything preventing me from getting it on with this man? My inner bitch pulled out her boxing gloves and got ready to take down the next intruder.

"You sure have a lot of people in your personal space. Doesn't that get annoying?" Hank stroked my breast and let out a low chuckle, his thumb swirling around my nipple in maddeningly accurate circles.

London strolled through the door, and we both turned our heads toward her.

She pointed a manicured finger at the both of us. "I knew it!" she screamed with glee.

I closed my eyes and Hank shifted, placing a hand on each hip as she entered. I was never going to live this down. The interrogation wouldn't end until she got blood.

She glided into the room smelling of cinnamon and looking like she just walked off a Hawaiian Tropics calendar. Her hand jutted out toward Hank. He smiled and shook hers. "I'm London Kelley. You must be the hunk—I mean Hank." She grinned at her own slipup. My intuition told me she did it on purpose.

Hank looked her up and down. "Damn, good genes in the Reynolds family."

I rolled my eyes.

"You're the dark version of my angel here." Hank clasped my neck in a possessive maneuver my sister zeroed in on in two seconds flat.

"Angel?" London queried with a sly smile, her gaze falling on the hand at my nape.

"London, what are you doing here?" A deep sigh slipped past my lips.

"What? I can't just pop by and see my sister?"

"No." My glare was a large block of ice, and she fidgeted under its weight.

"I wanted to meet your friend," she announced boldly. "He saved your life. I owe him a great deal."

"Sweetie, you don't owe me nothin'. I'm just glad I was in the right place at the right time." His hands caressed my hips, either to solidify his point or just to touch me. The man liked to touch me. All the time. I sure as hell wasn't going to complain.

My sister melted into a pool of mush at Hank's proclamation. She was being taken over by the Southern charm. Easy to fall under. I was damn near drowning in it after three days.

"*Middag serveras!*" Gustav shouted once more from down the hall, sounding very irritated.

"Oh! Dinner. I'm starving. Can I stay?" London asked.

Thou shalt not throttle thy sister was the mantra I repeated over and over internally.

"Yes, of course you can."

Hank pulled back the sheet and stood. His frame was enormous and swallowed up the space. He had on plain black boxer shorts that hugged and accentuated his hips and thighs' mouth-watering proportions. Both London and I were transfixed at the sight of his mostly naked body.

"Damn, Sis. You're one lucky bitch."

I stood there, biting my lip and nodding at the perfect specimen that was Hank Jensen. He was all man, and I wanted to lick and suck on every inch.

Hank grinned. "Why, thank you, I think?" he said as he slipped into a pair of soft gray sweats. "Darlin', do you think you could help me with this here shirt?" He waggled his eyebrows suggestively.

"I'll just tell Gustav I'm staying. Piss him off a little. See you in the kitchen," London said and left.

"Sure." I squeezed my legs together as the raging lust that diminished with my sister's intrusion roared back to life. Staring at this perfect man's bare chest and sexy grin did all kinds of things to my lady bits. Hank presented the shirt to me as I tried to get hold of my hormones.

★ ★ ★ ★

After a few fumbles and laughs, we reapplied the sling and got my shirt on. It was fun to watch Aspen try not to touch me during the process. Every time her hands landed on an exposed part of my skin, she'd jump as if burned by a hot poker. I got what I wanted in the end, though. Before we entered the kitchen, I had her little body pinned against the wall with my mouth on hers, kissing the daylights out of her.

She rubbed at her kiss-swollen, reddened lips as we entered the kitchen. I couldn't wipe the shit-eating grin off my face. I loved making this woman blush, and right now, she was three shades of pink. Her sister, London, was a looker and had a matching knowing smile plastered across her face. She looked exactly like Aspen, only with dark hair and skin. Same gray-blue eyes and facial structure, too. Based on the flowing clothes and chipper personality, she seemed a lot more easygoing, more free-spirited than Aspen. Didn't matter.

There was something special about Aspen that had me in a full-body twist. 'Sides her beauty, there was a little extra sparkle in her eyes when I looked at her, something that drew me to her, made me ache to be near her. Damn if I wasn't going to figure it out.

Dinner was incredible. That gourmet chef of hers definitely had talent in the kitchen. He served us some type of bird with a fancy glaze I couldn't pronounce, and an interesting side dish that looked like tiny little balls.

"What's this called again?" I pointed at the yellow balls.

Aspen smiled. "Couscous."

"Say what?"

"It's a rolled wheat type pasta," London offered. "Do you like it?"

"I do. Different," I managed around a big bite of the stuff.

"So, Hank, I want to thank you for saving my sister. Pen's important to me. Hell, she's important to the world. I can't believe you just jumped in front of her like that. So brave."

"Ah, it was nothin' really. I'd do it again in a heartbeat." Aspen's gaze held mine, burning with intensity. Her beauty was unexplainable. Waiting to be with her was as if a ton of bricks was dropping onto my chest, taking away my ability to breathe.

"Well, I'm glad you were there. So you'll be staying with Pen then?" she asked.

"That's the plan. Seems as though her uptight lawyers are worried I'm going to sue, so she's holding me hostage."

Aspen looked shocked. "That's not true! I want you to have the best care." Her tone held a twinge of hurt.

"So she says," I tried to joke. London gave a half laugh but focused her attention back and forth between us. I wasn't sure what she was doing.

London set down her fork and clasped her hands at her chin. Her eyes, so similar to her sister's, turned a shade darker and the edges tightened a hair. "But you're obviously into one another." She held my gaze, and then focused on Aspen. "The tension in here is so thick I could cut it with a knife."

"London! None of your prophecies tonight," Aspen warned.

"What? Anyone in a five-mile radius could sense how badly you two need to get it on."

I choked on my couscous and laughed. Her sister was as straightforward as they came. "I'm liking you more and more, London. You're good people."

She smiled sweetly. "Thank you." Then she stood and straightened her dress. "I can't be in the room with you two anymore. It's making me hot and bothered. I'm going to go hang out with Tripp. Maybe see a movie."

"Good. Do that," Aspen begged.

"Who's Tripp?" I asked.

"Her bisexual boyfriend."

London threw her napkin at her sister. "That is not true and you know it! He's my best friend." Her voice was strained, and then she fired back a scathing retort. "Are you fucking Ollie?"

I paid very close attention to this part. She'd brushed it off like nothing today and made me promise to apologize to him, but that little pip-squeak had his hands all over my angel.

"No, never have." Aspen's voice was as confident as when I heard her speaking to the doctor yesterday. "How about you and Tripp? Ever slept with your best friend? Hmmm?" Aspen shot back.

"That's not fair, Pen, and you know it." London's eyes narrowed.

"You started it," Aspen said, sounding like a five-year-old would after tattle-telling.

"Whatever. I'm outta here. Hank, you're hot. And it's obvious you're head over heels for my sister."

Was it that obvious?

"Can you please fuck her into oblivion so she'll get her head out of her ass and start enjoying life for once?"

Yup. This woman was tops for sure.

"I'm not talking to you for a month, London!" Aspen yelled.

"Don't care," she said flippantly. "I have a client for the next six weeks starting tomorrow, anyway. Not that you care."

"Oh, I didn't realize you had your next client lined up so quickly." Aspen sounded sad.

"Yeah, well, you would have if you'd cared to answer my calls or maybe lived a little. Instead you chose to throw yourself into work the last few months trying to forget about the asshole that cheated on you...twice!" she added.

Holy smokes! Her sister was putting all her dirty laundry out there. I felt wrong for being stuck in the middle of it, but I could see Aspen's eyes well up with tears and that was the end for me.

"Hey, hey now. London, that was uncalled for," I stated.

Her sister turned around and hugged me out of the blue. My mother was the same way, so it didn't bother me. Made me feel important. "Hank, I can feel how good you are for her. Even if she's a bitch." That part was slung over her shoulder in Aspen's direction. "She deserves a man who will treat her right. Don't screw her over. I don't want to pick up the pieces of her broken heart again."

"Got it," I said and meant it. I looked into the same blue-gray eyes and silently vowed not to hurt my blond angel.

She searched my eyes for a few moments. "I believe you." I don't know what she saw when she looked at me, but whatever it was, I got the green light from her sister. I'd just passed some type of squirrelly test only women had the answer key to.

With a turn of her heel, she went over to her sister and hugged her. A few tears built in Aspen's eyes and threatened to tumble over her cheek. I clutched my fingers into a fist. I didn't want to see her cry...ever.

"Be safe, Sis. I love you. And...I'm sorry. I shouldn't

have said what I said about Tripp," Aspen told London.

"Me too. It wasn't cool of me to try to get a rise out of you by bringing up your ex." She looked over at me. Her cheeks reddened in embarrassment.

"Please have Tripp send Oliver the specifics of your next client. You know I worry, even if you don't think so."

"I will." Then the dark woman was gone and Aspen had her head in her hands.

"Hey, darlin', what the hell was that?"

She sighed. "It was a long time coming."

"'Fess up? One moment we were eating supper and the next you two were fit to be tied."

"Yeah, it's been brewing awhile. She's been upset with me for ignoring her calls, not being a part of her life the past few months."

"Because of some jerk with shit for brains?"

She laughed, and it was the most precious sound. "You could say that, yes. A man did a number on me, but I'm fine."

"Tell me about him."

"Hank, you don't want to know about my ex. Really." She looked tired and drained.

"All right then, but one day you will talk about it. I want to know everything about you."

Her gaze searched mine. I had no idea what was going on in that head of hers.

"For now, though, how about we watch a movie together."

She squinted. "Like you did with the pretty nurse today?"

Looked like the green-eyed monster had a hold of my angel. Love this side of her. "She offered to watch a movie with me because I was stuck here all day. We'd just started watching something when you came home."

I could see the wheels turning in her head. Lying with her in a bed was exactly what I wanted to do. With a little guilt, I pressed on my bandaged shoulder and groaned.

She laughed. "Okay, okay, fine."

We got up from the table, and I led the way, holding her hand, warm and soft in mine. I could feel her heartbeat as our palms touched. We walked past my room and entered the master. The room was classy but warm. The sleigh-style bed sat proudly in the center of the room with wooden end tables on each side. The comforter looked like a burgundy cloud. I could hardly wait to get into it and snuggle up to the woman I was quickly becoming enamored with.

There were a variety of art pieces hung strategically throughout the room. One of the pictures above the bed had textured fabric and sequins in an Indian sari-inspired design. Another picture showed a seated Buddha, hands held in a strange pose. I didn't know anything about Indian art, but the room was definitely inspired by the culture. Heavy fabrics in rich maroons and golds were placed elegantly throughout the space.

Letting go of her hand, I walked to the side of the bed and pulled off my sweats. She watched me pull back the covers and slip into the bed. I patted the other side.

She pulled at the zipper behind her head and contorted her body. I could see the dress start to loosen in front.

"That's my side of the bed," she said, and continued to pull at the zipper behind her. The fabric pooled and hung forward even more.

"Not anymore."

Her head cocked to the side as she let the blue fabric slide down her form and pool at her feet. "We'll see about that, caveman."

"Fuck!" I lost my ability to breathe. She was right out of a wet dream, standing there in a black lace bra and panties. The low lighting from behind provided an incandescent glow around her silhouette. Black stockings were held up by magic halfway between milky thighs.

I felt my heartbeat stop as she sauntered across the room and turned, her back to me providing the most delectable view of her scantily clad ass. She was beyond beautiful. Emotions mixed with lust and a little of something else I wasn't ready to name. Then they all got together and prevented me from speaking or making a sound. No woman had ever put me in such a state. Though I knew I'd never liked a woman as much as I did Aspen. She was the entire package.

Smart, drop-dead gorgeous, a beautiful laugh, and a personality I wanted to know more of. Overall, she fascinated me and did more than turn me on. She broke me down to the base level where a man hid his savage beast. The one that kept me from all logic, zeroing in on only one thing.

Aspen.

When all my faculties got back on board, I called out to her. "Jesus Christ! Angel, get over here now," I demanded.

She shook her head and pilfered through her drawers. With a shirt clutched to her hand, she made to slip it over her head. I was out of the bed and gripping her wrist before she had the opportunity to slide it over her head.

"You gonna prance around in this, taunt me with your perfect body, and not let me touch?" I gripped her waist and thrust my erection against her behind.

She leaned back against me and moaned. I slid a hand up her ribs and over her breast. I took hold, sliding down one cup to tug and pull at the rigid nipple. She made a sound that was a cross between a moan and a plea. The sound went straight to my dick, hardening it further. "Hank, you can't. You just had surgery."

I thrust against her ass again more roughly. "My cock *feel* broken to you, darlin'? You do things to me. I need to show you what I'm feelin'. Let me," I whispered into her ear from behind.

She shivered and gasped, "Oh God. I want you so much." The words were a whisper, almost a cry.

I kissed along her bare neck, sweeping her hair off to one shoulder. She trembled as I licked and feasted on the skin of her neck up to her ear. My good arm slid around her front and down her body, enjoying the luscious curves and soft skin. She mewled and moaned when I slipped my fingers between her panties and bare skin and found her wet and wanting.

"So ready for me, angel? Mmm, I like that. So much." I plunged two fingers in while I trailed hot kisses all over her neck and back. She arched, and I added another finger. Her body was searing hot as I used my fingers in and out, in and out, again and again. I fucked her until she was gasping for air and begging for more. Her responsiveness shattered me.

I gloried in every little moan, gasp, and utterance of pleasure she bestowed. She was heaven, and I wanted to taste every inch of it. I plucked her core and spun my thumb around her tight little nub until she screamed out, her orgasm taking her in violent spasms coating my fingers with her honey. I held on the best I could with one arm. Her body bucked against my chest as the last of her pleasure slowed.

When she calmed, she turned around and slanted her mouth over mine, kissing me so thoroughly that I forgot about anything but the precious bundle I had half-naked in my arms.

CHAPTER SEVEN

Hank's right hand gripped and squeezed my ass as I sucked at the skin of his neck.

"Help me get this shirt off," he requested.

Having put the shirt on him, I had the trick down pat. I pulled the good arm though the shirt first, then his head, then carefully slipped his wounded arm through the armhole. He had me remove the sling, even though I disagreed profusely.

Once he was stripped of everything but his boxers, he turned abruptly and sat in the center of my bed. I was left feeling cold and bereft, yet insanely turned on.

"Take off your panties…slowly." His demanding tone sent heat throughout my body, warming me from the top of my head to the tip of my nylon-covered toes. I did what he asked, making a real meal of the process. "Now your bra." His voice was deeper, roughened by desire.

I twisted my arms behind my back and unclipped the hook. I shrugged and let the lace drop to the floor alongside my underwear.

"Fucking perfect," he whispered. I preened at his compliment. "Come here."

Taking long, slow strides, I walked to the foot of the bed. Putting my hands on the edge, I crawled up to where he sat, straddling his hips bravely. My black stockings were a stark contrast to my white flesh and his tanned skin. His hand came out and pulled me to his lap roughly. His mouth went straight for my breast, sucking my nipple with long, deep tugs of lips and teeth.

After a few minutes, he'd moan and flick just the tip playfully with the end of his tongue, sending a fresh bout of arousal to my core. He moved to my other breast, giving it the same attention. Heat rose within me, tipping the world on edge as his talented fingers and the wet heat of him possessed me. Before long, I was grinding against his erection, dizzy with the need to feel him inside.

Dragging his head away from my breasts, I plunged my tongue into his warm mouth. He groaned and sucked my tongue, thrilling me to no end. With great skill, that enchanting tongue feasted on every surface. He made kissing a full-on banquet of sensation. Every nerve ending was on high alert. Even the slightest touch of his skin against mine had me moaning with need. He was driving me to the edge of insanity with lust.

"Hank, more, I need more," I breathed into his mouth, tugging on his full bottom lip and waiting for the satisfying "plop" when I yanked away.

My hand snaked down between our bodies as both his hands cupped my bare bottom possessively. I could feel the difference in his wounded side. That hand merely held on, whereas his right gripped me with force. A pained expression came over his face.

"You okay?" The man just had surgery, and here I was trying to hop on pop.

"Don't you worry none. I'm more than okay now that I have you." His words egged me on. I found my target and squirmed onto his lap, backing up only to pull his erect cock out of his boxers.

"Oh, darlin', take my shorts off. I want nothin' between us." His eyes were smoldering as he stared at my body, licking his lips sinfully. I shimmied and tugged his boxers completely off him —rather ungracefully, but he didn't care. His hands were all over me, touching, caressing, and squeezing in perfect unison with my need to feel him. His deep sighs as he gripped a particular part made me feel like the sexiest woman in the world. With Hank, I didn't feel lacking. With Grant, I wasn't enough.

I nestled back over him. He had a beautiful cock that was rigid and proudly straining up to meet my body. I fondled it, slicking the wetness at the tip over and down the full length, watching his face, trying to catalogue what he liked best. He groaned and gritted his teeth when I played with the little patch of skin behind the wide knob of his dick.

He gestured for me to lift up to where I was holding my weight on my knees. His mouth came down and licked and kissed my belly with reverence. He inhaled deeply as he nuzzled my skin. Cherished. He made feel special, maybe even loved. I was loath to define it as such. It was too soon— much too soon—for mixing love and desire.

"I can't get over your scent. It's so… God, angel, everything about you is a dream come true." He licked and grazed his teeth along my ribs before taking a nipple and sucking hard. "Delicious." His teeth bit down and sent a surge of electric heat through my body. Wetness flooded my core. "You ready, darlin'? I feel like I'm ready to explode."

"God, yes, Hank. Now, please."

Every touch, every nibble was more succulent then next. Drugged. I felt as high as a kite with no desire to ever come down. Hank did that to me. Made me lose my mind. Since the moment I looked into his eyes, there was something there, something I couldn't define. A connection perhaps that led us to this very moment. He was everything I shouldn't want, but I did want him. Badly. It was impossible to deny this current running through my body, mind, even my soul. He was there and hell if he didn't fit perfectly.

"Condom…we, uh…" His voice was shredded with desire and emotion. He was affected, too.

Something was happening and it was bigger than both of us. Call it fate, call it passion, even lust was too weak a word to describe this bone-crushing need to be closer, to be more. His hips bucked up toward my core, hitting the tender bundle of nerves throbbing for his attention. I cried out, tipping my head back with the joy of feeling him exactly where I wanted him most.

Resurfacing from the pleasure of grinding down against his cock, I managed to whisper between long drawn-out pulls of his lips and tongue, "Pill. On it."

"I'm clean. Never have relations without…but with you…Christ, angel, I'm dying to take you bare. Jesus, you're killing me, here," Hank growled and gnashed his teeth against mine.

I smiled against his lips. "Just had a physical…" My tongue tangled with his. He chased my lips tugging on the bottom one as I tried to pull away to speak. The slight pinch of pain sent a jolt of pleasure between my legs. "I'm healthy. Take me, God, please. Now. I want you so much."

Hank dragged his thick cock along the seam between my thighs, wetting his dick with my essence and teasing me in the process. I tunneled my hands in his hair as he toyed with my sex, bringing me to the pinnacle of lust. Without preamble, he positioned himself right at the center of my sex and slammed me down on his cock. I screamed out. Underused muscles ached with the pleasure and pain of our coupling.

"Fuck!" he roared.

He stilled to give me time to adjust. His length stretched me wide, more so than I'd ever been before. The pressure was exquisite, mind-bending, with just a hint of pain. It was huge buried within me. His breath tickled the hair around my neck as I leaned back and looked down to where we were joined. There were still two inches left of his thick stalk visible between us. My eyes widened in shock.

"Oh yes, angel. There's more for you. Now lift up, baby." He smoothed a hand up my spine in a sweet caress as I lifted up, his cock sliding almost all the way out. The strong arm around my back cupped the crook of my shoulder for leverage, bringing us nose to nose. His eyes searched mine. I could see so much behind his gaze.

He swallowed, took a steadying breath, and then kissed my face. Small little presses of his lips across every inch of skin until he landed on my lips, taking them in a searing mash of wet tissue. He pulled back, his gaze sliding over my naked body and between us.

"So pretty. Seeing you on my cock, trusting me with your body. Angel, there's nothin' better."

His lips crushed mine as he surged up into me powerfully at the same moment he pulled down. He was everywhere all at once, splitting me in half in the most pleasurable way possible. The orgasm overtook me so fast I didn't recognize the sound of my wail into his mouth, but my entire body lit and tingled everywhere. I'd lost time, but he was there holding me with one strong arm, keeping me there with him.

"That's it, darlin'. I love seeing you come apart. But we're just getting started." Those words sent shivers through me. Even my hair tingled with anticipation.

His hips retreated and then plowed into me, barreling that massive cock into my tight channel over and over, ruthlessly fucking me. I was out of my mind—it blasted off into space and left me a needy, wanton hussy. I rode Hank like no tomorrow, aching for more pleasure, more of him. I wanted to be closer, needed to be. Mindful of his wounded shoulder, I squeezed my legs around and behind his body, bringing that glorious member of his deeper. He moaned and gritted his teeth.

Just when I thought I had his rhythm down, he'd throw in a twist of his hips and grind his pelvis against mine, crushing my clit in the process. Shock waves of pleasure ricocheted in every direction. He had me at the peak of orgasm again.

"Jesus, angel. Your perfect little body makes me fall apart!" Hank whispered in my ear and then bit down on the sensitive flesh just behind it. He lifted his knees and pressed my chest back, changing the angle. I braced myself on his muscular thighs, arching toward him teasingly. His hands tweaked and rolled my nipples into hard nubs. He used the new angle to his advantage, bringing his weaker hand down to my aching clit to rub it in juicy little circles.

I couldn't speak, only feel the way he played my body like a well-tuned instrument. He overpowered my senses, controlled my body, and made me forget that anything else existed. Everything I had yielded to him, spinning willingly into his vortex of pleasure.

"Give it to me, angel," he said through gritted teeth. I caught his gaze. Hank's eyes were intensely focused. His jaw was held tight, teeth clenched, sweat dusted his forehead and hairline as he hammered into me.

I tilted my hips back just as he took his thumb and forefinger and pinched my clit, pleasure and pain collided, and then he thrust his hefty cock into me. I saw stars, my orgasm shooting through every pore, overtaking me, escaping in a guttural cry. His mouth swallowed my scream as he pumped into me, roaring wildly, finding his own release. Deep flutters of warm liquid filled my womb, heating my lower half from the inside out.

"Angel," he breathed into my mouth while the last of his essence spilled into me.

He rolled his hips salaciously, prolonging our pleasure to the last possible second. I was completely boneless, my body draped over his like a ragdoll, utterly spent and sated. His cock, once thick and rigid, had softened, throbbing and nestled safely within me.

"Hank, that was..." I couldn't find the words, instead nuzzling into the crook of his neck on his good side.

"Everything. That was everything," he whispered against my neck, kissing and nibbling the skin there. His hands caressed up and down my back in a soothing calming rhythm.

We spent long minutes that way, clutching one another while coming down from our combined highs. I was as certain as the sun would rise tomorrow that the man had ruined me for other men. That was possibly the best sexual experience I'd ever had in my life and he wasn't even completely up to par, being hindered by his shoulder. I could only imagine what he'd be like with both arms in good working order. I could already picture being under him, his huge body surrounding me completely. Flutters of desire started to stir within my belly.

"Angel, I can feel your wheels spinning. What are you thinking about?" he asked, yearning evident in his voice.

"You. About how incredible this was. How I can't wait to experience you when you're healed." I grinned and bit my lip.

"Oh, darlin', you have no idea the ways I'm going to take you," he said before he kissed me, his soft lips and tongue overwhelming me. Deep affection was building between us so quickly it was hard to mask the rising feelings.

His tongue searched and played within mine in a saucy little dance. I moaned deeply, from the furthest recesses of my soul. I could feel him getting hard within me once more.

"Ride me, angel. Nice and slow this time." Hank was bossy in bed, but I found that I rather enjoyed it. His dominant nature, the sheer size of him in all ways, made me giddy with the need to have him and relinquish control.

Together we found a slow, sensual rhythm. I could tell his shoulder was hurting him because a grimace overtook his lovely face now and then. Sliding up and down, I put everything I had into making unhurried quiet love to him. With my body, I showed him how much I desired him. With punch-drunk kisses, I proved I wanted him and only him. Up and down, flesh to flesh, we melded our bodies and minds. Before long, we were both withering and crying out in combined release. I'd never come with a man at the same time. With Hank, I had twice. Being with him sexually was magical, unlike any connection I'd ever known. The thought excited and frightened me in equal measure.

Without trying, I was becoming attached. Physically and mentally, Hank had wiggled his way into my body and mind. At this very moment in time, it felt right.

★ ★ ★ ★

It's official. The woman was a goddess. Sex in my book was always good, sometimes great, but never like this. Ab-so-fucking-lutely mind-blowing. Her body drove me wild. She was damn near perfect, and I told her as much. The legs were finely sculpted and went on for days. Her lengthy, slim body fit mine like no other. Her breasts were mouth-wateringly tasty, and her ass—Jesus Christ, her ass made me weak. It was an ass you bowed down and worshiped, and I planned to…often.

I almost blew my load when she turned around in those sexy little panties. Honestly, I had planned on waiting to take her to bed. Wanted to heal up a bit, play with her a little, and build up the anticipation between us. That all ended the moment her dress hit the floor. My angel had a body that screamed *take me!* So I did. I'm not sorry, either.

Being with Aspen filled me with light. Made me whole. Finally, after weeks in this godforsaken city, I had something to hold onto. That something was several inches over five feet and had me wrapped around her delicate little baby finger.

After tonight, making love to her, there was nothin' that was going to keep me from being near her. It wasn't just the physical, either, though she damn near killed me with her knockout shape. I knew when I saw her weeks ago that she had a beautiful body, but seeing her bare, riding my cock… holy hell. I'd have to keep her close. There was no way in hell any man was ever going to look at my perfect angel ever again. She was mine. In time, I'd make her so, body, heart, and soul.

Finally, our breathing calmed to a normal rate. She lay naked, draped over my chest. Right where I needed her. She pulled her body back and my dick slipped out of her, both of us moaning in unison.

"I need to clean up," she said shyly, her hair falling over her face like a golden fan.

"I rather like you dirty." I couldn't keep the grit out of my voice. She shot me a knowing smile as she sauntered into the restroom, a little extra sway to those sexy hips.

Good Lord, the woman made me crazy. She did things to me. Feelings I hadn't felt in years were cropping up and demanding they be let out. Instead of dealing with them, my resident caveman came to the forefront, making me want to knock her over the head, drag her to my bed, and never let anyone have her. Wanted to keep her for my very own.

She returned in a dark purple satin nightgown, sans the stockings. My dick started to stir and I mentally tried to think of my mom and dad, my brother's two monsters, anything that would prevent me from the urge to take her again.

We both needed rest and I needed a pain pill. I got out of bed, went to my room, and took my pain remedy. Though a couple more rounds with my angel, and I wouldn't give a shit how much the shoulder hurt. The sweet bliss I felt inside her was intoxicating and all encompassing. I'd suffer through the pain willingly for another taste of her honey.

After cleaning up in the bathroom, I went back into her room. She had turned on the TV and was coyly looking away every time I tried to catch her blue-gray eyes.

"Um, I thought we could watch a movie now." She twisted her fingers together and gripped the comforter to her chest tightly.

"Sounds good, darlin'." Shyness was new and lovely on her. Unexpected after three orgasms, but cute nonetheless.

She watched me walk naked across the room.

"See something you like?" I asked her, standing unmoving at the side of the bed. Her eyes scoured my form greedily.

"You are a work of art, Hank," slipped past her pretty lips. I boldly stroked my dick for her pleasure more than mine. "Oh, God," she mewled as my cock grew to full mast.

Before I could say anything, she had scurried along the bed and my cock was down her throat. "Fuck, angel! Warn a man next time!" Her hands palmed my ass as she sucked and swirled her little pink tongue around and around the fat head.

I watched her with adoration. She was a beautiful sight, bobbing up and down over my cock.

That tongue of hers lapped at the fluid leaking from the tip, and I thought I'd died and gone to heaven. My vision blurred, and I had to reach out and hold onto the bedpost to keep from passing out. Seeing her small hand encase my length, her haunting eyes stared at mine as if she was reaching through to my soul.

The sight almost undid me. Almost.

Still, I couldn't look away. Didn't want to. She put such effort into pleasing me I damn near fell to my knees to beg for mercy. It was impossible that a woman so perfect, so ungodly beautiful, existed and wanted me. Big ol' Hank from Texas, playing building blocks in the big city.

She took me deep and hummed around my hard flesh. "God, fuck!" If I didn't take control of this, I was going to lavish her with words she wasn't ready to hear. Words that were meant for long-term lovers who were devoted to one another. I wanted to be devoted to her. Hell, I already was, even if she didn't want me for the long run. Somehow, I'd find a way to make her mine for good.

As she sucked me into oblivion, I gripped the sides of her head, fingers tunneling into her silky hair. "Let me." I gestured, thrusting my dick. Her eyes turned big and rolled back, closing of their own volition. She breathed deeply through her nose as I slid my cock down her throat, fucking her the way I wanted to from the moment I saw her in front of the building weeks ago. I twisted her long hair in my good hand, roughly tipped her head back, perfecting the angle as I plowed into her eager mouth.

One of her hands held her balance, the other came up to her creamy white breast where she cupped and pinched the nipple much harder than I would have. She moaned, and I watched astonished as she hungrily took my length down her throat over and over.

"Touch yourself…C-come with me, angel," I urged.

She slid her right hand down her gorgeous body, lifted her purple gown up to give me a nice view of her bare ass. She held herself up on her knees, one hand keeping balance on the bed. She leaned her weight onto her balancing arm and slid her other hand down to delve into her heat. I had the perfect position to see her fingers twirl around her clit.

The sight ripped through my body, sending jolts of pleasure where her pretty cheeks hollowed out around my cock. She moved faster and faster, following the pattern of my thrusts. I had been on the edge of coming since the second her lips touched me, but this, this was unbelievable. I was about to blow. Her fingers between her legs were a blur of activity; her ass tipped up and arched while she moaned, a shot of electricity sizzled through me. She removed her hand from her wet heat and brought it up to pinch and elongate her right nipple. With nimble fingers, she squeezed and yanked on it until it was the color of a ripe raspberry. I knew it tasted just as good.

Watching her stroke herself and take my cock down her throat at the same time did me in.

She jerked in orgasm the same time I pumped into her mouth, howling as the pleasure became too much. My seed jetted down her throat, a little dribbled out the side of her mouth. I took my thumb and brushed it off, wanting her skin unmarked. She swallowed my essence and then gripped my hand and licked off the remnants, like a cat sipping its milk from a bowl. Aspen was by far the sexiest woman I'd ever been with. Everything about her tore at my heart and ripped it open wide for her to steal.

She lapped at my softening dick, licking me clean. I cupped her face, fingertips lightly flowing along the ridges and planes. So many emotions were openly visible as her gaze held mine. The way she nuzzled against my shaft as if she were worshiping me stole my breath. My angel was too good to be true. None of the women I'd ever been with made me feel as if they owned me, but this one did. A small blink of her perfect lashes and I was done. A lift of her swollen lips and I was a goner. She straight owned me. It was more than the sex. It was the way she looked at me. As if she saw...me. Not just a hunk of meat or a body to fuck.

Her hands slid up and down my thighs and heavy bursts of air left me. She came up on her knees and held me. A hug. Something so simple held so much meaning. This wasn't just a roll in the hay. It was more. She knew it and I knew it. Now I just had to make sure she didn't try to escape it.

Leaning down, I kissed her deeply, wanting her to know how much this night had meant to me. I could taste myself in her kiss, and it was one of the most exotic things I'd ever experienced. I devoured her mouth and lips until we were both out of breath.

She removed her nighty, pulled back the covers, and slid under, leaving the space next to her open in invitation. I tilted on my good side and pulled her against me, her ass nestled against my groin. I lobbed the bum arm over her waist. "Is this okay?" I asked, a little uncertain.

"More than, okay. I'm tired, Hank. Go to sleep."

I fell asleep dreaming of all the wicked things I was going to do to my angel the very next chance I got.

★ ★ ★ ★

Turned out, we went at it like rabbits again first thing in the morning. She was riding my cock like a champion thoroughbred when her bedroom door flew open.

Her head tilted back and she came with a loud scream. The sound was louder than usual, and I realized after spurting hotly into her pussy that it wasn't just her screaming.

Standing with his hand still on the door was a stunned Oliver. Mouth opening and closing like a fish out of water. His eyes were wide and the size of dinner plates.

I covered Aspen's breasts protectively; they were the perfect size and filled my palms nicely, but I didn't want his eyes on 'em.

"Get on outta here, boy!" I yelled in anger at her friend.

His mouth hung open, catching flies. Then he abruptly turned on his heel and scampered away.

"Fuck! Why the hell does he come into your private chambers unannounced? How the hell did he get into the house?" A thousand questions formed, but I could only spurt out a couple of them. "Are you okay?" was my last question when I realized that she wasn't answering. I cooled my jets and smiled. Teasingly I asked, "Angel, did I fuck you dumb?"

She nodded against my neck, smiling wide, and I rubbed her back, then palmed her ass. Her knees were gripping my hips domineeringly, and if she didn't get up, I was going to take her again. All of a sudden, her shoulders started to shake and I worried that she was crying. Bone-breaking fear took over—I had screwed up something again.

Howling laughter barreled out of her as she slid off me and to her side, clutching her middle. Thank God it wasn't me messin' something up!

"I think you shocked the hell out of Ollie! Did you see his face? Oh, Hank, that was fucking perfect."

She was confusing the hell out of me, but I went with it. "Well, yeah, I thought the fucking was perfect, too." I grinned and she just laughed harder.

She smacked my chest playfully and tried to calm her

laughter. It was no use. She'd looked at me and started the whole bout over again. I let her finish her hysterics, enjoying the sight of her so carefree. Once done, her lips locked on mine in a long sweet kiss.

"Thank you."

"I'd never been thanked for sex before, but you're welcome. Anytime."

"No, Hank, thank you for freaking out Ollie. That was the perfect payback for a couple of his transgressions. He'll be mortified for a week...hell, maybe even a month!" Her smile was bright and lit up the room. It seemed it was easy to please my angel.

"Glad to be of service. Anytime you want to fuck me to freak out your little friend, I'm your guy," I assured her, hugging her sexy body tightly.

After a few moments, she leaned up. "Don't call him little. It's derogatory and it will hurt his feelings. I want payback, but I don't want you offending him. Okay?" I was reminded that regardless of our mating it didn't change the fact that Oliver had top billing. I needed a new plan to ensure I got top status.

"Got it, darlin'. Note to self. Do not piss off your assistant."

"He's not just my assistant. He's my best friend and only I get to piss him off. Got it?" She poked at my chest to make her point.

I nodded, still annoyed that he came and went as he pleased. Then my whole world went bright with her next comment.

"I have the entire day free."

"Really?" I tried not to sound too hopeful. "Whatever

shall we do?" I used my most eloquent accent and thrust my hips.

She hit my chest again and got out of bed swaying her delectable ass in the process. "I was thinking we start with a bath. You game, stud?"

"A bath?" I crinkled my nose. "What about your friend?"

"You can't get your bandage wet, so a shower's out." My angel thought of everything. "And Ollie can wait, the little punk."

"Oh, so you can call him little, but I can't?"

"Exactly!" She smiled. I didn't think I'd ever understand her relationship with that man. Boy. Man-boy. Whatever.

A brisk knock came at the door. She moved to open it, completely naked. "Don't you dare flaunt that body in front of him."

She looked at me in confusion and then just shrugged. I walked over to the door and opened it, bare-ass naked, instead.

Oliver's eyes traced my body from top to bottom. His mouth hung open again. "What is it?" I asked. He continued to stare.

Behind me, Aspen wedged her way around with that sexy purple nightgown back on. She stepped in front of me to hide my manhood. I put my arm around her shoulders and cupped her satin-clad breast, then kissed her neck. She leaned it to the side, giving me better access. She wanted to make her friend uncomfortable? I was her guy. If I got to touch her in the process, that was just fine with me.

"Oliver, when Hank's here, he'd prefer you knock."

"So it starts already?" The man's eyes narrowed

into slits; his lips held a hard line. She shrugged and he continued, "The nurse is here, and I've cancelled your afternoon appointments so that you could have the day as you requested. Is that going to be all, *Ms. Reynolds?*"

Heated looks were exchanged between the two and then a smile crept across Aspen's face. "Gotcha! Payback's a bitch!" she screamed with laughter. "I can't believe the look on your face, Ollie. You looked like you had wet your pants!"

His face softened. "I just saw my best friend being fucked! Though it was damn hot seeing you ride a sexy cowboy"—he looked me up and down and continued—"that was just twisted and evil. You knew I would be coming to wake you up like I do every day!"

"Actually, I was a little busy with the stud here to remember that you'd be making your morning wake-up call. But I'm not sorry I forgot. That was too good." They both laughed. "You gotta admit it was a good burn."

"I think I need a shower now. Seeing Hank in all his cowboy yumminess, I need to go home and spank Dean." Spank Dean? More information than I needed to hear about the pip-squeak and his sexual preferences.

"Well, you do that. I'm going to take my angel here and dirty her up some more. Tell the nurse to come back in an hour. Thanks, buddy, and sorry for yelling at ya. I was as surprised as you were by her joke," I said, trying to make a small effort with her friend. Seemed as though the way to her happiness was a wicked orgasm and making this guy happy.

His smile split across his entire face. His teeth were a startling white. "Buddy? I like it," he mused and then turned to leave.

"That was good of you, Hank. You're going to have to get over some of your jealousy toward Oliver. He's very gay and very in love with his boyfriend, Dean. Actually, you might like Dean. He's a firefighter."

"I don't have any gay friends, so it's not every day that I see a guy openly talking about being with one. I don't really care what he does in his personal time, but he doesn't need to be seeing you naked. That's reserved for me, and me alone."

"Is that right?" Her eyes were swirling with heat.

"Damn straight!" I smacked her on the ass. "Now about that bath." She laughed and ran to the bathroom.

"Come on, stud. The water's mighty fine," she called from the bathroom, butchering a Southern accent.

CHAPTER EIGHT

We spent the next two weeks in a similar routine. I'd go to work; Hank would wreak havoc on my home staff and check in with me and his crew by mobile. Gustav, my chef, didn't understand the relationship between Hank and I, but neither did I.

Spending time really analyzing it hadn't been at the top of my list of things to do. Instead, I preferred to enjoy the easy relationship we'd grown accustomed to, even though I kept waiting for the shoe to drop. I knew one day it would.

Every day Hank would greet me with an earth-shattering kiss, leaving me breathless and ready for him in mere seconds. We'd discuss our day, chat about different things we didn't know about one another, eat whatever Gustav prepared, and spend our evenings making love like wild animals. I rather enjoyed the routine. Having someone to come home to was new to me. Even Butch wormed his way into my heart.

"Tomorrow I'm gettin' outta here." Hank took a monster-sized bite of his garlic bread. The man was just so damned big. Everything he did seemed monumental.

Panic started to rise, my heart pounding out of my chest. "What do you mean? You're leaving? But…"

Hank cut me off before I could start in. "Darlin', don't worry your pretty little head. I'm not leaving you—I'm leaving the house. It's been over two weeks and I'm going crazy, shoulder-bitin' crazy." My entire body physically relaxed. "'Sides, I need to check in on my men. Make sure they're keeping up their end of the work."

"Okay, I'll have my driver take you."

"Nope. I can drive myself. My truck's automatic, and the therapist thinks it would be a good idea for me to start stretchin' myself a bit. Push the limits, ya know?"

"Really? So soon? You just started showing real improvement in your mobility." I thought back to earlier that morning when he fully gripped my hips and rammed into my body from behind, making me scream out in pleasure. He was definitely getting better. I could feel the warm blush spread across my cheeks and down my neck.

"Yup. I'd love to drive you to work tomorrow." His eyes were close to pleading.

Smiling, I agreed, knowing my security team would not appreciate this option. Having a lot of money had its disadvantages, and concern for my safety was one of them. Between disgruntled employees and the everyday wacko, I couldn't be too careful, and getting into a truck not manned by my security team was risky. Hank would keep me safe though. If anything, our concern for one another was growing in spades over the past couple weeks. Besides, if he'd throw his body under a sky raining metal pipes, I think he'd ensure I got safely to my building.

"So it's settled then."

"What's settled?" a voice called from the entryway to the dining room. I knew that voice. I grew up hearing the shrill tone, so high at times it could pierce an eardrum.

Hank looked confused. "Who the hell are you? Jesus, angel! Your security in this place needs some fixin'!" He stood up from the dining table and put himself between me and the she-devil.

I turned slowly as my mother's shocked face looked Hank up and down before her stoic exterior wall went back up. *Yeah, he's that impressive.*

"Hello, Mother," I said with no endearment. I needed to talk to the clerk managing the doors. Remove family members from having immediate access to my home. Now that Hank was here, you never knew what position we'd be in. That thought put a little smile on my face.

"Aspen, darling. I just heard about your accident"—*even though it happened two weeks ago,* I wanted to add— "and wanted to come and check on you." She looked between Hank's imposing form and then back to me. "I see you have company. I apologize for intruding." Her long over-trained manners made her sound almost polite and concerned for my welfare. I knew better.

"I'm fine, Mother, as you can see. This is Hank Jensen. He's the man who saved my life."

"Oh?" Her eyebrows rose to the ceiling. "So I am in your debt then." She thrust out a hand. Hank lifted it to his lips and kissed her knuckles in a move that was very old-fashioned. His Southern ways were quite charming.

"Pleasure to meet you, ma'am." He gestured to a seat and pulled it out for my mother. Damn Hank and his gentlemanly behavior. I wanted the woman out of my house, not sitting at my table.

"Don't mind if I do, Hank. Thank you." She sat ramrod straight and delicately placed her hands into her lap.

"Would you like some dinner, Mother? I can have Gustav bring you something." *Please say no, please say no, please say no...*

"No, thank you. A lady has to keep her girlish figure." Her eyes grazed over my huge plate of pasta. Normally I didn't eat this way, but I did work out a lot and Hank had been working me double-time in the bedroom. "I would love a martini though, darling."

"Sure. Just a moment." I got up and went to the kitchen to request the martini and another bottle of wine for me. I had a feeling this unannounced visit had more to it than motherly concern. She was not the type to fawn over her children.

While London, Rio, and I were growing up, she never cleaned a wound, kissed a boo-boo better, or stayed up with us when we'd had nightmares. None of that. All of the normal things a good mother did were done by highly paid nannies. London and I still spent time with ours and bought Christmas presents for them, celebrated our birthdays together, but Rio probably couldn't even remember their names. He had always been self-absorbed. Just like my mother.

I made my way back to the dining room and could hear her highness grilling Hank. *If she ruins this relationship for me, I'll disown her.* Relationship? I came to a screeching halt. Thinking about Hank and me as anything more than friends with benefits was going to get me in a world of hurt. Besides the jealous outbursts with Oliver and the possessiveness of my body between the sheets, he'd never so much as hinted at anything more.

I wasn't even sure I wanted more.

Yes, things between us had been great—fantastic even— but how long would that last? Until he recovered? Probably.

He was a cowboy from Texas. His business happened to be doing work in New York. That didn't mean he'd be here indefinitely, and there was no way I'd be able to leave the city. Leave AIR Bright for what? A man. Even in my head, it sounded ludicrous. We were having fun. A lot of fun.

We were compatible physically and I genuinely enjoyed his company. He was different from anyone else I knew, better somehow. His honesty, character, and moral values were appealing, but that wasn't enough. You actually needed to live the in the same state. Everyone knew long distance relationships never worked out, and trying to make it work with people from two different classes was an added knife in the shit cake that was my love life. Confused and downtrodden, I entered the dining room.

"So you'll come, then?" were the dreaded words I heard come from my mother's perfect crimson-stained lips.

"Sure thing. I was just telling Aspen here that I was going stir crazy on account I'd been stuck here for two weeks. Dinner with the family sounds great!"

"You've been staying here for two weeks?" It was the first time in a long time I'd seen my mother at a loss for words. Her perfect temperament slid off balance. Her fingers gripped the seat of the chair cushion and her lips formed a tight line. It gave me a great deal of pleasure to see her slip off her pedestal. Point for Hank!

"Yes, ma'am! Aspen's been taking real good care of me." He threw a wink my way. "So don't you worry yourself none." Oh, Hank. She didn't give a damn about him and his health. She was worried about what it would look like for others to find out that he was staying with me. To her, it was as if I'd taken in a filthy stray.

"Excuse me…" I butted in.

"Oh, it's settled then. Darling, your friend Mr. Jensen is going to attend our dinner party at the estate."

"You know, I don't think that's such a good idea. Hank's treatments have been exhausting and…"

"Oh nonsense. The man obviously wants to get out, don't you, dear?" The sweet man ate it up. It was like watching the evil witch give Snow White the poisoned apple.

"Absolutely. Angel, you know I'm doing heaps better. 'Sides, I'd love to meet your family." He dug into his pasta, happy as a clam. Poor guy just didn't know any better. She was planning to feed him to the society mavens and make a spectacle of him. My mother was nothing if not imaginative in her attacks.

Her plastic smile was on full display, her emotionless mask making her appear even colder.

"Angel?" she asked, her eyes pointed and squinting.

"Hank likes nicknames." I didn't really need to defend his pet name for me, but my mother brings out the psycho in anyone within a ten-foot radius. Hank seemed completely immune, just eating his dinner with fervor.

I pushed my plate away, no longer hungry.

"I'm glad you didn't eat all of those carbs. You're not as young as you used to be. You're close to thirty. A good man doesn't want a fat wife—remember that, dear."

I held my breath and counted to ten so I wouldn't throttle her.

"Hey now, she's got nothin' to worry about in that department." His eyes bored into mine, heated desire pooling in those honeyed depths. "Her body is fantastic." His gaze scanned my plate. "You're not hungry, darlin'?"

My mother was stunned, mouth agape and eyes wide. If there was a doubt to the extent of our "relationship" before, there definitely wasn't now. The thought actually thrilled me. Knowing she'd spend hours on end fretting over my lack of social class and snubbing my nose at my proper upbringing would give her a heavy dose of anxiety. Maybe she'd rethink that invitation and call it off.

"Not anymore, thank you, Hank. Mother, if that's all, I'll see you out." Hank stood when I did, the consummate gentleman. He walked us both to the door.

"Mrs. Reynolds, it was good to meet ya." Hank brought her hand to his lips for the second time that evening. I made a mental note to have him wash his face before he kissed me again.

"It sure was a surprise meeting you. Thank you for assisting Aspen. I look forward to seeing you tomorrow, Mr. Jensen." Her saccharine sweet tone made me want to gag.

"Good-bye, Mother," I said, trying to close the door. She air-kissed both sides of my cheeks. When she was gone, I leaned against the door with a heavy thud and closed my eyes.

"What's the matter, darlin'?" Hank's fingers traced the edges of my hairline. Home. His touch was becoming a necessity, something I craved and I leaned into it until his large hand was cupping my jaw.

"Hank, what's happening between us?"

"What do you mean? We're enjoying each other's company. Immensely, I might add." He waggled his eyebrows suggestively, and his hands gripped my hips. "And I'm healing up. Gettin' stronger every day." He thrust his pelvis against me playfully.

His response was exactly why I hadn't allowed myself to fall, to feel something more for this beautiful man. When he was healed, he'd go back home to his ranch, to his real life.

"I'll make excuses about the event tomorrow. There really is no need for you to attend. I, on the other hand, will not be able to avoid it. If she paid a visit, that means my father will be next if I don't show."

His face scrunched up, his mouth twisting into a grimace. "Why wouldn't I go? I meant what I said. I'd love to meet the rest of your family. I met your wacky sister and your mother seemed nice enough."

"Don't let her fool you. She's a wolf in sheep's clothing. She only came here to check you out."

He shrugged. "Don't care. Doesn't bother me none. But we're going to that shindig."

This was going to be a disaster. Hank would be his fun-loving, straightforward cowboy self, and my family would be ready to pounce. It was like throwing a steak in a tank of piranhas.

"Hank, this is not like a family barbeque." I blew a frustrated breath over my forehead. "It's a high-society social gathering. The place will be chock full of high-powered executives, politicians, people with more money than God…"

"Are you saying I won't fit in, darlin'? I can hold my own." His gaze searched mine. The next four words shook me to my core. "Do I embarrass you?"

"Of course not! No, I…no. I just don't think you'll enjoy yourself."

"And you will?"

"Well, no. But I never do. Being with my family is a necessary evil." I slid my hands over his broad torso, trying to express how very much I didn't want him to be near that kind of evil. He gripped my hands to his chest.

"Angel, I'm going to escort you to that party. I'm going to dance with you in front of your family. I'm going to show you that you can have fun anywhere as long as you're with the right person." Was he even real? It wasn't possible that there was something so good in the world.

"God, Hank, I could get used to you so easily." *But I won't.*

He laughed and kissed me, tentatively at first, then pulled an inch away, our breath still mingling. "I should hope the hell so. I'm not going anywhere anytime soon. You're stuck with me, angel."

"Do you mean that?" I whispered, keeping my eyes closed tight, not wanting to see his response. He kissed each eyelid and leaned his forehead against mine.

"I wouldn't have said it if I didn't."

★ ★ ★ ★

Ever since her mom visited yesterday, Aspen acted differently. She seemed almost sad when she got ready for work this morning and left for the office. We didn't make love. She said she had a headache and scampered off like a scared kitten to the washroom to shower and get ready for work.

Alone.

She barely pecked me on the lips as she left. That might have been the first morning we hadn't made love since I moved in. Had I really moved in, or was I just staying here?

I thought things were progressing nicely between us. When I wasn't with her, I wanted to be. But maybe she didn't feel that way.

Something was off. When she left this morning, it felt like she was stepping back from me. All I knew is that she held my heart in a vise and my balls in her grip. All she had to do was bat those pretty eyelashes and I was damn near putty in her tiny hands. Whatever it was, I was gettin' to the bottom of it tonight.

A knock sounded on my bedroom door. Technically, I hadn't actually slept in the room yet, but it held all my clothes and things. It was probably the therapist. That girl was a looker, but nothin' like my girl. One thing they had in common though was the overachieving. She was set on pushing me just to my breaking point every day with my treatments, and Aspen encouraged her. I didn't look forward to it, but if I was honest with myself, the progress I was making did give me something to smile about.

"Come in," I hollered, a smile plastered across my face. Thinking about my girl did that.

"Hello, Hank." Oliver strode in, a fierce set to his thin lips. He went straight to my closet without a word and swung the hangers on the rod from left to right with a quick, practiced hand.

Such a strange fella. He'd pause a moment on one piece or another, then continue smacking the hangers around. He was Aspen's best man-friend, not mine. I was making an effort, though. Seemed as if the guy was happy, my woman was happy. So, I did what any hot-blooded American man who wanted to keep getting laid would do: I decided to befriend the guy. Well, sort of.

"Mind telling me what you're doing there, buddy? Aspen's already at work. Shouldn't you know that?" He smiled secretively. I didn't particularly like his face, especially not when he was hiding something.

"Well, cowboy, our Aspen tells me you are going to the Bright-Reynolds estate to attend a social gathering. Everyone who's anyone will be in attendance, including yours truly." He pulled at my clothes, a deep frown set to his pinched features. "You don't have anything suitable. Just as I thought. We're going shopping. I'm rescheduling your therapy for this afternoon."

"Shopping's pretty much the last thing I want to do today." I crossed my arms over my chest as best as I could with a busted shoulder and tried to look menacing.

"Too bad." His eyes turned to look me up and down. "What, pray tell, do you plan on wearing to a formal social event? Aspen will be dressed in Versace. You can't be a prince going to the ball dressed in Wranglers."

"And why the hell not?" Who was this guy anyway? Just because he dressed my girl didn't mean that rolled down the chain of command to dressing me now.

"Because you'll embarrass her. Is that what you want?" His words ripped right through my heart. That was the absolute last thing I wanted to happen. I was certain that when I met her family I'd win them over with my Southern charm and chest full of party jokes. I had a good one planned for the evening, too. Either way, it was important that I impress her family tonight. Being from different worlds was hard on any relationship, but more so on women because they tended to have the innate need to please. Boy, did I want to please my angel.

"No, I don't. Lead the way, buddy."

"Thank you." He seemed to relax. Then he sized me up with a bright white smile. I wondered if he used those toothpaste strips that were meant to make your teeth so bright they could glow in the dark. "Now, I know exactly what designer we can have tailored to fit that broad chest and those massive biceps in a jam. Jeez, how much do you work out, anyway?"

I laughed aloud as he led me out of the apartment and into the elevator. Before long, we were pulling up to a store smack dab in the middle of Fifth Avenue, the heart of New York City. I looked over the building. Oliver was grinning so much I worried that his face would stick that way.

The building was gray stone with bars running down the first story. Golden letters popped out of the building's side, prominently displaying ARMANI / 5TH AVENUE in big block letters.

"Looks like a jail," I said. Oliver looked like he'd forgotten I was with him.

"If that's jail, then lock me up, honey, and throw away the key!" He grabbed onto my forearm and tugged me toward the entrance. He was obviously excited. Reminded me of when Butch was about to get a meaty bone. He'd wag his tail and turn around in furious circles landing in a heap at my feet when his excitement ebbed. Oliver was kind of like Butch, but I feared I was the meaty bone in this scenario.

After trying on six suits, I'd about had it. I was at my boiling point. Aspen was going to pay dearly for this—preferably on her back with her thighs around my ears.

"Oh, Hank, this is the one. This is it!" Oliver screeched.

I stood on a raised circle facing three large mirrors. They were tilted so that one could see the clothes from every angle. A small, hairy looking fella was standing in front of me measuring my inseam. He gripped my balls and shoved them to the side.

"What the heck, partner?" I jumped back, covering my crown jewels. "This ain't no doctor's office. Touch me again and I'll punch your teeth out!" The man rattled off something in a foreign language. Oliver went over and appeased the man.

Oliver rolled his eyes and came back over to me. "Hank, he's a tailor. They have to measure your inseam or your, um, bits will be uncomfortable. He got what he needed on the pant, so can he finish with the shoulders, arms, and waist? You going to be a good boy and keep your paws to yourself?" I squinted my eyes at him but got back on the circle. "We don't have a lot of time as it is." He sounded completely exasperated. The feeling was mutual.

"Sorry. Not used to this type of thing. Just get it done, then," I told the man with the accent. He hemmed and hawed until he finished sizing me up. Lord knows what the hell he had to do. The suit fit just fine; a little tight in the chest and shoulders, but I could remedy that by leaving it unbuttoned. It was the largest size they had on hand. I could make do, but Oliver was not okay with that option. He said I had to look the part. Whatever that meant. It wasn't like I was trying out for a Broadway show.

Oliver picked out several shirts, more than I needed for the evening. Instead, I scrolled through my phone and texted Aspen.

To: Aspen Reynolds

Your boy is dressing me up nice for the evening. You owe me. Big time.

I watched Oliver grab several ties and match them up with the brightly colored dress shirts. I overheard him telling the sales girl that we wanted the same suit in black and a pinstriped pattern and to charge everything to Aspen Reynolds's account. Before I could disagree, my phone pinged.

From: Aspen Reynolds

Are you being nice to him? How shall I pay up?

Oh, she wanted to play. Very nice. It took me a few moments, but I decided honesty was always the best policy.

To: Aspen Reynolds

You. Naked. I'll handle the rest.

Without even a chance to put the cell phone into my pocket, it pinged once more.

From: Aspen Reynolds

Deal, stud.

"Okay, Hank. Put your clothes back on. We'll have lunch while the tailor alters the gray suit. The other two will be finished later."

Time to get the hell out of there. I could pay Aspen back later for the clothes. It was a nice enough store, but nothin' had price tags and there were very few things hanging on the racks. When you walked in, you were met by someone who assessed your clothes, discussed your needs and such. Oliver called it a personal consultant.

If this was how the other half lived, I didn't want any part of it. What I did want, though, was a tall blond angel with the most beautiful eyes I'd ever seen and a body that wouldn't quit. God, she made my mouth water and my dick spring to attention. I couldn't get enough of her. I'd had her every day for weeks and, if anything, the need for her got stronger as the days went on. It wasn't possible to explain. She was just what I wanted, all the time.

My phone rang, and I picked it up, thinking it would be my girl. "Hello, angel. I was just thinking 'bout you."

"Angel? That's a new one, Punky," Ma's voice rang through the line loud and cheery as usual.

"Ma, it's good to hear your voice."

"Really? Is that so? 'Cause you haven't heard it in weeks!" Her tone was bitter with a hint of sarcasm.

"Oh, Ma, I'm sorry. Things got kinda crazy at the job. There was an accident and I got hurt." Shit, she was going to be pissed when she realized this happened weeks ago.

"Oh my God! My baby. What happened? Tell me everything!" I laughed. She was going to tar and feather me.

"Now, Ma, I'm fine. Just got stuck with a pipe is all. Went straight into my shoulder. The doctors fixed me up real good. Now I'm almost three weeks out on recovery."

"You had surgery? Hank!" she cried. Then she yelled over the receiver, "Henry, Henry, my baby's been hurt. Had to have surgery and everythin'!" I could hear mumbled words through the hand I knew she had held over the speaker while she updated Old Man Henry. My mother wasn't typically a dramatic woman, but the moment one of her children got hurt, she was like a mama bear with her cubs. All worked up and worried over nothin' at all.

Oh, man. Now I'd done it. Telling my family about the accident slipped my mind. She was going on and on. I answered each of her questions, telling her every detail as I remembered it.

"Well I'll be coming out there. I have to see my baby!" I could hear her tears and sniffles all the way across the states. When Julia Jensen got her mind set on something, there was no changing it.

"Okay, okay, Ma. I'll buy you a ticket and make arrangements, but it's really unnecessary. Aspen and her team of helpers really have been great. I'm healing up nicely."

"Aspen?" Her tone was curious, so I just plowed through and told her as much as I could while I threw on my clothes. I glazed over some parts and left her wondering about others. She'd hound me when she visited anyway. No need to go into it all now.

"Well, I'll only believe you're okay if I see it with my own eyes. Wait until your father sees you, Punky. He's liable to blister your bum for not telling us sooner."

I knew she was joking. Mom and Dad had never so much as laid a finger on us boys growin' up, but the fear of my father busting out his belt or using his big hand on our rears had me and Heath running for the hills.

"I'm sorry, Ma. Really, I'm fine. You'll see. I love you."

"To the moon and back, Punky. I love you to the moon and back."

Just hearing my ma's voice made me homesick. Looks

like I'd have news to share with Aspen. This ought to make for an interesting evening. I wondered how she would take it.

"Come on, Hank. I'm wasting away out here!" Oliver's squeaky voice came from beyond the dressing room door. "How long could it possibly take to put on a pair of jeans?"

"Hold your horses, boy!" He was like an angry mosquito that you couldn't shake.

I left the solace of the dressing room.

"You ready, cowboy?"

"As ready as I'll ever be."

CHAPTER NINE

Oliver put the finishing touches on my hair. He had pulled it into a sleek bun with loose tendrils of hair framing my face delicately and a few dime-sized crystals pinned around the bun. They matched the earrings and bracelet he chose for the evening. The dress wasn't new, but one of my favorites. It was simple: a strapless bodice and a hemline that hung just to my knees, deep royal blue, and, at the waist, a satin gray belt.

The look was definitely a newer trend, almost a play on a business suit but with a lux fabric and sheen. Oliver paired it with sky-high gray suede platforms. They had crystals capped at the back that continued along down the line of the heel. Sexy as hell.

After checking myself out in the mirror, Oliver and I both agreed that I looked hot. This was the first time in a long time that I'd dressed to please a man instead of the guest list. It made me feel young and girlie—two ways I would have never described myself. Ever.

As I stepped out of my room, Hank was just leaving his.

"Damn, angel. You're the prettiest woman I've ever seen. C'mere, let me look atcha."

He grabbed my hand and twirled me around slowly. I allowed it, captivated by the spell he had me under. Once I'd finished the spin, he laid his big paws on my hips, encircling my waist. His hands could almost touch each other. He made me feel so small and dainty. Most men I'd dated were only an inch or two taller and I had to keep myself really lean in order to not look out of place standing in pictures next to them. The last thing I'd needed in the society pages was fat commentary. My mother would never let me live it down. Hank, though, he was enormous. I looked downright petite with him, and I loved it.

"You sure clean up nice, stud." I fingered his royal-blue tie. He stood before me in a steel-gray suit. His eyes bore more of the green than caramel hue this evening. His dress shirt was bright white and lightly lined with tiny blue pinstripes.

Oliver was damned good at his job. The overall effect was drop-dead gorgeous. With looks like these, I'd need to keep my eyes on him all night. Otherwise, he'd be bombarded by all the slutty socialites with nothing to do but play Monopoly with their trust funds and squander away hot men.

"Oh, the two of you make the perfect couple. You two should be on the first cover of *Bright Magazine*!" Oliver gushed.

The doorbell rang, and Hank held his arm out for me to take. I loved his old world charm. "If I had half a brain, I'd blow off this event and take you back into that room and have my wicked way with ya," he whispered in my ear. His breath made the hair on the back of my neck tingle.

I smiled coyly at him as we made our way to the foyer. Oliver was kissing Dean when we approached. When Hank saw the PDA between Oliver and Dean, he turned a tad pink. Oliver didn't care who saw him with Dean. Never had. He'd only ever been in the closet long enough to kiss boys that were still in there.

Hank cleared his throat. Dean smiled and pulled away first. Oliver stared into Dean's eyes, obviously love-struck. They made for a great team; I was thrilled that my Ollie had a mate. If only I were so lucky.

Dean held his hand out to Hank. "You must be the hunk I've heard so much about." Dean gave him a sly grin.

He was tall, much taller than Oliver. He had a large enough build to tuck Oliver into his side to shake hands, but he was not quite as large as Hank. His thick black hair was slicked back into a sleek cut, and he had dazzling blue eyes that swirled with mirth as he held Oliver close.

It was obvious that Dean was the alpha male in this relationship, but the man was a complete dichotomy. Most of his career had been spent doing makeup and hair for the modeling industry. That's how he and Oliver met. Then one day, he up and left it to become a firefighter. He was definitely one of the prettiest firemen I'd ever seen. He'd recently appeared in a sexy fireman's calendar "showcasing his assets," as Oliver put it.

"It's Hank, but never hurts the ego to be called a hunk!" Hank shook Dean's hand as they both laughed. "Hear you're a firefighter? Back home I used to volunteer with the fire department to help out now and again." Hank had never mentioned that. There was still so much we didn't know about one another. I enjoyed finding out these little tidbits.

"Guilty. I love getting my hands dirty. Men's work, you know?"

"Abso-fucking-lutely, bro!" Hank clapped a hand on Dean's shoulder. He seemed to take to Dean so quickly. Made me wonder why he didn't have the same ease with my Ollie.

The two continued their "men talk" as we entered the elevator. Oliver came to me and hugged me tight. "Our boyfriends are getting along. Isn't this so exciting? Dean hated Grant with a passion."

"Dean hates me with a passion, not Grant," I reminded him.

"Oh yeah, I forgot about that," he snickered. "He actually hated Grant, too." He laughed louder, and then turned to Dean. "Hey, baby, do you still hate Aspen?"

"Are you still working eighteen-hour days, not excluding weekends?"

"Yes, snookums," Oliver said.

"Then yes." But his face held a smile I knew all too well. We always joked that Dean hated me. It was part of our everyday conversation, though a small part of me believed that he did resent me a little for how much I needed Oliver's attention. I knew since he made a firefighter's wage and not the high salary he used to bring home working in the fashion industry, that he appreciated how much I paid Ollie in the end.

We made it to my parent's estate on the outskirts of the city in good time, considering Friday rush hour traffic. The stretch limo pulled around the circular drive. My parents were standing at the threshold greeting everyone as they strolled up. A small get-together for my mother was around hundred and fifty people. As we approached, I saw the Senator and her husband, previously the President of the United States, air-kiss my mother and shake hands with my father.

"Is that who I think it is?" Hank whispered in my ear.

"Yes."

"Whoa, Nelly. When you said a bunch of fancy-dancy folks were going to be here tonight, I hadn't expected one of our past presidents. I can't wait to meet him!"

His joy made me smile. We approached my mother and father, Dean and Oliver right on our heels. Hank immediately took my mother's hands and kissed her knuckles and then shook my father's hand.

"Evenin', Mr. and Mrs. Reynolds."

"Mr. Jensen, it's an honor to meet the man that saved my darling Pen. I owe you a great deal." My father addressed Hank, smiling wide. My mother was an evil she-bitch, but I adored my father. He was the one person aside from London and Oliver who told me to reach for the stars and pursue my dreams.

"Hello, Daddy." I kissed his cheek and he hugged me tightly. I turned to my mother. "Mother." My mother gave me her standard double air-kiss. I tamped down the desire to make a jab at her.

We moved out of the line of guests and stood off to the side to wait for Dean and Oliver. I wanted Hank to feel comfortable tonight, so I'd made Oliver swear to stay close. Even if they weren't the best of friends, at least Hank knew him and Ollie knew everyone. Though it didn't look like it would matter one way or the other with the way Dean and Hank were carrying on as if they were long-lost brothers.

They'd moved from firefighting to sports teams and betting on who would make the playoffs this year. Of course, Dean was on the side of the New York Giants, and Hank was a firm believer in the Dallas Cowboys.

We found a table out in the garden next to the pool

where the four of us could sit; two chairs were left open. Large Japanese lanterns were hanging from invisible wires over the entire area. Twinkling candles sat on the tables next to a beautiful display of hydrangeas. The pool had floating lily pads with candles in the centers. Each of the trees was circled with twinkling white lights.

The entire theme was ethereal. Soft orchestral music played from a small quartet off to the side of the yard. Mother was a perfect party planner. No detail was left undone. Maybe if I paid her a huge compliment, let her plan an event for me, she'd lay off the marriage talk. It could work, but it was doubtful.

Ever since Grant and I broke up, she'd been hounding me to get back with him. According to her, he was the perfect man—regardless of the fact that he'd cheated on me...twice! She believed cheating was to be expected from a man of his pedigree. I disagreed with her and that's been at the crux of our dysfunctional relationship ever since.

We sat and enjoyed comfortable conversation before Hank and Dean took off to get us drinks from the bar.

"Oh, princess, our princes are besties. Isn't this great?" I couldn't help but get caught up in his happiness.

"I know, Ollie. But what if mine turns out to be a frog?"

Oliver's face snapped back to attention, his eyes squinting. "What do you mean? I thought you and Hank were getting along great. From what I saw in the bedroom a couple weeks ago, he seemed to satisfy those needs."

"Yes. He's incredible in the bedroom." I thought back to the other day when he surprised me in my dressing closet by sliding his cock into me from behind. We left quite a mess in the closet, clothes strewn everywhere. I almost felt bad for the maid. "Oh, Oliver. I just don't know where this thing with him is going. We're so different. Just because we're compatible physically doesn't mean we're right for each other."

"Why not? I don't understand. He looks at you like the entire world just stopped because you were in his line of vision. That cowboy is falling for you, princess. I know it like I know my labels. You *know* I know my labels!"

"I just don't see how it could really work in the long run. He lives in Texas. I live in New York."

"So he moves here or you move to Texas. Oh, no, that would mean I'd have to move to Texas. I don't know if my hair could handle that heat!" He patted his perfectly coiffed hair to make sure even mentioning it didn't mess it up.

"Stop being a drama queen. I'm not moving to Texas."

"You don't think you're moving to Texas. You don't know what the future holds, Pen. Just let the coming weeks happen. I've never seen you happier. Enjoy being with Hank. He seems to enjoy the hell out of you."

★ ★ ★ ★

"Who enjoys the hell out of you, angel?" I set the white wine in front of her. It amazed me how quickly I picked up and socked away information about her likes and dislikes. In previous relationships, those details just didn't matter to me. With Aspen, I wanted to know everything about her. Dean handed me the small plate of food, and I set that down in between us to share.

"You, stud." That sparkle in her eyes when she'd said it made me want to bow at her pretty feet.

"Well, ain't that the truth." I leaned over and pecked her on the lips. She gripped my neck and pressed our lips together harder. Just when I was starting to get into it, she pulled away, looking shy.

Everyone at the table laughed. So far, the party had been great. I'd met the ex-President of the United States, and a few other muckety-mucks. Also, I enjoyed talking with Dean. He was nothing like his prissy boyfriend. He was cool. I liked the fella a great deal. Could see myself watching the games with him on occasion in Aspen's TV room. Maybe we could even go to a live game. I briefly wondered if Aspen liked sports.

"Hey, darlin', you like sports?" She cringed. That pretty much gave me my answer.

"Pen! I can't believe you're here!" London yelled as she ran over. A lanky fella smoothly followed in her wake. London threw her arms around her sister. Aspen smiled brightly. I loved seeing that smile on her face. Looked like whatever disagreement they'd had back at the house a couple weeks ago had come and gone.

"London, Tripp, I'm surprised you're here! Don't you have a client?" she asked as she hugged her sister back.

"Yes. But this one's a couple! So I'm actually free to do what I want on the weekends unless I tag along with them. The wife wasn't too pleased with my unconventional methods. She's the jealous type. Can't blame her though. Her hubs is a hottie!" she squealed. I made a mental note to ask Aspen more about her sister's job.

Aspen hugged the tall man. I gripped my hands into fists as the man squeezed her with too much familiarity. "Tripp, I want you to meet Hank." She put her pretty hand on my shoulder and glided it down my good arm. The movement sent chills through me.

God, just a small touch and she had me almost painfully hard. It didn't help that we hadn't made love today. I wanted to fuck her into next week, the longing for her soft body so strong.

"Hank, this is Tripp Devereaux. He's London's best friend and assistant." *The one she beds on occasion*, I thought.

"Some of the time, beautiful. Only when she needs the help. Which has been more often with business booming."

Beautiful? The ease with which he said the nickname sent prickles of jealousy up my spine.

Tripp held out his hand. "Good to meet you, Hank. I understand you're the man that saved our Pen's life. Thank you for that. I couldn't imagine dealing with Bridge if anything had happened to her sister."

Our Pen? I shook the man's hand making sure to squeeze it harder than someone would who's being polite. Tripp's eyes squinted at the gesture. Message received. Good.

"Bridge? Who's that? Your wife?"

"Wife?" The man laughed a full-bellied laugh that caught on to the rest of the group. "No, big guy. Bridge is what I call London. You know, kind of like 'London Bridge Is Falling Down.' You see?"

"Uh, sure. Okay." To each his own.

The two newcomers joined the group and the drinking started in earnest. I hadn't had so much as a sip of alcohol since my accident, so by the time I'd had three beers, in a glass no less, I was feeling pretty good.

"Hey, stud, this is fun. You're fun," a tipsy Aspen slurred.

"I'm feeling mighty fine myself, angel." I laid a beer-laced kiss on her lips. She hummed in appreciation and smacked her chops.

"I love how he calls her angel. Isn't that so sweet?" London spoke to the group. She leaned on the table, face in her hand, as Tripp rubbed a hand up and down her back. I hadn't figured them out yet. They were close—really close. But then again, so were Oliver and Aspen, but they were not sexual in any way. Tripp and London, on the other hand, seemed very familiar with one another. "Why do you call her angel, Hank?" London asked.

Aspen looked over at me, a huge smile on her beautiful face. "Because when daggers were raining from the sky, she was there. All golden and white and keepin' me centered."

There was a collective "aww" from everyone at the table. Everyone except Aspen. She had her perfect little pink bottom lip snared between her teeth. I knew that face. That look could bring a team of football players to their knees in an instant. She was turned on. Fuck me, she looked good enough to eat too.

"Hank, will you escort me to the restroom, please? Tall heels and all?" I looked down at her heels. They were very sparkly and high. Connected to the best set of gams I'd ever seen, too.

"Of course, darlin'. Lead the way." I'd follow her to the ends of the earth if her ass were my view.

On the way to the washroom, Aspen was stopped at least a dozen times. Everyone seemed to want a piece of her. Hell, I wanted a piece of her. We made it to our destination, and I was about to turn around and get settled against the wall when she tugged my tie and pulled me into the room with her.

Her lips covered mine the second she pushed me against the door. I was bathed in the smell of vanilla and honey, good enough to eat. At this moment, I was starved.

"Hank, I want you. Now." Her lips singed mine. They were so hot, slick, and delicious. Our tongues tangled in deep strokes. The wine she was drinking earlier awakened my taste buds with hints of cherry, plum, and my angel. She pulled away, and her slippery little tongue licked a trail from my ear, down my neck, and back up again. Fuck, the woman knew how to twist me up into knots.

I shoved my hands into her hair, diamond pins flying everywhere, letting her hair fall in curling waves over the softest bare shoulders. "Christ! You're perfect." And she was. Every facet of her blew me away. The way her body arched toward mine as if she couldn't control it. How her breasts heaved waiting for me to handle them. The absolute heaven between her thighs that wept for my touch. These things combined had me spinning with want and need.

Her nimble fingers pulled and plucked at my belt. I heard the telltale signs of my zipper going down in the all-too-quiet room. I slapped the switches near my hand. The fan whirred to life, helping to mask some of the sound. My angel was not a quiet woman in the sack. I ate up every sound she made, but I didn't think the rest of the party would want to hear her—especially not her mother.

"Hank, I need you to fuck me. Right here, right now."

A low growl exited my throat as I pulled up her dress and she freed my cock. She was wearing those fucking black stockings again. I slipped my fingers in the tiny scrap of fabric at her hips. They shredded against my onslaught in seconds.

She groaned as I tucked them into my pocket and walked her backward over to the sink. Her mouth hung onto my neck like a leech. When her ass butted against the counter, she lifted herself up on the edge. I would have loved nothing more than to pin her against the door and fuck her, but my shoulder was not up to the task of holding her weight...yet.

Soon I'd be wall-banging her. With little finesse, I yanked her thighs wide apart to accommodate my body between them. She was dripping wet. Soaked. Her juices coated my fingers.

As I slipped two fingers into her channel, her tongue trailed along the part of my chest she'd exposed. When she had undone the buttons of my shirt was lost on me. All I could focus on was her wet heat, her scent like warm honey on a summer's day. She was so damned hot for me. Her lips down low coated my hand, ready to accept me.

"Oh, angel, so eager for my cock."

She nodded against my throat, teeth piercing my skin. I'm sure she'd just marked me. "Ah, fuck!" I lined up my cock, pulled on her ass, and rammed into her in one hard thrust.

"Oh God!" I tried to drown out the sound by kissing her. She was too wild. "Harder, Hank. Please. Fuck me, hard." She bit the tender cartilage of my ear, and I pounded into her. My thrusts were relentless in rhythm; I had her begging and pleading to God. She held onto me so tight I wasn't sure I could breathe, so caught up in all that was her.

The way her body smelled and tasted, the pull and clench of her pussy around my cock, the heated breath against my neck. The woman was my kryptonite.

When we were connected physically, she owned me body and soul. I couldn't get close enough. Twisting my hips, I pinned her clit between us, grinding against her. Her inner walls clamped down like a fist around my cock, shooting pleasure through the thick staff between my thighs.

She was going over the edge. I wanted more. "More, angel. Always more. Give me everything."

I bit at her lips, pushed down the top of her strapless dress her bra with it and pinched her rosy nipples, tugging them into tight aching little points. She liked it a little rough. I sucked on her right breast and plunged my hand down between our bodies. It was intoxicating to feel myself pushing in and out of her wet heat.

I felt like I was ripping her apart. Hell, she was ripping me apart.

She bit into the tender flesh at my neck once more, and I held back my own cry, trying my damndest to keep quiet, but it was too much. She was too much. I pounded ruthlessly into her body. She started making these little whimpering noises, and I knew she was on the precipice of a monster orgasm.

Swirling my thumb on her hot little wad of nerves and biting down on her nipple had her arching and screaming out her release. I held my other hand over her mouth to muffle the sound as best I could. She bit my hand but I held on, pumping into her roughly, extending her pleasure, and finding my own.

"I love fucking you," I whispered through clenched teeth.

A few more thrusts and I was coming into her hot tunnel. Her legs held tight around my waist pulling at my body. It was a good five minutes of taking huge gasping breaths before we both calmed.

"Jesus, Hank. You undo me," she whispered, placing light kisses along my neck and face.

"Good. I want to be the only one who does. You got that?" I rubbed my softening dick against her. "Only me from now on." I punctuated with a thrust and a deep kiss, fucking her with my mouth as my lower half relaxed.

She kissed me and tugged on my body. "Keep that up, angel, and I'll be fucking you again." My dick was already getting hard within her. That's how much this woman affected me. Once wasn't nearly enough.

"You're crazy, you know that?" She laughed and pushed me away. My cock slipped out of her along with a gush of our combined fluids.

"Crazy 'bout you, darlin'." I grinned while buttoning up my shirt, and then fixed my tie.

She cleaned herself up and put herself back together sans panties. Those were in my pocket for safekeeping. I had a duffle bag full of these ripped pieces of lace. Her hair was a lost cause though.

Aspen inspected herself in the bathroom mirror. Long fingers tugged through her sex-hair. "Oliver's going to be pissed that you pulled my hair down."

"I don't give a shit what he thinks. I'll sick Dean on 'em."

"You really like Dean?" she asked. Her fingers ran through her golden hair. It still looked perfect to me. Then again, everything about her did.

"I do. He's a good guy. Man's man, you know?"

"Yeah, I get it. You have more in common with Dean

than with Oliver. I'm glad you've made a new friend. I think you'd really like Tripp, too. He's a mix between a manly man and a chick. You never really know either way. One moment he's kissing a woman, the next he's taking it in the ass from a hot male model."

"Whoa, angel, too much info. Jeez. You gotta keep that shit to yourself," I told her, smiling wickedly and squeezing her ass.

We exited the bathroom and went back to our group. Food had been served, and there were two plates sitting at our table. After the bathroom acrobatics, I was starving and the pain in my shoulder was thrumming. Nothing another beer wouldn't fix. 'Sides, I'd gladly take a little pain for a lot of Aspen.

"You had to fuck with her hair, didn't you, Hank? Damn it! That took me forever to get just right." Oliver pouted and gave me the evil eye.

"I'd say I was sorry, but we both know I'd be lying, so I won't. Had to be done," I told him as I pulled out Aspen's chair for her to sit.

Dean, London, and Tripp laughed so loud other tables were staring.

"It had to be done or she had to be done?" he quipped. Oh, my buddy wanted to play. Yeah, I was definitely warming to the fella.

"Both." I grinned and he gave me a fish face.

"I'll take note that you prefer her hair be down when you're going to go all macho on her." He harrumphed and took a sip of his wine.

"Are you kidding? Aspen, tell him it was you who attacked me!" I clasped my beer and chugged the entire thing down, smiling like a loon.

"Shut the hell up, Ollie." Aspen pinched Oliver in the shoulder.

"Ouch!" He moved closer to Dean and out of her reach.

"Such language, Aspen. You realize who's here tonight. You should be minding your manners," said the cool voice of Aspen's mother from behind her.

"Oh, Mother. Not everyone is as perfect as you are." Aspen downed the rest of her wine and held the glass out to me. "Another, please."

I jumped up, not wanting to participate in a battle of words with Aspen and her mother. I wanted to take my angel home and fuck her until morning, and then start all over again. Fighting with her about her mother was not going to fit into that plan.

Dean and Tripp followed me to the bar.

"God, that woman is insufferable." Tripp was the first to break the silence.

"I've never understood why she is such a bitch to Aspen. Out of the three children, Aspen is by far the most successful. You'd think she'd be singing her praises, but instead she finds every opportunity to prod her." Dean jumped into the first seat on the Hate Aspen's Mother train.

I just let the two men vent, listening intently to their opinions on the mother–daughter dynamic.

"Oh great, and then the party takes a complete nose dive." Dean gestured over to Aspen. A nice-lookin' fella in a suit was standing next to my angel. His hand was on her shoulder, his thumb creeping along her bare neck. I could see her visibly shrink back.

Oh, hell no. I saw only red.

I made my way through the crowd coming up behind Aspen. With my good arm, I flicked the man's hand off Aspen and circled her waist with my hands possessively. I pulled her tight against my front. She leaned against me willingly. Kissing the soft flesh of her neck where the man had touched her gave the added oomph I needed to make the man's eyes widen in shock.

"I missed you, angel." I kissed her neck once more.

Her mother's eyes were blistering with anger as she took in our comfortable body language. Instead of letting her go, I reached out my hand to the space invader. "Hank Jensen. And you are…?"

The man's composure turned from shock to perfectly composed in mere seconds. "Grant. Grant Campbell, I'm Aspen's —"

"Business partner on *Bright Magazine.*" Aspen completed his sentence. I knew who the fucker was, and I already hated him with a passion. He had hurt her not once, but twice. That alone was worthy of a beatdown, but his smug "I'm better than you" tone was a close second contender. Though at that moment, I wanted to hurt him just for shits and giggles.

"So who are you to Aspen, Mr. Jensen?" the man asked, a sneer twisting his lips.

"I'm the boyfriend."

CHAPTER TEN

My eyes must have been the size of baby elephants. Hank just announced in no uncertain terms that he was my boyfriend. *Holy shit!* Grant's reaction almost matched my mother's horrified expression, except hers was delivered with a gasp. Next time she'd think pretty hard about inviting my houseguests to her events in the future.

"I can't help but say that I'm surprised to hear such news." Grant was always good under pressure, but his jaw was his tell. He had a tic and a small vein that ran up his neck that proved his anger.

Something about the way he said he was surprised made my own jaw twitch. "And why's that? It took no time at all for you to choose a new flavor of the month."

Grants mouth twisted into a scowl. That's right, buddy, suck on that. I held Grant's gaze as his eyes shone bright with fire.

Hank's arms squeezed my waist. "Hank, are you ready to go home?" I asked over my shoulder. One of his hands met the tender skin at the nape of my neck, really sealing the deal of his possession. I still wasn't sure if he'd claimed boyfriend status to help me save face in front of Grant, or because he'd genuinely meant it. One way or the other, we would discuss it. First, I needed to get away from Grant and Mommy Dearest.

"You live together?" Grant snorted in disgust.

"You got a problem with that, pretty boy?" I didn't like the sound of that. Hank physically moved me to the side; Dean placed an arm around my waist.

"What makes you think you have any right to her? You've known her what? All of two weeks?" Grant hedged. Hank stopped dead in his tracks. Grant knew he had the upper hand and continued to press his luck by coming closer to Hank's face. "You're just a convenient fuck to her. She spreads those legs nice and pretty, doesn't she?" Hank gritted his teeth, his hands turning to fists. The tendons in his strong hands popped out and showed white as he clenched them. I stared in horror, completely taken aback by Grant's harsh words.

His eyes were cold and his lips curled into a snarl. "What are you going to give a woman like Aspen? Or maybe it's not about what you can give her, but about what she can give you—with her mouth and her money."

Oh no. This is not good.

"I'm sorry, angel. But he had it comin'," Hank said as he pulled back and decked Grant in the jaw. Hard. I think I heard Grant's jaw crack at the blow. The man fell back and was knocked out cold, barely missing the pool's edge by an inch. My mother jumped to Grant's aid, but knowing full well the power behind Hank, the man might have a concussion. He'd need a doctor.

"You barbarian!" my mother shouted.

"Jesus, Hank! What the hell were you thinking?" I covered my face in my hands.

Even if Grant deserved it and the nice fat bruised face to go with it, this reaction was completely undignified. The former President of the United States was sitting at a table just behind us, bodyguards off to the side, ready to jump in if the situation worsened. So many of the city's elite were watching the show, all aware that Aspen Reynolds's ex, the Senator's son, was decked by her date.

This night started out so perfectly. Had me believing in the possibility of something more for Hank and me. This spectacle just proved how different we were.

Out of nowhere, my father joined the group. He clasped Hank on the shoulder, and I thought for sure he was going to escort him out. Instead, he jerked out his hand and gripped Hank's in a firm handshake. "Hank, it seems I owe you again. Rumor was that jerk broke my baby girl's heart some time ago by being unfaithful to her. I think you have honor and know how to treat a lady."

"I'd never stray from Aspen, sir. You have my word." Hank's smile melted my heart a little. "I'm sorry about causing a scene at your party, Mr. and Mrs. Reynolds. I'd understand if you want me to leave." God, Hank was such a kind and caring man. He was also possessive, ornery, reactionary, and completely untamable. A life with him would include more occurrences like this.

"Are you kidding? I'd been hoping someone would shake up the party! Let's have a drink together, son." *Son.* My dad was falling for Hank's charm and charisma. It was really hard not to. There was just something so special about him.

Hank turned around to me, his gaze searing mine. There was such sadness and apology in his now bright green eyes that I physically couldn't move, caught once again under his cowboy spell. His eyes also held adoration, fear that I was angry, and something else. Something I was not yet ready to even attempt to decipher. I couldn't help but smile at his beautiful rugged face, a shadow of hair darkening the skin around his jaw.

"Angel?"

"Go, Hank. It's okay. We'll talk later."

He pulled me against his chest and rested his forehead against mine. "Tell me we're okay?" he whispered against my lips. Tears pooled at my eyes. I'd never had a man care so much, worry about what I was thinking and feeling.

I nodded against him, and he kissed me in front of the entire party. It wasn't a heated kiss at first, but it held so much promise. His hands twined into my hair, gripping me at the nape as he kissed me with more intent. I pulled away first, knowing that if I didn't, we'd both be lost to the sensation. The two of us pressed together was a heady mixture that intoxicated us both beyond reason.

He stepped out of my arms and gestured to Oliver. "I like the hair down," he said, with a sexy grit to his voice. I laughed out loud.

"I see that, Macho Man," Oliver snapped with the slightest hint of mirth in his tone.

I looked over at my father, who had the biggest grin on his face I'd ever seen. He looked utterly thrilled. My mother looked like she'd eaten something raunchy. My inner bitch was hooting and hollering in the background, lifting a trophy above her head proudly.

Even though I didn't approve of Hank's approach, Grant did have it coming. The things he'd said were vile. I only wished Hank had been able to control himself at a social event. If we were going to consider being an official couple, he'd be attending countless charity events and galas.

It was just part of my world.

Even as we spoke there were photographers quietly snapping pictures from a distance, their giant camera lenses pointed at Grant's sprawled form. Hank didn't understand what this would amount to. I'm certain that the second Grant came to, he'd contact his lawyers.

"Ollie, call Legal."

He flipped out his phone and snapped some pictures of Grant lying on the ground. He then typed quickly into the keyboard and started talking. He'd take care of the repercussions, though it was going to cost me a pretty penny. There was no doubt Grant would want to make me pay.

"Jeez, Pen, if I knew you'd be this much fun at parties I'd have invited you to more of mine." London laughed. Tripp gave her a dirty look but silently agreed with her by way of nodding.

Dean came over to me and pulled me into a hug. He spoke softly into my ear, "He means well, you know that right? He wouldn't have done it if he hadn't been provoked and your honor at stake." I closed my eyes and breathed in Dean's sweet-smelling cologne. It matched Oliver's. "Don't break his heart, Pen. He's more fragile than he looks."

I pulled back and Dean's eyes held no accusation, nothing in those pearly blues but concern. "You think *I'm* going to hurt *him*?"

"You're easy to love. My Oliver is hopelessly in love with you." I opened my mouth to object. "He is in love with you. He'd do anything for you, as would I by extension of his love. You're just lucky I'm willing to share." I nodded, realizing that this was by far the most honest Dean had ever been with his emotions and affections in all the years he'd been with Oliver.

"You know it's not physical?" I started to assure him.

He tipped his head back and laughed, still holding me close. "Of course I know that. But love is love and I take Oliver's love very seriously, and I know you do, too. So I'm warning you: That big lug is smitten. You better figure out soon what it is you want out of your time with him, or you may miss the boat." My best friend's boyfriend was giving *me* a love lecture. There was something oddly dysfunctional about that.

"I'm falling, too." The words left my mouth so swiftly that I wasn't sure I'd even said them.

"I know. Oh, honey, I know. You look at Hank the way I look at Oliver. It's unmistakable. Only the two of you are blind to it." He smiled and I hugged him tightly.

"Hey now! You trying to steal my girl?" Hank said from behind us. My father must have moved on to another group. Probably telling everyone at the party about how his daughter's boyfriend decked a congressman's son.

"Sharing is caring, Hank." Dean's mouth twitched but his face stayed serious.

"The hell it is. Didn't you get a gander at the other fella who talked about my angel? Want to join him?" He hooked a thumb behind his back for emphasis.

Dean couldn't hold it in any longer. They both started to crack up. Hank brought over a beer for the man and a new glass of wine for me. It was startling how quickly these two men had bonded.

Just a moment ago, I was getting the "watch out for Hank's heart" lecture from *my* friend, a man Hank met only a few hours ago! I felt like I was in the Twilight Zone.

Nothing in my perfectly calculated and planned-out world continued to add up. Everything was spinning out of control, specifically circling around a man well over six feet tall who controlled me and my lady parts with just the sound of his breath against the open skin of my neck.

My mother had Grant's passed-out body taken to one of the guest rooms. I was certain she'd have one of the many doctors in attendance look him over. The group settled back into an easy commentary after the spectacle though I didn't participate.

So much of my life was out of whack. Ever since Hank entered, things had been off balance and messy. Though the last three weeks had most certainly not been predictable, I'd still never been happier.

It dawned on me that maybe I was trying too hard to keep every facet of my life the same. Trying to fit Hank into my everyday life was like trying to fit a square peg into a round hole. Yes, Hank would have to adapt to my obligations with work and up his social grace, but it didn't mean I wanted to change who he was. I adored him.

I looked over at Hank. A huge smile was plastered across his face. A five o'clock shadow just grazed the surface of his chin, making him look more rugged and handsome by the second. His green-brown eyes darted between my friends. I realized while watching him how perfectly he fit in with the only people in the world who actually mattered. He even was getting along more easily with Oliver, and it warmed my heart to see them joking with one another. Could I see myself with him in the long run? I didn't know. We needed more time. Three weeks was hardly enough to determine what the future would hold.

Hank leaned back in his chair and laughed at the story London was telling about how her current clients wanted a stripper pole in their master bedroom. She was completely against it but had one put in because the wife was adamant. The first time the female client tried to use the pole she fell off and broke her wrist.

Needless to say, the pole was removed the next day, and the client was now letting London make the decisions about home décor. Hank gripped my hand, picked it up, and brought it to his lips, never swaying from the conversation before us. He kissed each one of my knuckles, and then placed a warm kiss at the center of my palm. My entire body shivered and ached with desire.

I pulled both of our hands down to my lap. He surprised me by placing his large hand over my thigh and inching up my skirt, just enough so that the act wasn't indecent. His fingers toyed with my nylons and made endless circles over my knee and around the tender skin just above. He looked over at me; his full lips displayed a small smile before he sent me an air kiss.

The man was full of surprises.

★ ★ ★ ★

Punching out Aspen's ex-boyfriend in the middle of a forced family fun event was not my best moment. The dick had it comin'. He was downright disrespectful to my angel, and someone needed to teach the pretty boy a lesson about respecting a lady. Especially if said lady was on my arm.

Growing up I'd gotten into my fair share of trouble, stealing Farmer McMann's tractor on account of a dare

ANGEL FALLING

from my brother. Old Man Henry let me stay a full night
in the local clink for that. It was never reported, though,
because my father was friends with both Farmer McMann
and the sheriff. I ended up doing a month's worth of hay
baling and cleaning up pig shit for that offense.

A few other times I'd gotten into a raucous fight with
a couple of jocks, then again when I beat up my girlfriend's
cousin for touching her inappropriately. Hell, now that I
looked back on it, I'd gotten in a heap of trouble. I'd just
hoped that my pattern of solving problems with my fists
wouldn't push Aspen away. For her I could find a way to
keep my cool. At least I'd try my damnedest.

"So, I hear your new beau took out Grant this evening."
A fella with a very smart suit and a slutty-looking filly
attached to his arm spoke over Tripp's current tale.

Aspen rolled her eyes. "Good to see you, too, Rio."
London jumped up and hugged the man, picking the tart
off his arm so she could hug him more fully. Rio smiled a
slick grin at London, and the filly frowned.

"London, dear sister, how are you?" he asked. The tart's
smile returned. So this was Rio. I could see the resemblance
to their father, but his demeanor said smarmy—nothing like
London's carefree nature and Aspen's quiet elegance. No,
this man thought his shit didn't stink.

Aspen rose and hugged her brother, patting him
lightly on the back. I could see their bodies didn't even
touch. Nothin' like back home. Ma would strangle a family
member until they couldn't breathe when she hugged. I
stood and put out a hand. "Hank Jensen. Good to finally
meet you, Mr. Reynolds."

"Rio, please. May I call you Hank?"

164

"It is my name." I smiled, hoping to get a reaction out of him. A smile, anything. It didn't work.

"So tell me, Mr Jensen, what on earth would make you raise your fists to Mr. Campbell? The rumors are spreading like wildfire. I thought it best to come ask the source." Rio leaned against the back of London's chair.

"Well, I don't take kindly to people disrespecting my girl. That includes stuck-up, rich pretty boys like Mr. Campbell. 'Sides, he wasn't good to your sister when they were datin'. That alone was reason enough." I couldn't figure out this guy's angle. He showed no facial expression whatsoever. He must have practiced the stink face for hours on end to perfect it the way he had.

"Such strong provocation for someone so new to the fold."

"Let it go, Rio. It's really none of your business," Aspen jumped in.

"Father is going on and on about how 'Hank the Hero' knocked out the little prick. It's becoming legendary. At least now I can say I've met the man and heard the legend firsthand." Aspen rolled her eyes and huffed. "It will be entertaining reading about it in the papers tomorrow." He turned to his date. "Shall we?" He gestured to the barely dressed brunette. "Until next time, ladies, gents." His arm candy followed him blindly.

"What's he mean, he'll read about it in the papers?"

Everyone looked at one another until Oliver spoke, "Hank, the entire scene will be front-page news in the society pages. Don't worry though; our lawyers are already handling it. You'll come out on top, and Aspen will take care of any reparations."

"Reparations. What're you gettin' at?" I could feel the anger rise through my chest and out my arms.

"She will compensate Grant for any damages."

"Are you kidding me? You're going to pay that bastard off because I hit him?"

Aspen's eyes went wide. "Hank, we can talk about this later."

"The hell we are. We'll talk about this now!" I pointed a finger hard onto the crisp linen tablecloth.

Dean leaned over and gripped my forearm. "Hank, now is not the time or the place to have this conversation. Once again, people are starting to stare. This does not look good for Pen or her family."

I looked around the yard and several people were staring, probably waiting for the next show to start. I nodded and stood.

"Darlin', you ready to blow this Popsicle stand?" I held out a hand to her. She took it and allowed me to lead her. The guys stood and followed us.

"Never a dull moment with you, stud." She leaned into my side. I could tell she was trying to lighten the mood, but I was good and pissed. Unfortunately, her shoulders were stiff, held back into a perfect arrow. I'd relax her nice and good back home. A few well-given orgasms and she'd forget all about tonight's happenings.

Home.

Without realizing it, her penthouse was becoming more like home to me than the ranch. My men were still here on the job, and I was improving quicker than expected. Doctor said I'd be back to work in two to three more weeks, at least doing desk duty. Maybe then I wouldn't feel such restlessness.

We made good time back to the city from her parent's mansion, but the ride was quiet. I could feel the tension in Aspen's shoulders. She stared out the window the entire time. Every so often, I'd catch a glance from Oliver or Dean.

Once back home, Aspen went straight to the bathroom and started the shower. I sat on her bed, thinking about my next move. She was quiet, not exactly mad. She seemed… sad. Of all the things I'd seen her feel, sad hadn't been one of them. I didn't like it one bit.

Deciding to eat crow, I ventured into the bathroom. She was standing under the spray, her body porcelain and perfect through the clear glass. I removed my clothes and entered the shower. She barely registered my presence. Her shoulders sagged and her head tipped low in defeat.

I kissed the warm skin between her shoulder blades. She sighed. I slowly started to massage her neck, working out the kinks and knots I found there.

"You going to talk to me, angel? You've been pretty quiet." I continued to knead her muscles and smooth my hands down her back.

"It shouldn't be this hard," she whispered.

"What shouldn't be, darlin'?"

"This. A relationship. We're so…"

"So what, angel?" I pulled her back until her slick body melded to mine.

"Different," she finished on an exhale.

I slid my hands up her wet body; one hand cupped her breast, the other her neck. I tilted her chin to the side and trailed kisses up the white column from behind. She moaned when my fingers rolled her nipple, elongating the tender flesh.

"Different can be good," I told her, my hands continuing to caress and stroke.

"You think so?" Her response was almost lost to the sound of rushing water as it poured over our bodies.

"I know so." I slid my hands down her body and pushed my knee between her legs, encouraging her to widen them. Leaning down, I lined up my cock with her entrance. In one thrust, I was embedded deep inside her slick heat.

"Oh God, Hank!" she cried out.

"See, angel." *Thrust.* "Has it ever—" *Thrust.* "Been like this—" *Thrust.* "Before?" *Thrust.*

She shook her head, bit her lip, and clenched me internally. "I'm going to come," she whispered.

"Yes, you are, and I'm going to make it happen again." *Thrust.* "And again. Until you know damn sure that no man will ever fulfill you physically or emotionally like I do, angel."

After that last statement, I pounded into her. Her hands slammed against the wall in front of her as I took her roughly from behind. I had a point to make. She came over and over again as I hammered into her core. "You feel that? You feel your body succumbing to it. Let it happen, angel. I'm here. I'll always be here." I wanted her to beg me to stop. Beg me to never leave.

"Hank, I can't, I can't, no more," she cried, then moaned as I reached around and found her clit.

"Another. Just one more. I want you to come with me, angel." That did her in. Her pussy clamped down around my length so tight it sucked all the air from my lungs. My cock jerked, pouring my seed into her.

We both tumbled into a heap of naked limbs and arms to the floor. I caught her listless form as she slid into my lap. My shoulder screamed like hell, but I didn't care. That was one of the most intense experiences of my life. I knew at that moment that we could never be apart. She was it for me. There would be no other like her. Now I just needed to convince *her* of it.

CHAPTER ELEVEN

Something about Hank was off. All week he'd been less demanding of my time, more attentive to what he perceived were my needs. Instead of rushing to bed, he wanted to talk each night. Really talk about my day, about life, about random things. It was nice, normal even. We watched movies together, went for walks, got ice cream, he even went so far as to make me breakfast in bed one morning. I doubt Gustav was thrilled with that. The Swede didn't take kindly to anyone cooking in my kitchen but him.

Even the sex was different this week. I couldn't put my finger on exactly what it was, but it seemed as though it held more meaning.

I wondered briefly if it had anything to do with the fact that his mother was coming into town this evening and would be here for a few days.

Excitement and dread took over my thoughts in equal parts. What if she didn't like me? What if she made Hank go back home? He held his mother on a pedestal, something I was completely unaccustomed to.

My mother was an evil she-devil who didn't deserve more than a fleeting thought. He doted on his mother and talked about her as if she were made of sugar and spice and everything nice. I pictured a Mary Poppins type. A real do-gooder. I was doomed.

Oliver entered my office. "I've got reservations at

Bellissimo scheduled for seven for the three of you. Are you ready to meet Hank's mother?"

"Not really. What if she hates me?"

"Pen, seriously? She's not going to hate you." He started messing with my hair, wrapping locks around his fingers to refresh the curls. Hank liked it best when he could run his fingers through my hair, so it was down. I'd been wearing it down a lot more lately. I loved having Hank's hands on me and would go to great lengths to make sure he did as often as possible.

"You don't know that. My own mother hates me!"

"Your mother is a stuck-up bitch. She doesn't even like herself." We both smiled, knowing that his words held a great deal of truth

I leaned against my desk, chewing my lip until it hurt. A headache was starting at my temples and I rubbed at it uselessly.

"You're really worried?" His voice held a twinge of surprise.

"Yes, I am." I took a deep breath. "Hank adores his mother. If she doesn't like me, there's no hope for us."

"I can't believe that. Honey, you don't give yourself enough credit. You're beautiful, obscenely rich, and most importantly, Hank loves you," he finished.

"Shut your mouth! He doesn't love me. He loves fucking me. Big difference!" The words flew from my mouth, but even I didn't believe them a hundred percent.

"Pen, he does, too. He's been living in your home for what, five weeks now? Sleeping in your bed. You've spent every single free moment together." His eyebrows knit together. "You owe me for that one by the way. And at the end of the day, you've never been happier." He tipped my chin until my eyes met his. "The cowboy loves you. You'd better accept that and start taking responsibility for it. And you need to tell him."

"I have nothing to give a man like him."

"You have everything to give and his love to gain. He's not Grant. He's not going to screw you over. He's Hank the Hunk. A fucking cowboy from Texas. I should be so lucky!"

"You have Dean, asshat!"

"You've got a point. I do have Dean and...mmm, he's yummy." He looked off into the distance with one of his dreamy-eyed stares.

"I'm just not used to feeling nervous about meeting the family. In my past relationships, their families knew my family and my reputation spoke for itself. With Hank's mom, she doesn't know me from Adam." I sank into my leather office chair and banged my head on the desk.

Oliver rubbed my back and shoulders and pulled me up. "Stop that, you'll leave a mark," he laughed. "Look, you're going to be great. Let your beauty and sparkling personality win her over. It did for me. You had nothing but frizzy hair and a trust fund when we met, and I just knew I had to share a life with you."

"Thank you, Ollie." Tears pooled at the corner of my eyes, and I used the pad of my ringer fingers to stop the flow. The last thing I wanted was to look like a raccoon when I met his mom.

"Yeah, well, who else was going to fix that mop of hair and burn your scrunchies?" He mock shivered and pretended to vomit.

"Oh, cut it out. I wasn't that bad."

He looked at me pointedly, eyebrows sky-high.

"Okay, maybe I was."

We finished up the day focusing solely on business. I texted Hank to ensure that he was ready.

To: Hank Jensen
Dinner's at 7:00 at Bellissimo. Is she here?
From: Hank Jensen
Precious cargo arrived. We'll meet you there, angel.

Of course, my five o'clock meeting ran late. I hadn't notified Hank, but I was meeting with Grant and his lawyers about the incident at the estate last weekend. After a week of legal hell, I was prepared to offer the bastard a settlement. I didn't want any of this to get between Hank's healing or his excitement over his mother coming.

My lawyer, Nathaniel Walker, was a shrewd businessman with a lovely British accent, and he was easy on the eyes. We'd actually been introduced and went on a couple dates a few years ago. Nothing more than a chaste kiss ever occurred; we realized that we were better suited to a friendship and professional relationship than a romantic one.

With Nate, there just wasn't a spark. Initially he had hounded me mercilessly for months to get me to agree to the first date. Now he was using the mercilessness to save me a few hundred thousand dollars on a mistake I wish I'd never made.

Grant was being utterly ridiculous. He wanted to hurt me, and he was using his legal arms in an attempt to batter and embarrass me. With Nate on my side, he wouldn't win. Stone, Walker & Associates were known for their success rates, not their losses.

We left the meeting having not come to an agreement. Grant officially wanted to press charges, but was holding back, waiting to see what I'd offer him.

"God, he's such a creep! I can't believe I ever thought I loved him. What the hell was I thinking?" I rubbed at my eyes as Nate and I headed toward the elevator.

"'Creep' sure does fit the bill. Don't worry though, love." He gripped my shoulder and squeezed it. "Before long, I'll have his arse in a sling," he said with conviction and a wicked hot British accent.

"Oh, Nate, I believe you. If anyone can get past his bull, it will be you and Collier. How is your brother, anyway?"

His brother was also a fine specimen of the opposite sex. Good-looking, smart, very kind eyes. And he had the charming British accent that made women melt on the spot. Though as of late, it was a Southern accent that made my panties drop.

Nate walked me to my limo and opened the door. "Can I drop you anywhere?" I asked him.

"Maybe. You up or downtown?"

"Up."

"Brilliant! I'd fancy a lift then. Thank you, love."

Nathaniel Walker was a good guy, charming, with movie star looks. I wondered why he was still single. "Nate, you seeing anyone?"

He waggled his eyebrows and his mouth turned into a sexy grin. "Is that an invitation?" he joked.

"You know it's not. I'm just curious. What's a single guy, good-looking, British no less, doing without a beautiful bombshell on his arm?"

"Just because there's not one on my arm right this moment doesn't mean there isn't one," he chided.

"Oh! I'm sorry. You're right."

He laughed. "No, you're dead on, love. I'm not officially seeing anyone. Just dating here and there. Pretty busy to find the right bird, as it were."

"Bird?"

"A lady friend. We Brits often call our women birds," he clarified.

"You Brits are strange."

"No more strange than you Yanks! Here, men call their ladies by terrible names in comparison. I hear 'my bitch' or 'my old lady' constantly. Can't fathom that a woman would rather be addressed as a bitch or old versus a lovely bird in any context."

I rolled around his logic. "Good point. Bird it is."

We both laughed. I leaned over and poured myself two fingers of scotch.

"Whoa, love. That's a lot for a little thing like you."

"Liquid courage." I hesitated and took a sip, letting the alcohol warm my belly and calm my nerves.

"Aspen, darling, you've never been afraid of anything in the few years we've known each other. Would you care to share?"

"My significant other's mother is coming to town for the first time."

"Ah, I see. Say no more. My mum would interrogate any woman I brought home. Just be yourself. And if that doesn't work, buy her a car." He grinned wickedly.

I smacked him on the shoulder and laughed with him.

My stop was first and with the best of manners, Nate

got out and helped me out of the car and gave me a hug. Then he kissed both cheeks, slid his hands down my arms to clasp my hands, squeezing them. "You'll do great, my love." He lightly kissed my forehead.

I smiled up at him and turned away. My nose bumped into a solid mass. *Ouch!* I could recognize that manly scent mixed with citrus anywhere. I looked into the smoldering green eyes of my cowboy. His jaw was clenched and his gaze glacial.

"Who's your friend, angel?"

It took me a moment to comprehend his question, so taken aback by the electricity and anger I felt sizzling off him. Nate heard the question and immediately introduced himself.

"You must be the significant other she mentioned in the car. 'Right-hook Hank'!" Nate put out his hand and Hank's eyebrows knit together, his eyes scrunching into tight points. "I'm Nathaniel Walker, Aspen's friend and attorney. It's good to meet you."

Hank shook his hand. "Right-hook Hank? That's a first. Hank Jensen." He seemed to relax a little. His arm came around my shoulders and I burrowed into his side. "I wanted to be outside when you arrived so that you knew where to find our table." His eyes softened as he looked into mine.

"Right-o, well then, mate, I best be on my way. We'll have to get together sometime." I nodded, and Hank just hugged me tighter to his chest. "Cheers."

★ ★ ★ ★

Seeing that man's hands on Aspen had me fit to be tied. "I don't care for another man's hands on my woman." The tension was building within me, and I was not capable of stopping it until I had my answers. With a hand on her waist, I ushered her into the restaurant.

"Hank, don't be silly. He's my lawyer and an old friend. There's nothing between us," she tried to assure me unconvincingly. In a short time, I knew my angel well enough to know she was holding something back.

"Have you slept with him?" I had to know if that man had put his paws on my girl.

"No!" she half-whispered, half-yelled.

"Ever date him?" I don't know why I was choosing to torture myself, but he had his hands on her. He was a good-looking man, and he seemed way too familiar with her. She groaned.

"Yes, two dates. Enough to realize we were never going to be anything more than friends." She sighed and searched my eyes.

"Did he kiss you?" She stopped dead in her tracks, and I knew the answer.

"Can we not do this now?"

I gripped her chin and held her gaze. "Answer the question."

"Seriously?" She rolled her eyes. "Technically, yes, we'd kissed...once! It felt like kissing my brother. Happy?"

"Not especially. Your lips are mine now. I don't want anyone ever getting to taste the pleasure of what's mine." With that, I cupped her face in both of my hands. "You got it?"

She stared intently, her gray-blue eyes swirling. I saw the

very moment she understood. Her eyes closed and a slow breath left her lips. God, she was so beautiful. "Hank…" she started, but I stopped her with my lips. She tasted like honey and cherry lip gloss.

She sighed into my mouth, and I dipped my tongue in, tasting her more fully. I could feel people walking past us and I didn't care. I kissed my angel like it was my meal ticket. Like a good solid day's work. She returned my kiss with a ferocity I didn't expect. My hand went down and cradled her ass, pulling her up and against me. She moaned. Damn, she was perfect. She pulled away first, her eyes a deep blue now.

"That's more like it, stud."

Damn, I loved when she called me that. It made my heart warm and my dick hard. I couldn't wait to get her back home.

"Stop looking at me like that," she chastised.

I smiled. "Like what?"

"Like you're thinking of all the naughty things you're going to do to me."

I cupped and squeezed her ass, pecking her on the lips one more time. "You know me too well, darlin'."

"Come on, Hank, your mom is waiting."

Holy shit! "I damn near forgot! Shit!" I pushed her on into the room where my mother was happily rearranging the centerpiece flowers. Her eyes jumped up, and she smiled when she saw me. "Mom, this here is Aspen Reynolds."

"Lovely to meet you, Mrs. Jensen." Aspen reached her hand out, but my mother jumped out of her chair and threw her arms around her.

"Just call me Julia or Mom, everyone does!"

"Thank you, Julia. My friends call me Pen." Aspen returned the hug and moved away.

I pulled out my mother's seat and then Aspen's.

We ordered drinks and stuffed mushrooms to start. I let Aspen choose the wine since she actually knew something about the stuff.

Out of nowhere, the most beautiful words came out of my angel's mouth directed at our waiter. "*Ci piacerebbe avere vino rosso questa sera. Che cosa mi consiglia?*"

My mother and I looked on in awe as Aspen spoke to the waiter in fluent Italian ordering the wine.

"Angel? You speak Italian?" I know my smile was as infectious as my mom's, who also couldn't hold back her own surprise.

"I do. Spanish, French, and a touch of German, as well." She smiled. I looked at her, completely astonished. "What?" She grinned.

"You amaze me, angel."

"In my line of work, I wouldn't be able to speak to half of the models and talent if I didn't know enough of their languages. I mean, most speak English, but it can be very hard to understand them. When I'm negotiating a contract, I want them to be fully aware of what they are signing up for."

"You're so smart. I bet you have a great job!" my mother gushed. "Who do you work for?"

"I do," she answered without finishing.

"Don't be shy, darlin'. Tell Ma here what you do." I was proud of my girl and wanted her to be proud of herself, too.

"Oh, Hank, your mom's really not interested in my work." At that moment, the wine arrived, and she swirled it around her glass, stuck her nose in, and took a sniff. Then she sipped and nodded to the waiter. He poured three glasses, and she took a huge gulp. She was acting strange, knotting her fingers together in her lap and rubbing them together. Then it dawned on me. The confident, take-charge businesswoman was nervous.

"Ma, Aspen's being shy. She's actually a real big deal. You know she owns the very building that I'm adding to. Her account is the one I bid on and won." I smiled wide and Aspen hung her head.

Strange behavior for her. She'd always been really confident and screamed powerful woman in a "hear me roar" way since we'd met. Especially when talking 'bout her work. She normally was a regular stick of dynamite going off if you so much as mentioned something she was working on.

Tonight she was trying to downplay her job, and I didn't understand why.

"Wow! Such a young little thing like you, speaking all those languages and owning buildings? Amazing." Ma placed her head in the hand leaning on the table. She smiled brightly at Aspen, and it made me feel tall, bigger somehow.

"Told you, Ma. My angel is as smart as she is beautiful."

Her eyes scanned Aspen's face and body. "She will make pretty babies for sure!" Mom hinted and winked.

Aspen's mouth opened and her eyes widened. "Mom! None of that talk. You've got two grandsons already. Don't be greedy." Aspen visibly relaxed. Did she not want children? I wanted kids. I didn't expect them right away but in the future, a couple years down the road maybe. I was already thirty-four. I didn't want to wait too much longer.

Looks like we had yet another thing to add to the growing list of things to talk about later.

The meal was extremely filling and the wine had been flowing. Aspen drank more than she usually did and was starting to slur her words together. I didn't mind, though, because when she started to drink she couldn't keep her hands off me. She was very affectionate and loose-lipped when she drank, and I planned to take advantage of it once Ma was settled in for the night.

I took my two best girls home. Of course, Aspen had her limo pick us up, and my mom was thrilled to no end. She had never been in a limo before and went on and on about how exciting and fancy it was. Aspen just smiled and snuggled into my side, sneaking kisses on my neck when she thought my mom wasn't looking. She'd had more to drink than she thought. She wasn't inconspicuous at all, but Mom seemed to enjoy the scene. There was no reason to bring home a woman to my family when I wasn't planning on keeping her around. Aspen I planned on keeping around for good. Every so often Mom would look over at us, a knowing look in her eye.

"You remind me of your father, Punky."

"Ma, you say that all the time." I shook my head and continued pulling my fingers through Aspen's silky hair.

"I know I do, but seeing you with her reminds me of your father and I years ago when we were young and only had eyes for each other."

I tensed and looked down, but I needn't worry about what my mother was saying. Aspen was fast asleep against my side.

"What do you think, Ma?" I whispered.

"She's very beautiful," she said, looking at her.

"She is. And smart too," I added.

She nodded. "And you love her," she stated flatly. Never could get one past my mother. When Heath and I were young rascals, she always knew when we were gettin' into mischief or trying to sneak extra cookies. She'd even told Heath on his first date with Jess that he "was gonna marry that girl" and low and behold, he did. Now she was reading me like an open book. No use trying to put off the inevitable.

"I do, Ma."

"And she doesn't know yet?" Perceptive my ma was.

I shook my head.

"Why haven't you told her?" She wasn't judging me. I could tell she was concerned.

"It hasn't been the right time. I've been healin' up. She's been working a lot. I met her family last weekend. It was a disaster."

"Well, she's still here with you, so it couldn't have been that bad. Obviously that means something." I shrugged. "Do you think she loves you, dear?"

I closed my eyes. That was the magic question of the year. Did Aspen love me? And if she did, why? I wasn't rich. I couldn't give her the lifestyle she was used to. Hell, I didn't even know if I could stay in New York and not go back home. She'd never leave her company. It was too successful. So if I wanted her, I'd have to make some sacrifices. Was I prepared to do that? I didn't know.

There was a lot still to work through. I know if she loved me, though, we could get through it all. We'd make it work, somehow.

"I don't know," I finally said. "I just don't know."

"Well, son, looks like you need to buck up and get yourself the girl then."

"You're right, Ma. But how?"

"We'll figure it out, baby. Don't you worry none. Mama's here now."

Somehow, I knew my mother was going to get all up in my business with Aspen. It was surprising how little I cared. I could use all the help I could get. I did worry about her methods, though.

"Lord help us all," I whispered into Aspen's hairline. She snuggled in deeper and my mother laughed.

CHAPTER TWELVE

Put in grounds. Check. Add water. Good. Press start. Okay. I can do this.

Gustav was allowed a sick day; I could handle coffee. Hopefully. If Hank hadn't woken me after the car ride and proceeded to ravage me through the night, I wouldn't be so damned tired. The man was insatiable. I mean, sure, I went through a huge dry spell and have been pretty satisfied over the past several weeks, but a girl has got to get some sleep. Last night was something else. It was as if he were starved and I was his first meal in weeks. The things Hank did to me could be considered illegal in some countries. The man was going to kill me.

Death by orgasm.

The thought gave me a little chuckle. My thighs quivered at the memory of how many times he brought me to release with his mouth alone. *Jesus!*

The coffee dripped slowly as I enjoyed the memories of last night.

"Mornin', pretty girl." I heard the sweet voice of Hank's mother.

Hank's mother...crap!

The fact that we had company had been lost on me in my sex-induced, sleep-deprived haze. I closed my eyes and tried not to look completely mortified by my appearance— my hair up haphazardly thrown into a messy bun, braless, and standing there in nothing but black lace panties, easily visible through Hank's white buttoned-down dress shirt. The one he wore to dinner last night. It was the first thing I found when I climbed out of bed this morning. I could feel the flame of embarrassment creep up and across my chest. Not only was his mother going to hate me, but she was going to think I was a hoochie, too. Way to make a great impression.

Gripping the edges of the shirt, I tried in vain to pull it down to cover up more of my bare legs. It didn't work. Fate sealed, I turned around. She looked bright and chipper, perfectly put together this sunny morning. God, I wanted to hate her so bad. "Good morning. Coffee?"

"Sure, thanks." She beamed a full glowing megawatt smile. *Did everyone in his family wake up happy?* Hank was the same way. Her eyes took in my clothing or lack thereof. "Looks like you had quite the evening."

A flush swept across my entire body. My skin must have been bright pink. "I'm so sorry. Honestly, I forgot you were here. This is highly inappropriate…"

She cut me off. "Are you kidding? I'm married to a Jensen, honey. If Hank is anything like my Henry, and based on what you're wearin'"—she pointed a finger up and down and then stopped at the collar of my shirt—"and that huge love bite there on your neck says he is, you could end up permanently bowlegged."

There was only one way to handle this conversation. Laughter. Deep, huge bouts of belly aching guffaws overtook me. Tears sluiced down my face. Hank entered, wearing only pajama bottoms, his massive body and beautifully honey-colored skin on perfect display. He came over to me and patted my back.

"I'm guessing you're responsible for this?" He gestured to his mom while I tried and failed to contain my hysterics.

"That one's a hair trigger." She shrugged, smiling.

"In more ways than one," he whispered sexily in my ear, which only brought on a new bout of tears and snorts.

Hank lifted me up from my bent over position. His hand landed on my waist, the other on my neck. "Better, darlin'?" he asked, wiping away the errant tears. I nodded. "You're so purdy when you cry." He kissed me full on the mouth in front of his mother. He pulled back and searched my face. "Also real purdy when you blush." He smirked and winked, then let me go to pull out three mugs.

"No need to be embarrassed, Pen. You both are adults. Ain't no judgment here. I just love seein' my boy smile."

I looked over at Hank. He was leaning his large form against the counter, absently strumming his fingers against the granite, waiting for the coffee to finish dripping. His chest shone bright with a sprinkling of hair that I loved to scratch my nails through.

Without realizing it, I had reached over and ran my hand down his chest and back up to inspect his scar from the surgery. I leaned my lips against the puckered flesh and gave it a soft kiss. Loving this scar, kissing it was now part of my daily routine. He walked around bare-chested, and I looked and touched my fill.

Each morning it was my duty to bathe his scar with kisses sending up a silent prayer to God for his sacrifice. His groan at the feel of my lips against his skin was matched by a gasp from behind us. I ventured a look over at his mother. Her eyes were pooling with unshed tears.

"I'm okay, Mom, really."

"I can see that. It's just I've waited for a long time to see this." Her statement made absolutely no sense to me, but Hank smiled and pulled me closer.

The day continued on just like that, except Hank's mother doted on him all day. Jumped up every chance she could to get him drinks, or a snack. He was eating it up, literally and figuratively. She rehashed old stories of Hank growing up. I paid close attention to the tales of him hiding girls in the barn and sneaking out after dark.

Laughed so hard I cried when she told the story of Hank making out with a girl in his dad's old Chevy. Things had gotten a little heated with the girl, and they knocked the gearshift and the truck backed into a ditch. Of course, Hank tried to recant her version of the story and said it was an accident. They weren't making out like lovesick teenagers.

"That was little Susie Q, right? Your high school sweetheart?" his mother asked.

"It was." Hank stopped talking and looked introspective for a moment.

"Oh, Hank was so smitten with Susie Shoemaker. I was convinced you two were going to marry. You know, I just heard she got divorced recently." She pinched her lips to the side in thought.

"Is that so?" Hank asked, his interest piqued.

"What ever happened between you to?" I asked. Curious as to why he didn't stay with his high-school sweetheart.

"Nothin'." Hank stiffened and pulled his arm from behind my shoulders. "I really don't want to talk about Susie. It was a long time ago. How're my brother and his rug rats?"

Hank steered the conversation back to safer territory.

Both his mother and I picked up on his discomfort and let it go. If he wasn't comfortable talking about it, I didn't really want to know. Technically, I was lying to myself. I did want to know what had him in a snit and planned on asking about it when we were alone.

I left Hank and his mother mid-afternoon to catch a nap and give them some time alone. A few hours had passed and the sun was setting on the horizon when I woke to the sound of my belly grumbling. I took a quick shower and threw on a comfy jersey housedress. It was formfitting in the way that yoga pants were, but nothing overtly sexual. It was a soft gray and felt more like a long T-shirt than a dress. Slowly, I made my way through the house to where I could hear Hank and his mother talking. I heard my name, so I held back to listen a few moments.

"Aspen's lovely, Punky, and it's obvious how she feels about you."

I strained to hear his reply. "I like her, too, Ma. More than I should." His voice seemed sad, not like himself. *Why would he say it like that? More than he should? What did it mean?*

"Are you going to bring her back home when the job is done?" she asked.

"I don't know if she'd want to come. Ma, it's not like you and Dad. We haven't even had a discussion about what this is between us."

Dread trickled its way up my spine landing on the tiny hairs behind my neck. The feeling was unfamiliar with an extra dose of unpleasant.

"Punky, as much as you seem to like this girl and she you, I mean, you're a Jensen, what's not to like?" She laughed and then continued, "A long distance relationship would never work. You know that, right?"

Hank grumbled his agreement, defeat ringing clearly in the tone. "I do know that."

The wall was cold against my palms. The thought of Hank going home, us not seeing each other every day, was like sticking a sharp knife into my gut. In such a small amount of time, this man had become a regular fixture in my world. Something I could count on seeing when I got home. The person I could vent to, laugh with, make love to. But it couldn't work.

His home, his ranch, his beautiful family were in Texas. Mine were here. Would he give it up to be with me in an undefined relationship? Could I for him? We hadn't even shared how we felt about one another. How was I supposed to wrap my mind around my feelings for him when all I could think about now was that we only had a few short weeks left?

Instead of continuing to listen, I took a deep breath and entered the living room.

"Hey, darlin'. Did you get a good nap in?" Hank clasped my hand and pulled me into his lap, not the seat on the couch next to him. I squealed like a little girl and tried to keep my dress from showing my lady bits. His skin was warm when he snuggled into my neck. I could feel the small prickly hairs that had grown on his chin as it abraded my skin. It didn't hurt, quite the opposite actually.

"I did, thank you. Sorry I was out for so long."

"You were tired." His corresponding grin spoke volumes. He whispered in my ear, "Oh, angel, the things I plan to do to you tonight..." he trailed off and then placed a wet smack against my ear.

"Gross!" I cringed and wiped at the wet spot.

Hank and his mother both laughed at my expense.

"Get used to it, pretty girl. The Jensen men are notorious pranksters."

"Duly noted."

Hank hugged me to him. "We're not that bad."

"I'm going to leave you two for a bit and get supper started," Julia said.

"Oh, no, you don't have to cook. Even though Gustav's not here, we can go out or call in."

"Now that the pesky fella isn't here, I'm dyin' to get into that kitchen. That see-through fridge alone is something right out of the movies! And a six-burner stove! Punky, can you imagine the meals I could've cooked with something like that when you boys were young?"

"Just leave her. This is fun for her. She's a really great cook and I could use a home-cooked meal," Hank said.

"What do you mean? You have one every night." I made certain we spent more meals in than out because I knew how much Hank liked to eat in.

"Darlin', you can't really call that gourmet stuff Gusto cooks a home-cooked meal, could ya?"

"Yes, I could and I do. What do you call it?"

"It tastes like food you get at a restaurant. You'll see after you've had Ma's cooking."

"Ma," Hank screamed. "Whatcha cookin'?"

They continued to talk through the walls. The sound was deafening. Screaming at one another through walls did not happen in the Bright-Reynolds home. As in, ever.

"Your favorite!" Julia hollered back.

"Oh, my. You are in for a real treat, angel. She's 'bout

to blow your mind with her famous fried chicken and cornbread." Hank was by far the most excited I'd seen him. Well, aside from when I was naked and splayed out for his enjoyment. It was funny to see that same excitement about a meal. As long as he was happy, my world seemed good.

★ ★ ★ ★

"Oh God, oh…holy, mmmm," Aspen moaned around a bite of fried chicken. Every bite she took she seemed to have a small orgasm. It was making me hard as steel and having trouble paying attention to anything else. All I wanted to do was throw her on top of the table and have my wicked way with her. If she kept up the foodgasms I just might, Ma be damned.

"Good, angel?"

She smiled around a mouthful of food. She was shoveling it in like it was her last meal. I loved watching my angel eat…really eat. She was always so finicky about how much she ate, what the calories, carbs, and fat intake were. Then she would spend hours in the house gym if she felt she over did it. Couldn't complain though, her body was right out of *Sports Illustrated* and I enjoyed every inch of it.

"Oh man, Julia. This is… I don't think I've ever had anything like it. It's literally the best chicken I've ever had. I'm not sure I've ever had fried chicken. You have to share this recipe with Gustav!" She plopped in a bite of cornbread.

"Nuh-uh! Nope. Ain't gonna happen, pretty girl. You want my chicken you have to come to Texas to get it. Of course, you could move there and I'd promise to make it for you and Hank every week."

Aspen's eyes closed, and she patted her mouth with her napkin. "Julia, I don't think that's a possibility at this time. My work…" She sighed, and it hurt to see my girl struggling. "My work is important. I employ tens of thousands of people, and if I didn't keep the company running the way it is, a lot of people would be out of work."

"Holy smokes. You employ that many people? Hell, Hank, that's a lot of families that could be hurt if our pretty girl picked up and left. I had no idea. Wow…" Ma trailed off.

Aspen no longer looked interested in her food, just pushed the potatoes around her plate.

"No one's asking you to leave, angel." Aspen's gaze jumped up to meet mine. Hurt and pain swirled in those shimmery blue depths. "I mean, uh, shit…" I didn't know how to finish telling her. The situation seemed impossible.

Tears welled up in her eyes and she stood. "Thank you so much, Julia, for a lovely meal. The best I've ever had. I have some work to do in my study. Just leave the dishes. The maid will take care of it." And then she was gone without a look back, a peck on the cheek, nothing. She was hurt, and I had no idea how to fix it.

"Hank, what the hell were you thinking?" Ma was red with anger.

"What was I supposed to do? She's not going to leave and come home to Texas."

"Have you considered staying here?"

"In New York?"

"Don't be thick, son. The woman is clearly in love with you and you with her."

"You don't know that, Ma."

"Oh, yes, I do. Call it mother's intuition. That pretty girl loves you and she's devastated right now. Who works on a Saturday?" She doesn't know Aspen. My girl works all the time. That's why she's so successful. It never completely leaves her. "You need to tell her that you're going to work this situation out."

"How can I promise her that?"

"You tell her you're going to stay in New York. You're going to figure out what to do about your business. Maybe this is the time to expand it. You were talking about having another branch. This is the perfect opportunity."

My mom had a good point. I had been talking to Mac, my most trusted employee, about expanding the business. He'd never leave Texas for longer than necessary, though. His wife and three kids were back home waiting anxiously for his return. This job was the longest we'd been away and I was flying him home every other weekend to be with his family. What if I did set up a branch in New York? Mac could run the Texas office just fine without me.

"It's something to consider, Ma. But I'd need an office and investors here to expand. I don't have enough capital yet to open an office in such an expensive place."

"Didn't you say your girlfriend owned a building?" She tilted her head and looked at me as if I were deaf, dumb, and blind. "Maybe you could rent a space from her? She's also got lots of money. Bet she knows some investors."

Again, the woman was smart. She didn't run the backend of the cattle business because she was dumb.

"Maybe I could talk to Aspen about it. But if she doesn't feel the same way, I..."

"Shut it, Punky. You tell that woman how you feel

and I'd bet every dollar in my bank account she feels the same. Have a little faith, dear. You're a Jensen. My boys are irresistible. You're the most loveable men in the world."

"Ma, you're biased."

"That's right, and with good reason. You will take perfect care of her. She needs a real man around. If you don't give her that, I'm telling you, she's a catch. Someone will..." She left off.

To hell with that! There was no way on God's green earth that I'd let another man so much as touch a hair on her purdy head. The thought of someone kissing or making love to my girl made me crazy. Insane. Downright certifiable.

"Ma, good night."

"Go get her, baby!" she yelled as I headed to Aspen's study.

She was standing staring out the window, arms crossed protectively over her chest. She didn't hear me come in. I took in her form as she stood facing the New York skyline. I could tell she was lost in thought. She was so beautiful.

The gray dress she wore clung to her hips and ass. The light from her desk lamp highlighted the gold in her long blond hair. Her head was tipped to the side, exposing the creamy column of her neck. That neck made me weak. I wanted to brand her, mark her there so everyone could see that she was taken, that she was mine.

Slowly, I crept up and slid my arms around her waist and set my head in that lovely crook in her neck. She sighed and curved her form against mine. She filled all my spaces perfectly.

"Angel, we're going to work out our living situation—" I started, but she cut me off.

"How? It's impossible, Hank. This has all been great, but it's not reality. It isn't real."

White-hot anger spiraled through me. How could she blow this off so easy? My entire body tensed around her, fingers digging into her hips.

"You don't mean that, this is very real..."

She flipped around in my arms. Tears streaked down her angelic face. It killed me to see her hurting. I wanted to kiss away those tears, to make her happy, see her smile.

"Is it? Is it really? Because it feels like a dream. Like a perfect beautiful dream...but not real." Her voice broke into a sob on that last word.

Hands gripping her head to me, I crushed my mouth over hers. On her gasp, I pushed my tongue into the sweet cavern of her mouth, tasting the honey I knew I'd find there. My hands trailed down her back and to her ass, pressing her against me. "This feel real, angel?" I thrust my erection against her and she groaned. Turning us around, I lifted those sweet cheeks into the air and she clamped them around my waist in a vise grip.

I pushed the chair and documents from her desk and set her ass on the wood surface. Her mouth ravaged mine, our tongues swirled, teeth gnashed. When she sucked my tongue, I spread her thighs wide, opening her most private place to my need. Fumbling fingers found the edges of her panties, and I tore the material off her in a snap. I brought the soaking lace to my face. She watched me, her eyes dilated to the point where I could barely tell they were blue. I sniffed her sopping panties, her scent firing through my senses and settling at my cock, making me painfully hard.

"This real, angel? How wet you are for me, how fucking

good you smell!"

"Hank…" Her voice held so much need. A need only I could fill.

I shoved down my pajama bottoms as she lifted her dress up and off her body. My hands covered the supple round globes of her breasts, tugging the nipples into tight aching points. I laved one nipple, swirling my tongue around the surface. She moaned and arched her back, offering her breasts up as a gift. I worshipped each tender peak with my tongue, lips, and fingers.

"This real, angel?" I continued my rant as I sucked and lavished her breasts until she was rotating her hips hard against my cock, wetting it with her pleasure.

"Fuck, Hank…"

"Oh, I'm gonna fuck you. I'm gonna fuck you so hard you will never forget how real this is, Angel." I lined up my cock with her entrance, gripped her ass cheeks in both hands, and slammed into her. She screamed, throwing her head back. I pulled out and did it again. "Is this real, me buried balls deep in your perfect pussy? This is—" *Thrust.* "So fucking—" *Thrust.* "Real!"

She came hard against me, her cunt squeezing me in a viselike grip. Holding strong against my own desire, I tipped her back to lie fully on the desk. She arched with each aftershock, her beautiful pale body on display, ready for me to take her again. I pulled out of her and she groaned. I needed a taste.

"Hank, Hank…you…need." She was barely able to speak through her panting.

"Oh, angel, I'm not done with you."

CHAPTER THIRTEEN

Hank's hands were everywhere at once. Before I could even come down completely from the high, he had me spread out naked on my desk, legs splayed wide. He twirled his thick fingers into my sex, rubbing my clit with one hand while the other gripped my thigh. Sex had never been like this before Hank. It wasn't just sex or fucking, it was an experience. The man had incredible skills in the bedroom, and he used every one of them on me.

I moaned and tried to reach for him as the pad of his thumb rubbed the tight knot of pleasure at the apex of my thighs. He whispered, "Feel real to you, angel?"

Then he abruptly sat in my office chair, pulled my lower lips wide, and dipped his tongue in for a taste. He moaned in approval. His tongue licked and nipped, as if my center were a ripe peach. My eyes rolled back and closed, the pleasure too much to bear. He held my thighs wide open as he feasted, fucking me with his warm tongue. I could hear the wet suck and pull of his tongue and lips against my sex.

Before long, he added a couple fingers, tipping them up perfectly to my G-spot. He hooked that delectable spot with his fingers and yanked, hard. I came instantly, pushing my hips against his face, riding his mouth. I could feel his smile against my pussy. Then he wrapped those full lips over my clit and nibbled me into another mind-altering release.

I shoved and pushed at his face. "No more, I can't. No more…"

He stood up, pulled my thighs to his huge cock, and slowly entered me. The swollen tissue of my sex relented at his assault. So full. He reached deep, so far within me it was possible he was touching my very soul.

"You can handle more, angel, and you will. Feel me within you. My cock pressing you open…"

"So big, too much," I barely spoke as he pulled out and slammed his cock to the hilt, crushing my clit in the process. Shocks of desire spiraled down my spine and out my fingertips. When we were joined, my entire body hummed and tingled. I'd never felt more alive than when I was joined with this man.

"Never too much." He groaned and rotated his hips. I gasped at the pleasure. "This…right here. This is real. You feel it now, angel." He punctuated his statement with a deep thrust that made my teeth rattle.

"Yes, I feel it… Oh, Hank, I feel it," I screamed as he jackhammered me. He hooked my legs around his waist and pulled me up to him. Face-to-face, his lips devoured mine in a brutal kiss. His tongue entered and receded, simulating what our bodies were doing down below.

He sat down in the desk chair and his cock jutted higher into me, going impossibly deep. I could hardly breathe. He rubbed our noses together and kissed me softly. "Feel me, angel?"

I nodded.

"This is real…don't ever doubt that." I nodded again. "Now ride me." His voice cracked with the effort to speak. He was finally losing control. It made me hungry for him.

Powerful.

I clasped my hands behind his neck and twisted my fingers in his dark hair. It was slick with sweat. I kissed him, tugged on his bottom lip with my teeth, then soothed it better with my tongue. "I'm sorry... There has never been anything more real in my life," I whispered against his lips. "Only you." I punctuated my words by lifting up, using the leverage of my feet and what strength I had left to slide up and down his length.

Then, I rode my man like I was an award-winning horse jockey. His hands held my hips and thrust up into me on the down stroke. His hips would tilt up, his body arching to me. It was the sexist damn thing I'd ever seen. We set a perfect rhythm until both of us were clawing at the other, nails puncturing in little crescents against moist skin as we screamed out our combined release.

"Only you," Hank whispered into my ear as I lay in a heap on top of him, legs and arms dangling. A handful of orgasms would do that to any woman. His hands soothed up and down my back until I lost track of what was happening, too sated to do anything other than snooze against his warm, bare chest. His heart beat slowing provided the perfect music to lull me. He stood up with me still wrapped around him, our bodies forever connected. He exited the study. I was half-asleep, both of us completely naked as he headed toward *our* room.

"'Night, Ma," I heard him say. I didn't have the energy to worry about what this looked like.

"Oh my, son!" she said with a laugh. "I've covered my eyes, Aspen! Jeez, son, you could have warned me. You're going to make me miss my Henry something awful seein' you two like that."

"We worked it out," he said, continuing to walk to our room. Instead of being mortified, I just accepted it. Hank did what Hank wanted. If he chose to walk us both naked from room to room, that was his prerogative. At least she'd only seen our asses since our fronts were plastered together. Hopefully she wouldn't judge me too harshly in the morning.

"So you did. Well then, good night."

I woke up the next morning to something wet licking my hand and something poking my shoulder. I opened one eye to find Butch lapping happily at my hand that hung off the bed making it nice and slobbery. Oliver was the culprit poking my shoulder.

"Ollie, it's Sunday. What the hell are you doing here?" I sat up and the blankets pooled at my waist. Oliver covered his eyes, and it took me a moment to realize what he was doing.

"It's not like you've never seen me naked before. Hell, you've probably seen me naked more than Hank. A lot more than Hank."

That got Hank's attention. He sat up, his bed hair spiked all over the place. Oliver did not hide his eyes when Hank's naked chest came into view. Couldn't blame him there, the man was a remarkable sight.

"Lucky bitch." Ollie tsk-tsked and ogled Hank openly.

"True." I grinned. "What do you want? Why are you waking me up on a Sunday?" I asked as Hank tugged me to lean back against him and pulled the blanket up to my neck. He did not like another man seeing me naked. Made me feel special, coveted.

"This better be good, buddy." Hank kissed my bare shoulder.

"It's work, Pen. We've got a rogue model. This time I think she's overdosed. She's supposed to be at the shoot in Times Square right now."

I flung out of bed stark naked, jumping over Butch, who then jumped up on the bed. Hank groaned.

Ollie sat on the bed, petting the dog as I jetted into the bathroom to take a quick shower.

I could hear laughing, then Oliver entered the bathroom, heading to the walk-in closet. Hank was hot on his heels.

"Jesus, Oliver. I'm going to tear into you if you don't stop looking at my girl." Oliver just continued through the bathroom to the closet to choose my outfit.

"Hank, when are you going to learn that I have no interest in your girl's boobies or anything else?" Hank stood naked as a jaybird and stomped his foot. "You, on the other hand…" Ollie looked at Hank in all his glory.

His cock hung down thick and heavy along his thigh, tight dark hair nestled at the groin. Sculpted abs and chest. It took everything I had not to trail my hands down to my center to rub one out while watching him, angry and flustered, standing just outside the shower stall's glass door. The man was just too good to look at.

Ollie continued to openly stare at my man. "Damn, Hank. If I wasn't in a committed relationship with the world's sexiest fireman, I'd be all over you like white on rice, cowboy."

I laughed as Hank beat feet into the shower. "You've got freaky friends, darlin'."

"Believe me, I know," I said loud enough for Oliver to

hear. Hank's hands came around my back and cupped my breasts, pinching the nipples between his fingers.

"Buddy, if you don't want another show, I suggest you get movin' on outta here," Hank warned, his cock now erect and pressed against the seam of my ass.

A dark blur carrying something bright red rushed past. I heard the door snick shut a second later.

After a very productive shower—Hank liked to call it preserving water—I had my red suit on paired with a beige silk blouse and nude peep-toe slingbacks. Oliver had just put the final touches on a sleek chignon when Hank leaned against the vanity. His dark jeans hung low on his hips, a Dallas Cowboys T-shirt stretched tight against his broad chest. *Yum.*

"So, how long will you be gone today?" Hank asked, arms crossed over each other. He was still cradling the elbow on his wounded side, but it was barely perceptible. It was odd that he was asking how long I'd be. He'd never questioned when or how much I had to work before.

"I don't know," I countered honestly. "This model, Hank. She's incredible. The most sought after in the business right now, but she's young, dumb, makes terrible decisions, and needs help. She comes from a very broken family and has no one to help set her on the right path."

"And that person has to be you?" His voice wasn't judgmental or laced with anything other than curiosity.

"Maybe. Ultimately, I'm responsible for her completing the jobs I've contracted her for through AIR Bright Modeling Agency. If she's overdosed on drugs, I need to assess whether she can finish the job she's committed to this weekend or is off to rehab. Why?" I didn't mean for my tone to take on an accusatory edge, but I'd never had to answer to anyone before and it threw me off my game.

"No reason." He shrugged. "Hey, would you have a problem with me inviting some of the guys over for the game since you'll be out?" Immediately the tension I was prepared for ebbed and went away. He was so adorable asking permission to have his friends over. It was unnecessary—he didn't need my permission for anything, but I appreciated it.

"Are we done, Ollie?" He spritzed a few more times, capturing any stray flyaway hairs.

"Perfection. I'll be in the kitchen grabbing your cappuccino for the road."

"Thank you." I waited for him to leave the room, and then I turned to Hank and put my arms around his waist. He curved those large arms around me, hugging me close. The T-shirt he wore was baby soft against my cheek as if it had been washed a million times. It probably had, as much as Hank loved that football team. "Hank, you can have whomever you want over, whenever you want. For as long as you're here, I want you to feel like this is your home."

"I do feel at home, angel. Wherever you are is where I want to be," he said, his chin resting against the top of my head. I didn't want to hope it meant for good, and I didn't dare ask.

"Okay then. I have to go. Enjoy your game."

He walked me out into the kitchen; his mother was talking to Gustav. The tension was thick in the air. She wanted to make homemade pancakes, and Gustav had planned on making crepes. Oliver watched the two, completely fascinated as they argued. I tried to avoid making eye contact with Julia. Remembering how she saw Hank carrying me out of the study in my birthday suit last night sent a wave of heat across my face and neck. The skin of my neck probably matched the red of my suit.

"Here you go, pretty girl." Hank's mother handed me a ball of wrapped-up paper towels.

"What's this?"

"Homemade blueberry muffins. I made them early this morning for you." She smiled so bright it might have reached the edges of the sun. The woman was incredibly kind and unfazed at all by the happenings between Hank and me. Gustav scowled but kept quiet.

"Blueberry muffins are my favorite!" The muffin she prepped for me were still warm. I was baffled by her kindness.

"I know. I asked Hank yesterday during your nap what some of your favorite things were." I looked over at Hank. He smiled shyly and looked down, then shuffled his feet.

"Hank, how did you know that blueberry muffins were my favorite? We haven't had them together."

"You mentioned it once when we walked past a bakery. Said you don't have them much because you only liked fresh-baked ones. Ma makes the best in Texas." He preened for his mother's benefit. It was probably one of the nicest things a man had ever done for me.

★ ★ ★ ★

The door rang out, and I rushed over to answer it. Dean's smiling face greeted me. "Your Cowboys are going down, man!" Dean smack-talked the second I opened the door.

He was wearing a New York Giants shirt, not a Jets shirt. His longish black hair was hanging loose around his face. He'd be an imposing fella if I didn't know better.

Another guy I recognized pulled in behind him. It was that lawyer friend of Aspen's. My eyes narrowed at his presence, but I tried not to let it get to me.

"The hell they are. Your Jets are going to flap their girlie wings and fly away after my Cowboys hog-tie their asses!"

"Hank, you said I could bring a friend. This is Nate Walker. He does all the legal work for Aspen and Oleander." He always called Oliver by his pet name. I could relate. I rarely called my angel by her God-given name.

"We've met." I put out my hand to shake his hand.

"Yeah, Hank here thought I was putting the moves on his bird," he joked and shook my hand. I squeezed it tight to remind him that I could take him out in a second if provoked.

"Damn! Mate, settle down. I need that hand!" He pulled away and shook it, clearly in pain. I grinned happily.

"Didn't you date Aspen, Nate?" Dean asked, and I bristled, anger creeping up my spine.

"Bloody hell, Dean! You have a piss-poor way of introducing friends. If I didn't know any better, I'd suspect you were trying to get me killed!" Okay, so the man didn't have shit for brains.

"No bother. Aspen told me that you went on a couple dates, said you kissed somethin' awful. She compared you to her brother." I shivered and grimaced for fun.

"Put a sock in it. That's just bloody mean." He grinned, but I smacked him on the back to let him know we were good. Of course, I'd take every opportunity to insult the man's romancing skills every chance I could today. Paybacks and all that.

Just as I turned around to talk more shit to Dean, the

door rang again. This time it was Mac. "Good to see ya, Mac! Always good to have another Texan in the house!"

Mac was a large man, his Stetson firmly in place on his head, Cowboys jersey proudly displayed. He almost stood taller than me with his cowboy hat and boots. His brown eyes gleamed with mirth. "Nice digs, boss."

"Ah shucks, Mac. You know these digs are my lady's. Wait till you see the media room. You ain't never gonna want to leave!"

We entered the room and Mac whistled. There were eight individual leather recliners in a deep brown. At the front was a matching dark leather couch. I suspected that's where my girl lay down to watch movies. Entire room was painted red with gold girlie swirls and shit dangling here and there. The screen took up the entire far wall. It was as if we were in our own personal movie theater. Ma brought us popcorn and some snacks.

"Gusto! Thanks for the beers, man." He handed us chilled pints full of ice-cold beer. "Want to join the game?" Gustav looked at the guys and nodded. He sat in one of the chairs, and not too long after we were all screamin' and laughing at the screen. The Cowboys and Jets were tied at halftime.

The guys followed me into the kitchen where Ma was dishing out lunch. Gusto ran over to help.

"I got this, Gusto."

"What is this?" he asked, his accent thick.

"Pigs in a blanket, silly." Ma handed him one and he ate it.

His face screwed into what I think was pleasure. You could never really tell with the man. He always seemed pissed off.

"You must teach me this!" he exclaimed, his tone serious.

"All right, but only if you teach me how to make those crepe thingies," Ma offered.

The rest of us guys loaded our plates with food, grabbed fresh brewskies, more chips and dip, and then made our way onto the large outdoor balcony to grub. Dean broke out some cigars and we enjoyed them with our beers. The tobacco mixed with beer and guys made me feel right at home. I liked Dean and Nate, more than I thought I would. Dean was quieter than I was used to, but when he spoke, he had us all in stitches. The fella was funny.

Nate was an interesting fella, as well. He talked a lot and had tons of useless knowledge about football. Though in England, it actually was soccer. Turned out he preferred soccer to football and it took us a while to figure out he wasn't referring to the NFL game we enjoyed. He even wore a European team jersey in a bright green with white-and-black wording and stripes. Some of the things he said were hard to figure out. He spoke English but used words I'd never heard before. After a few beers, it didn't matter. When I didn't understand him, I just shrugged and let Dean translate.

Mac seemed to be having a good time. A couple times, he'd leave the room to take a call on his cell phone. It was the off weekend, so he spent a good deal of time on the phone with his wife. Lisa was great. She understood he had to work, but I could tell Mac missed her somethin' awful.

Seein' him sore about not being with his wife and kids helped solidify the idea about expanding the business.

I wasn't ready to tell Aspen about the idea yet. We hadn't talked about where this thing between us was going but one thing I knew for certain, I wanted to be where she was. Period.

At the third quarter, I asked Mac to follow me into Aspen's study. He looked concerned when I leaned against the desk. Memories of what I did to my angel last night were fresh, and I smiled like an idiot.

"What's up, man?" Mac asked.

"What would you say if I told ya I was thinking 'bout expanding Jensen Construction?"

Mac's eyes widened and a smile broke across his hairy face. The man didn't shave on the weekends. Said if he wasn't kissin' his wife, he could enjoy being a man. "I'd say it's about damn time, boss!"

I laughed. "So, I'm thinking about opening up an office here in New York City."

Mac's smile slipped off his face. "Hank, I really don't want to work for anyone else, but I can't move my family to NYC. It's not an option. Lisa would kill me for even suggestin' such a thing...and I—" He started to make excuses, but I shook my head.

"I'm thinking about movin' here and opening the office. Keeping the one back home and promoting someone to foreman and manager of the Texas branch. Know anyone who'd be good for it?" I grinned.

Mac's smile came back like a shot. "Shit, Hank. You offerin' me the opportunity to run the office back home?"

"If I can get the capital together and set up shop here, yes, I reckon I am."

Mac took off his cowboy hat and ruffled his fingers

through his hat hair. "Shoot, boss, I'd be honored and I wouldn't let you down. You're like a brother to me. And Lisa and the kids think you're family. I'd be proud to do it."

"All right then. I'll let you know in the next couple weeks what the plan is. Don't get too excited; nothin' has happened yet, but I trust you and couldn't do it if I didn't have a good man on the ground in Texas." I slapped him on the back as we made our way back to the game.

There was a commotion in the kitchen and I ran over. Aspen and Oliver had made it back and were laughing at Gusto and Ma, who were having a flour fight.

"Hey, hey, hey. What in God's name are you two up to?" They both turned to the growing group of onlookers. Ma's hair was white, flour coating the entire surface. Gusto was worse for the wear. He had flour and butter stuck all over his white jacket and a glob stuck to his cheek. His hair was also white from flour. Looks like Ma got some good shots in.

"My goodness, Gustav, I'm shocked!" Aspen said, and he looked down and shuffled his feet.

"Oh, she's just joshin' ya, Gusto. Relax, partner. You're not in trouble. Looks like you and Ma got the best of each other." We all laughed as the rest of the guys made their way into the kitchen.

"Commercial break," Dean said, and hooked a thumb over his shoulder at the media room. "The Jets got a field goal and it's back to a tied game."

"Thanks for the update, pal." Aspen snuggled in and I tipped her face up with a finger under her chin. "Afternoon, angel." I pecked her on the lips. "How was work?"

Oliver cringed and hugged Dean, rubbing his face

into Dean's chest. Dean wrapped his arms around the man, perfectly comfortable with being with Oliver in front of others. You didn't see it a lot back home, but it didn't bother me. You could tell that Dean felt very protective toward Oliver. 'Bout as much as I did for Aspen.

"Ugh, don't ask. Let's just say I'm going to lose a couple hundred thousand dollars and potentially a half-million-dollar campaign while the model detoxes for the next thirty days."

Nate jumped in. "Pen, you need me on this?"

She nodded and sighed. "Yeah, she's definitely in breach of her contract, but we'll talk later. I want to know about the game and what you guys have been up to."

We all went back to enjoy the last quarter. Aspen really got into it. She rooted for the Cowboys because she said her only preference was my happiness. If I didn't love her before, I most certainly did at that moment. She was everything I never knew I wanted in a woman. She was smart, distractingly beautiful, didn't know how to cook, probably clean either. She was not domestic, wouldn't make a good housewife in the ways Ma would want for me. And I could give two shits. I just wanted her, the workaholic debutante who rocked a men's suit better than I did.

She was all soft curves and luscious woman under those suits, and my angel was the perfect lady on the street and a freak in the bed. It was obvious to me and even my mother that she was it for me. There was never going to be another woman who could stand up to her. I was ready to tell her how I felt, but wanted to do it on my turf.

As the Cowboys took the game into the winning field goal that broke the tie, I kissed my girl. She tasted of popcorn and beer, and I ate it up. Before things got too heated, I pulled her chin up and searched her gaze. "Will you come home with me next weekend? Just a long weekend?"

"Of course. Everything okay?" Her gaze held mine. Those blue eyes seemed deeper than the ocean and just as purdy. I could get lost in 'em.

"I want to show you the ranch. Have you meet my brother, his wife, Jess, and the boys."

"I'd love to." She smiled shyly.

"Then it's settled. I'll book some tickets."

"No need." She tapped Oliver on the shoulder. He was busy in a lip-lock with Dean. It was strange seeing two men kiss and carry on, but it really was no different than me groping and lovin' on my girl. "Ollie, can you reserve my jet for this coming weekend? Hank and I are going to accompany his mother home and stay for a weekend. Plan for us to come back on Monday or Tuesday depending on my schedule." Oliver puffed out his bottom lip. "What, honey?" she asked.

"I wanna go, too." He continued to pout and then she turned her face to me, matching pout in place. Her glistening pink lip puffed out, ready for me to bite it, so I did. She deepened the kiss. Oh boy, I was in trouble with these two. One had my girl by the hair; my girl had me by the nuts. Not a good combination.

"Oliver, Dean, would you like to come to Texas? There's plenty of room at the ranch," I asked them. Oliver smiled like it was his birthday and he'd just been given the one present he'd always wanted.

"Could you get the time, baby?" Oliver asked Dean, practically jumping up and down.

"Well, technically I do have a million hours of vacation time since your boss is a slave driver and never lets you have time off," he said dryly, his eyes squinted at Aspen. We both knew by now that he was playing. Aspen rolled her eyes but pretended to look hurt.

"Oh, this is going to be so fun! Pen, I have to get us cowboy boots and sexy hot jeans… Oooh oooh and that new Ralph Lauren line has those fitted plaid shirts." The man squealed like a little girl.

"You've made him so happy, stud," Aspen whispered in my ear. "You know that means I'm going to be extra nice to you tonight," she promised with a flick of her tongue at the tender cartilage of my ear.

"All right, all right, you crazy kids. Gusto and I have made a feast!" Ma called from the doorway. The entire group shuffled out.

The display of food was staggering. There were homemade chili beans, corn on the cob, Ma's famous fried chicken, ribs, roasted veggies, and a ton of other fixins. We chowed down, barely a peep between us until the first round of drinks and food were taken care of. Then the smack talkin' started flying again about Cowboys kicking the Jets' asses. Really, the game was so close it could have ended in a tie, but that didn't stop me from shoving our win in their Jets' pansy-ass faces.

Aspen followed along, her bare feet with perfect pink toes in my lap. I rubbed her feet as we drank and enjoyed our time with friends. This time next week, I'd be home telling my angel exactly how I felt about her, as well as my plans for moving to the city. My only hope was that I wasn't wrong and she felt the same way.

CHAPTER FOURTEEN

The week flew by. Dealing with a high-profile, detoxing model, along with the *Bright Magazine* building addition, had its challenges. I was ready for a long weekend in the country. At least I thought I was. Oliver had laid out a ton of clothes he'd secured for the trip. I'd never seen so much plaid, paisley, or denim in my life. This was definitely going to be an interesting weekend at least style-wise. I fingered the opalescent button on one of the shirts.

"Ollie, are you sure about this stuff? This is not our normal wear," I called out to him. He was pulling stuff out of my closet at an alarming rate.

"Of course I'm sure, princess. How are you going to look like a cowgirl without it?"

"I'm not trying to look like a cowgirl. Hank likes me the way I am." At least I was pretty sure he did.

The past two weeks with Hank had been right out of a fairy tale. He was attentive emotionally and physically. We shared a living space as if we'd always lived together. It was relatively easy. Even Butch and his sloppy morning wake-up kisses were becoming the norm, something I now attributed to the comfort of being home.

Thinking about Hank and being at home with him was very dangerous territory—eventually he would go back to Texas. Pushing the thoughts from my mind, I filled my suitcase full of a few of the items Ollie had purchased and a few more things that were more my taste.

Oliver cringed as I placed dress slacks into the suitcase. "Seriously, Pen? When are you going to wear those?"

"I have no idea, but I want to be prepared just in case. I didn't get to where I am today by second-guessing myself. Now please, grab a silk blouse and a blazer to go with the trousers."

"Fine," he huffed.

Together we knocked out my packing in record time, which was a good thing since we'd waited until the last minute to get started.

Hank rushed into the bedroom, his mother hot on his heels. "You ready, angel?" He smiled when he saw my suitcase zipped up tight and ready to be hauled off. He pulled me against him and laid a wet kiss on my lips. "I can't wait to get you home." His accompanying smile was beautiful, but added to the pit that was building in my stomach. Home for Hank was his ranch, not the penthouse.

I sucked in a deep breath, locking my fears away. "Me, too." It was only a small lie, but Hank's eyes searched mine. The man could read me too well. "Really, let's go."

Hank's gaze held mine for a moment, and then he grabbed my luggage with his good arm and we were off. Julia about had a heart attack when she realized we were taking a private jet. She hopped from foot to foot with excitement as the plane sat on the tarmac.

"Oh, Punky, isn't this great!" Her hands were clasped together in front of her chest. Excitement buzzed in the air around her as she stared at my jet, AIR Bright Enterprises firmly emblazoned on the tail of the plane.

Hank and I both smiled. The stewards secured all of our

bags from the limo, and we boarded the plane.

"Welcome aboard, Ms. Reynolds. It's lovely to see you again." The captain kissed my cheek Hank's arm came around my waist and he tugged me to his side. *Caveman.*

"Hank, this is Captain Kirk."

Hank's eyes widened and he started laughing and slapped at his knee. "Captain Kirk? For real?"

"What's the matter with you? Yes, this is our captain."

The captain just stood there, a knowing smile on his thin lips. He had graying hair but was altogether nice enough to look at. Had to be in his early forties. Hank slowly calmed down enough to shake the man's hand.

"I'm sorry, partner, but I wasn't expecting that."

"I don't get it. What's so funny?" I looked between the two men. Captain Kirk just shook his head. Hank tried to control his sniggering.

"Oh, darlin', don't tell me you've never seen *Star Trek*?"

"Uh, no. Is this a movie or something?"

"It's a very popular TV show, and then later there were movies. Anyhoo, it's good to meet ya, Captain. Sorry about that."

"It's quite all right, Hank. It happens a lot." Captain Kirk was being gracious and kind. I, on the other hand, was still a little peeved at Hank's lack of consideration.

Several hours and a catnap later, we landed in Texas. We all hustled into the limo for the two-hour drive to Hank's ranch. As the limo sped down the freeway, the view turned from concrete and cinder block to serene rolling green landscapes. The road changed from pristine asphalt to chunky unattended roads with potholes, right down to pure dirt and gravel. Hank refused to leave Butch with Gustav.

Was convinced he'd be too lonely so we brought him with.

Butch happily enjoyed biting at the wind, head stuck completely out the window, jowls flapping. Eventually the limo turned off the dirt road and made its way through a tree-lined smaller path. At the end was a circular gravel driveway with a large two-story house. It was painted white with horizontal wooden slats across its face. Dark blue shutters hugged each window's side. There was an enticing wraparound porch that faced a wide expanse of luscious green land.

Butch practically jumped out the window in his haste to leave the car. Once we opened the door, he shot off like an arrow, his target a gaggle of geese in the distance. Hank laughed as we exited. The air around us smelled fresh with a hint of spring flowers. I heard a babbling brook or creek not far in the distance. It was incredible, and I stared in wonder at the large ranch home.

"Hank…this is, wow. It's stunning."

He pulled his hands around my waist from behind and snuggled his chin into the crook of my neck. "Welcome to your home away from home, angel. Come. I want to show you around."

He led me up the wooden stairs that creaked upon receiving our weight. Everyone followed us up the steps and into the home. The inside was dark, and Hank's mother rushed over to open the curtains, letting in the light.

"I asked that boy to come over and open them windows to let some air run through. Must've forgot." Julia shook her head and pulled open the windows, letting the summer breeze snake through the room.

It was a large living room with old furniture and

throw blankets everywhere. One wall was packed floor to ceiling with bookcases. I was surprised to see so many books gracing the shelves. I knew Hank liked to read by the amount of paperbacks he had stacked on dresser in the spare room back home. This though was half a room filled with different colored spines of books that looked to be well loved. Julia followed where I was looking. "My Hank here loves to read. Used to want to be a writer. He wrote the best detective novels as a youngster."

Hank shrugged and rolled his eyes. I placed a finger along the shelves and scanned some of the titles. A huge section was devoted to Grisham and Koontz novels, but two shelves were filled with books on architecture and design. Hank hooked my elbow with his large hand. "Hey, you can check out my collection later. I want to get your bags settled and show you something."

We were led up the stairs. The first room was a guest bathroom decorated in garish flowers. They covered every available surface with wallpaper to match. Oliver and I looked at one another horrified. "Ma designed it. She thought it needed a woman's touch." I nodded but didn't offer an opinion. Oliver kept his thoughts to himself as well. Dean didn't seem fazed by it at all. The man was gay with an eye for hair and makeup, but he definitely was not an effeminate male.

"This is one of the guest rooms you fellas could stay in…unless you want two?" Hank hedged.

Oliver looked at Hank like he'd grown horns. "You know we live together, right, cowboy?"

Dean shoved Oliver in the shoulder. "Hank, thank you. One room will be just fine." They entered the room.

I could hear Dean scolding Oliver playfully. "Southern charm. Manners, Oleander. I can't take you anywhere," was the last thing I heard Dean say when they shut the door to get settled in.

Hank and I both grinned at one another. "And this right here is our room." It was the way he said *our* room that made me melt into his side. He opened the double doors to a large room. The space was bright with dark chocolate plantation shutters. The room was denim blue with white baseboards and crown molding.

In the middle of the room sat a wooden mahogany four-poster bed. A polar opposite to my sleigh bed in the penthouse back in New York. Each spindle of the bed had an ornate carving. The grooves set deep into the wood when I ran my fingers against them.

"Beautiful bed," I gasped.

"My grandfather made it. One of the last things he made before he passed several years back." Hank's tone was tinged with sadness, but he smiled as I inspected the etchings more closely.

"It's lovely, Hank."

"I can't wait to get you into it," he smirked and I grinned.

Off to the side of the room was a bathroom. An old-fashioned claw foot tub sat next to an ultra-modern walk-in shower. The shower didn't have any doors. It only had three tiled walls, decorated with tiny little mosaic tiles in varying shades of crème and gold, and a rain-style showerhead dropped from the ceiling. I liked seeing something so antique as the tub proudly displayed along something so opulent and modern. It reminded me of Hank and me.

He was old-fashioned and I was contemporary. And in this circumstance, it fit so well. Could that be possible in life and love too? The answer was still lost on me.

"You ready to go downstairs? I want to show you something," he reminded me.

"Sure." Though I looked over at the bed with longing, wishing we were going to have a romp then a nap after a long travel day.

He caught onto what I was staring at. "Oh, darlin', I'm going to take you good and hard in that there bed tonight." His lips descended on mine, his tongue entering my mouth swiftly. I groaned and rolled my tongue against his. We had been right next to one another all day, but I still felt as though I missed him, clutching his broad chest to mine. Large hands cupped and massaged my bum, pressing his erection into my groin.

"Hank…" I warned with a stiff press of my own hips.

He grunted like an animal. "All right, all right. Let's go downstairs. I heard the truck roll up." I looked at him, mouth pinched in concentration. "Means my brother and his family are here," he said with excitement.

Hank clasped my hand and pulled me down the other side of the stairs. You could get to the upstairs through the living room or coming down the backside, which opened to the kitchen. The kitchen was a good size, again, not as large as mine but charming. It was a bright yellow with white distressed cabinets and twisted spurs for handles on each cupboard. Very shabby chic. He pulled open a set of French doors that opened onto a huge raised patio. *Oh. My. God.*

I stood there with my mouth hanging wide open. I'd never seen anything like it.

★ ★ ★ ★

She stood there, mouth agape, gasping like a fish. I pulled my arms around her from behind and hugged her back against my chest. "So, what do you think?"

"When can I move in?" she gasped and I laughed.

"Oh, angel. I told you, this is your home away from home."

"What does that mean to you, Hank?" she whispered as she took in the view of the entire ranch. I held her close and thought about it while looking out into the distance. The view is what sold the ranch for me. Green land spread out as far as the eye could see, dotted with trees and flowers galore. Rolling hills and a creek filled the landscape with texture. My red barn stood way off to one side, not polluting or obstructing the view but adding to its beauty. A big "J" was painted in white at the peak of it.

"Well, that means I want you with me wherever I am. Right now, home is here. When we're in New York, home is the penthouse." It seemed such a simple idea but not knowing how she perceived us, it did dampen things a little. "Angel, don't you know?"

She turned to face me, her blue eyes bouncing off the blue of the sky making them seem endless. "Know what, Hank?"

"You're it for me. I lo—" was cut off by my body being propelled forward. I knocked heads with Aspen briefly before I caught hold of the force that was pushing me into her. Two identical heads looked up at me all brown hair and big green eyes. Aspen and I both rubbed the spots on our foreheads where we collided. "You okay, darlin'?"

She laughed. "Yeah, stud. I'm fine. Who are these little rascals?" She patted both boys' heads at the same time.

"Uncle Hank, Uncle Hank!" they both screamed in unison, their bright smiles a sight for sore eyes.

I hefted them both up onto the crook of each arm. My wounded shoulder protested a little but not too much. They weren't that heavy. "This here is Hunter, and this little guy is Holt." I gestured to each boy.

"Wow, you two are surely identical. It's nice to meet you. Your uncle Hank has told me all about you!" Their eyes widened, and without a second thought, they both jumped down to the ground and clasped Aspen's legs in a hug. She gasped in surprise and then cuddled them against her small body. She looked damn fine with a couple of Jensen boys wrapped around her. Sent my imagination into a tailspin wondering what she'd look like with a couple of our own children clamoring for her attention.

Holt looked at Hunter and they whispered something. "You're purdy," they said, again in unison. Then they turned to me. "Any presents for us?" They started to hop up and down and squeal with delight.

I had forgotten to get the rug rats a gift. I looked up and bit my lip about to let them down cold. "Of course we have presents for the world's best little boys," Aspen chimed in. "And after we are all settled and dinner is served, you will be certain to have them."

My eyes sought hers. She winked and smiled. Shit. I was a goner. The woman was damned near perfect.

"Holt, Hunter, where in God's name are you!" a booming voice sounded through the open kitchen door.

"Out here," I yelled

My brother made his way out, tipping the large cowboy hat under the doorframe. He might have been my baby brother, but he was taller than I was by an inch—add the Stetson and he was a few inches taller. His long arms pulled me in for a hug slapping me on the back. I returned the hug, having missed my brother something awful.

"Damn near scared the dickens out of Ma," he scolded. "How's the shoulder healin' up anyhow?"

"Good. Real good. Ain't nothin' to worry 'bout. 'Sides, my girl has been takin' good care of me."

"So you're the purdy little thing Ma's been going on and on about. Come over here, girl!" He yanked Aspen into a hug. Her startled surprise was priceless. My brother was probably the only man I'd let manhandle my girl into a hug.

"It's good to meet you, Heath. Hank has said such nice things about you and your wife."

"You pay her to say that?" Heath hooked his thumb at Aspen.

Jess entered the patio in a flowing skirt and tank top. Long dark hair blowing in the wind. Her tanned athletic body and matching chocolate-brown eyes suited her just fine. My brother was a lucky man. Not as lucky as me but she was easy on the eyes. "Angel, this is Jess. Jess, this is Aspen."

"Pen, please. Everyone but Hank calls me Pen."

Everyone shook hands and then we settled in at the patio table. Ma was already in the kitchen. Before long, she brought out fresh lemonade and cheese and crackers.

"Jess, you're really beautiful, have you ever thought about modeling?" Aspen asked my brother's wife.

"Oh no, no. You're too kind. I'm just a country girl

living the country life. 'Sides, helping Heath run the family business is just fine. I get to be with the boys and participate in our livelihood."

"Well, if you ever change your mind, you have striking bone structure…" After a little while, I started to tune out the conversation. The shit women talked about was dead boring sometimes.

My dad finally made it over and another round of introductions were made. By this time, the men had made it down from their room looking freshly showered and content.

Aspen looked over at Oliver, a twinkle in her eye. The pip-squeak grinned from ear to ear. I knew what that meant. It meant I'd be burning those sheets in the guest room after they left. Aspen laughed and then pouted and shook her head. Oliver rolled his eyes and shrugged. The silent communication between them was much more interesting to watch. It was like they were having an entire conversation without ever having to open their mouths.

"So, Aspen, Ma here tells us that you're stinkin' rich," Old Man Henry said.

My gaze swung over to his. "What the hell, Pops?"

"Just makin' conversation is all." He took a pull from his Coors.

"It's okay, Hank." Her hand patted mine and then pulled it into her lap. "You know, I've worked really hard to get to where I am today and yes, it's paid off. It's paid off very well in fact."

"I saw your name in a magazine at the local supermarket. Said somethin' 'bout you being on some list of real important people in the fashion and entertainment industry," Jess added, eyes alight with admiration. I always did like that Jess.

"Probably true. Oliver could speak better to it since he plans and organizes all of my functions. I do photo shoots a couple of times a month for one magazine or another. Usually it's talking about an upcoming model, or agent, a new film star that type of thing." Aspen was answering without conceit or even malice, though I wanted to holler at Old Man Henry for starting such a conversation.

"So then, what's your thoughts on having a family and bein' a wife if you work so much?" My pops was going to get a punch to the gut. Of course, I'd pay dearly for it because he had a mean right hook, and my mother alone would kill me for striking Dad, but the man was off his rocker.

Aspen was finally affected. I saw her jaw clench and back stiffen. She let go of my hand, took a sip of her lemonade, and then I heard her suck in a steadying breath. Either she was going to let him have it or I was. "I haven't been in the position to really think about it, Henry. I'd never been in a relationship with a man that wanted such things." She looked up at me, her teeth biting down on her lip.

"Until now," I confirmed and looped my arm over her shoulders to sidle her in next to me.

She smiled. "Until now, yes." She relaxed a little and I rubbed the back of her neck the way she liked. I could hear a subtle hum at the back of her throat. The sound made my wranglers a bit too tight exciting other parts of my body.

"I see. Well, then you better get to thinkin' 'bout it then, 'cause I'm expecting some more grandbabies out of this lug." Henry laughed. It eased the tension throughout the table but not in my girl. She was still stiff as a board. She'd been here only a couple hours and was already asked about her money, her career, and whether or not she was ready to settle down and be my wife and give my parents grandbabies.

The fact that she was still here was a testament to her strength and courage. Any other woman in her position would have hightailed it outta here already.

Jess and Ma brought out some cold beers for the guys and some type of fruity wine concoction for the women.

"What's this?" Aspen asked.

"Spritzers," Jess confirmed.

Aspen took a small sip and then nodded with a smile. Oliver grabbed her glass and took a sip. "Mmm, I want the bitch drink," Oliver said, and both Ma and Jess laughed.

Oliver set his beer in front of Dean. Dean's arm came around Oliver then he nuzzled the side of his head and kissed his temple while listening to Heath go on and on about the cattle ranch.

"What the hell?" Pops said, his intent clear on Dean and Oliver. The man was about to blow his top. His face was red, and his chest puffed out to an intimidating degree.

I stood up quick, grabbed Old Man Henry's arm. "Pops, I need a word. Now!"

"Boy, this better be good." His tone held a clear warning.

I took Old Man Henry to another room and explained that Dean and Oliver were in a committed relationship. He was shocked. He'd never met "the gays" before. He didn't understand it. Wasn't happy about it, neither, but finally agreed to keep his mouth shut. These were friends of mine and Aspen's and guests in this house. He was to treat them with respect. I added the fact that Oliver had been making sure my recovery was top notch and that Dean enjoyed the NFL. At the table, I'd bring up that Dean was a fireman. Pops would like that. Men's work and all that shit.

It surprised me how quick I was to defend Oliver and Dean. The men had become true friends, and I enjoyed their company and their place in my life. Of course, it was obvious that Aspen loved Oliver in a brotherly way and would never accept a man who didn't accept him. So it didn't matter. If I wanted the girl, I had to take the man, too. They were a package deal—as long as he didn't hurt or try to fuck my angel, we were just fine.

Back at the patio, I found Aspen leaning on the ledge, looking out into the darkening sky. Lightning bugs flicked around in the distance, making a halo of light sparkle around her form. I was drawn to her. My body physically ached to be near her. I put my hands on her tiny waist and kissed the baby soft skin at the juncture of her neck.

"You wreck me with your beauty, angel." I bit at her neck and then soothed it with my tongue.

She pushed into me and twined her fingers with mine around her waist. "I love it here, Hank."

"I love you being here."

I could feel her tense up and sigh. Something was eating at her, but she wasn't sharing. I'd get it out of her when we were alone.

"Okay, you two, come on back. Dinner's ready!" Ma hollered.

I swung her around and pinned her to the railing. My hands cupped each side of her face and tipped her chin up, so I could gaze into her pretty blues. She smiled the instant

226

our eyes met. I couldn't help but lean down and kiss her. She was too much. Everything about her sucked me in and swallowed me whole. The tip of my tongue traced the seam of her lips and she gasped, allowing me entrance. I took it, sliding my tongue along hers. She tasted of cherries and wine. My new favorite flavor.

Our tongues tangled, lips pressed, and teeth nibbled until we both forgot where we were. I slid my hands down her sides to cup her heart-shaped fanny. She moaned and tipped her head to the side to delve deeper. Contentment spread through my veins as I kissed an angel.

Just as I was about to haul her legs up and around my waist, a voice broke through my lust-filled haze.

"Guys, you have an audience," Dean spoke from behind my back.

I pulled away and looked over my shoulder. Aspen tucked her head into my chest and shook her head, clearly embarrassed. The entire table was silent, watching our lack of decency. I shrugged.

"What can I say?" I laughed. "She's frickin' hot!" The entire table roared with laughter.

"Watch your mouth, son. Now stop manhandling the pretty little thing and get on over here. Your mama damn near slaved over this meal!" Pops was in true man-of-the-house mode, even though it was my home.

"You ready, darlin'?" She nodded, and I pulled her along the patio to her seat.

Before she sat, I clutched her to me, dipped her body back, and held her gaze, my intent clear as day. "One more for the road!" I said and then kissed the shit out of her, making a big deal out of it in front of my whole family and our friends. She gripped my biceps and dug her nails in. In no time, she relaxed into my embrace and kissed me back.

I hauled her back up and pulled out her chair and physically put her in it. The table was full of smiling faces.

"Caveman!" she spat, but her voice held nothing but joy. I knew it was the right thing to do. It took the embarrassment away from her and put it onto me.

Soon everyone was enjoying the pork chops, mashed potatoes, and corn Ma had whipped up. Oliver and Dean both cleared their plates, and Aspen did that humming foodgasm thing again. My dick was so hard by the end of the meal that I knew one touch of her pale hand would set me off. After dinner, Aspen followed the women into the kitchen to clean up.

"She's mighty fine, bro." Heath tipped his chin at the window where we could see the three women cleaning up after the meal. "You're a goner, aren't cha?"

I nodded. "Yup. The damn girl but ruined me." Pops, Oliver, and Dean listened, but didn't butt in.

"You haven't told her, have you?"

My brother knew me too well. Hiding wasn't an option with the Jensen clan. "Nah, we haven't discussed it yet. I plan to talk to her here. I wanted to see what she thought about the ranch."

Dean finally added his thoughts. "You know she's not going to move here." His voice sounded a bit sad.

"Yeah, I reckon I knew that the moment we met. I have some thoughts on that, but it's still in the works." I proceeded to tell the guys my concerns about getting the capital or investors to expand. Oliver had some ideas and said he would talk about it when we were alone. Pops bristled with anger, but kept his mouth shut. I knew he'd have his words with me when he could corner me alone.

"Oh, Hank, that plan… It's perfect. And so romantic," Oliver cooed and fell all over himself. Dean rubbed his back with one hand, the fingers of his other curled around a beer.

"Keep your mouths shut. I want to talk to my girl in private when the time is right." Everyone nodded, and the evening continued without further discussion. The women joined us with dessert in tow. Once we'd had our fill of Ma's cookin', everyone said their good-byes. The guys disappeared off to their room, and I grabbed my girl around the waist the second the door closed and my family had left.

"Now that you have me all to yourself, what are you going to do with me, stud?" Her purdy little lips puckered seductively.

"Oh, angel, I'm about to wreck you like you've wrecked me." She squealed as I knelt, clasped her around the waist, and hauled her over my good shoulder in a fireman's carry. Something I learned as a volunteer. Her hands gripped and smacked my ass as I made my way up the stairs.

CHAPTER FIFTEEN

Hank unceremoniously threw me on the bed. His hands traced my legs up my pants, then undid the buttons and removed them, leaving me in a lacy red thong. The man loved me in red. He groaned when the matching bra was revealed. The demi-cups barely concealed my heaving breasts.

"Fuck," he growled as he bit one peak. I arched my chest to gain more contact. He plucked and tugged on my other nipple, the lace adding a grating texture to the sensitive patch of skin.

He pulled down each cup, exposing them to the cool air. Each tip turned into a tight little peak of want and desire. Hank leaned down and flicked the tip of his tongue at one erect bud, swirling the wet muscle around the surface in endless, dizzying circles of heat. I fumbled with his shirt, pushing it up his body. He only released my breast to remove the garment. Skin to skin. *Perfect.*

I groaned. "God, Hank, I love feeling you."

"Darlin', you're about to feel a whole lot more of me." He accentuated with a thrust of his manhood between my thighs.

His hand traveled down over my breasts and flattened stomach, directly under the lace of my thong. Large fingers tickled my folds until he pressed two of them in.

"Shit!" He cursed a lot in the bedroom. "Oh, angel,

you're dripping wet. You don't know what that does to me."
His mouth continued to bite and nibble on each breast,
alternating between the two. Ribbons of electricity jolted
through my body; I hummed with need.

"Only you, Hank." I pressed hard into his fingers, losing
my breath in the process. "My body aches for your touch,"
I admitted on a particularly hard thrust of those amazing
fingers.

A deep guttural moan ripped through his chest right
before he used both hands at the edge of each hip and
shredded the fabric of my thong. Hank loved tearing my
panties to pieces. He tossed the ripped fabric over his
shoulder. Another hundred-dollar pair of panties gone with
the wind.

I didn't care. His need for me was exciting, and those
tattered remnants of his unconcealed lust would be tossed
in the trash with pride. Another casualty to our fevered ache
for one another. I lay there as his gaze roamed over every
inch of me. His breath labored.

Strong hands spread my quivering thighs open wide.
Those eyes were indescribable in the little bit of moonlight
coming through the room. It didn't hide the hunger, the
raw intensity of his desire for my body, for me. It shook me
to my core. Had I ever seen a man look at me like that? As
if I was the most beautiful woman in the world?

His hands cupped my knees then trailed down the
insides of each thigh. Shivers replaced need. I anticipated his
touch like a brand. When his thumbs separated my folds, he
tipped his face down and breathed against my sex.

Every pant was like he was breathing life back into
my sour life. I'd always thought that life was good. Work

was great, my home was magazine-worthy, and I had more money than I knew what to do with. Then I met this roguish, handsome cowboy who saved my life, and everything changed...for the better.

Before Hank, I had no idea how little I had. Now that I had the comfort of a man—this man—I knew that I was an empty shell of the woman I could be. Hank made anything feel possible: work, friends, family, a man to come home to. These are things I had right now, and I didn't know how I was going to hold onto them.

Hank broke me from my musing with a long wet lap of his tongue from my tight hole all the way up to my clit.

"Holy...oh God!" I screamed out.

My body twitched and stretched, spurring him on. He opened me like a flower and sucked the nectar until I was a screaming ball of pleasure. His tongue swirled through my opening, licking and sucking every last drop of my release. The contented sounds spilled from his throat in a deep hum that unraveled me.

"Fucking honey and vanilla. Christ, I'll never get enough of you," he whispered as he bit and licked his way up my body, dragging his tongue along the sensitive plane of my abdomen, dipping in and around my navel. He continued his path upward, taking a moment to graze his teeth along each delicate rib.

Shivers ran down my spine and goose bumps spanned the surface of overly heated flesh. He placed small nips and kisses against each breast until he reached my mouth. His tongue dipped in to feast and I made a huge meal of it. Sucking his tongue, tasting myself mixed with his unique flavor. The pleasure had me grinding my pelvis into his and wrapping my leg around him.

"Fuck me, stud." I sank my teeth into the crook of his neck. I wanted to mark him, make him mine.

"Not tonight, angel. Tonight, I make love to you in our bed, in our home away from home." His words reached the deepest recesses of my heart. The heart I thought had been broken to pieces by a cheating prick of a man. In reality, what I felt for Grant paled in comparison to what I felt for Hank. He made me feel alive, desired, needed.

Hank kicked his jeans off, settling his toned naked body in between my legs. I reached behind my back, undid my bra, and threw it to the side of the bed. He hiked up both of my legs and spread me wide. I resisted the urge to close my legs. The man had just licked me to oblivion; shyness was ludicrous at this point. There was just something about the way he looked at me in that moment when he lined up his cock with my moist opening. The gaze that searched mine was filled with reverence, with…love. Then he sank his thick length into me, inch by blessed inch. Slow as molasses. We both gasped, eyes burning fire into one another as he filled me with life.

"You still don't know?" he whispered against my lips, eyes never leaving mine.

"I think I do," I said nervously, not expecting to be here, with this man, at this time in my life. It was so surreal.

"You're everything, angel. Everything I ever wanted." He punctuated his words by pulling almost all the way out then slamming back in, grinding his hips at the end. *Oh, God!*

"Hank…" I moaned but couldn't look away from this beautiful man. His control barely contained, body shaking with the effort to go slow, hold back, say what he needed to say. He was struggling and my eyes pooled with tears. I lifted my hands to cup both cheeks, his stubble scratched against my open palms. I wrapped both legs around his waist and clasped my ankles at the dip in his lower back. Pulling his head down, I kissed him.

I left everything in that kiss. All my fears, my nerves, my past, everything that would prevent me from truly letting myself love this man.

He pulled away, kissed the entire surface of my face, and then searched out my eyes again. "I love you, angel." Tears welled and slid down the side of my face. He kissed them away and then kissed me. We sat there holding one another, completely entwined, he still long and hard, nestled deep within me.

I choked back a sob and buried my head into his neck. His citrus mixed with musky Hank invaded my senses. I never wanted anything else. This was it. He was my other half. "Make love to me," I whispered against his neck.

"I want nothing more," he said as he pulled his hips back, and on a tight snap shoved his steel length into me, filling my body and my heart. Over and over and over again. It healed me. Fulfilled me. It made me whole. He made me feel like a whole person.

"I love you. I love you. I love you. I love you. Oh God, I love you." The last part was whispered on a howl of ecstasy. I thought it was Hank saying those words as his hot seed coated my insides, burning me with his passion, chanting those words over and over. But it was me. The words spilled from my mouth as my entire body tightened and exploded around his pulsating cock.

We both came to sometime later. He had reversed our positions. I was now limp-limbed across his big body. His hands roamed up and down my back, down to my ass and back up. Every so often, he'd squeeze a handful of cheek and dip his pelvis up to massage me. He was insatiable, fully embedded deep within me almost every night since we met and still ready to go. I'd take a solid bet Hank could get it up piss-ass drunk. I'd have to investigate that theory.

"Hey, you dead?"

I giggled and rubbed my face into his broad chest, taking a moment to kiss around his nipple then lick and bite the tip gently. The rubbery texture of his nipple stirred the pot holding my desire. I could feel his dick hardening under me. Two orgasms down and my need for this man hadn't abated. I wanted him again. Plain and simple, I was a goner. Gyrating my hips against his growing member, I leaned up and caught his gaze.

"Did you mean it?" I asked.

He nodded. "Darlin', I'm downright crazy in love with ya," he said and pinched his lips together. "You mean it?" He cocked his head to the side.

"Every word, stud." His smile was all I needed. I sat up and settled over his burgeoning erection. "Again?" I rounded my ass against his need.

"You drive me wild, angel. I'll never have enough of you."

"Well, we can't have that, now can we?" Without much ado, I sat up, centered his member at my slick opening, and impaled him. He bucked wildly under me.

"Fuck, angel!" He gripped my hips and steadied me. I twisted and moved my hips in a small circle, relishing the feel of him buried so deep. "You're perfect. Meant for me. Only me, darlin'." He punctuated his thought by lifting me up and planting me back down, his hips rocking up into me.

"Oh, God!"

I thought I had the upper hand straddling him, but he took every advantage. When I'd rise up, he'd pull me down and lift his hips in punishing, mouth-watering thrusts. Before long, we were both screaming out to the heavens. I fell to his chest, wiped out. Sleep took me instantly.

★ ★ ★ ★

She loves me. Last night, my angel admitted she loved me. Her form lay across mine deep in sleep. Her skin was baby soft and smelled like warm, sugared toast. The woman was fully under my skin. I'd only ever told one other woman in my thirty-four years on this earth that I'd loved her, 'sides Ma and Jess. It was not a phrase I took lightly. The fact that I said it to a woman that on the outside was all kinds of wrong for me took the cake.

The differences in our upbringings, our jobs, our everyday lives, were as far and wide as the state of Texas itself. But none of that mattered. She made my heart thump, my mind dizzy with lust, and my body ache to be near her. Aspen was the bee's knees. I'd love her until the day I died, and I would spend the rest of my days making sure she knew it.

Her body started to stretch and nuzzle, purring softly like a baby kitten into the crook of my neck. The movement warmed and solidified my need for her. She pushed the wayward strands of hair away from her face. Her endless blue eyes found mine, a smile spread across her face.

"Morning, stud." That gravelly tone went straight to my dick, deepening the morning excitement.

"Angel. Sleep well?" I pivoted my hips against hers with a little tilt. She moaned and kissed my chest, humming in the back of her throat. That sound did things to me. Made me want to throw her under me and pin her to the sheets right quick.

"I did," she said, and then a heavy knock banged against the door, startling us both.

"Rise and shine, breakfast will be ready in twenty!" Ma's voice screeched through the door.

"Jesus H. Christ! Ma, go home!" I screamed back at her.

"Don't you take the Lord's name in vain, young man! 'Sides, your brother and the kids are already here, you best get up! We're not wasting our time with Aspen, and the boys want to ride the horses!" Her voice broke off. After that, it was silent. She must have left to tend to the cookin'.

Aspen was laughing against my chest. "Is it always like this?"

"Sometimes. But I think more so because you're here. They want to get to know the woman I'm in love with," I told her unashamed. Her breath caught as I said the words so easily that we'd spoken last night. I'd wondered if she was going to pretend like nothin' ever happened. If she was, it wasn't gonna happen. I planned to make her understand exactly where I wanted to be and that's where she was. Period. "How about we shower real quick?" I waggled my eyebrows and thrust my fully erect cock up at her.

"Yes, let's. After…" With that, she tilted her hips and sank down on my cock with a quickness I hadn't expected.

"Shit, fuck, angel!" I groaned and locked my hands at her waist. "You'll damn near kill a man with moves like that!"

We finished our business, had a quick five-minute shower, where I proceeded to wash me off her with a big ol' pout. She thought it funny that I liked her dirty. Really I just wanted any man within a three-foot radius to know she was spoken for. Men tended to sense these things, especially if I loaded her right full with my troopers. The thought made me smile. But she would have none of it, wanting to be squeaky clean for my family.

We made our way down and settled in the sun-room. Ma had served the guys, my brother, Jess, and the rug rats with eggs, bacon, and her homemade biscuits. If she had gravy for those biscuits, I would've kidnapped an angel and never gone back to New York. Lucky for Aspen she didn't.

We ate and enjoyed the easy company of my family. I couldn't be happier, and judging by the shy smile on my girl's face, she was damned content. Life was good.

"So, tonight's the Jensen barbecue. Y'all are comin', right?" Jess asked.

"What's that now?" I asked.

"Oh, Punky, you have to come to our summer barbecue. Remember, we have it every year at this time. You just surprised us by bein' home in time for it! Everyone's goin' to be there!" She was alight with excitement. I liked seeing Ma so happy.

"Angel?"

"Of course. We're here, let's party!" She picked up her biscuit and took a huge bite. The dreaded foodgasms started again. She really loved Ma's cookin'. I couldn't blame her, though; there was none better in my opinion.

I leaned over and whispered in her ear. "You keep up those sounds and I'm going to be doing something real indecent to you here directly." She grinned and took another huge bite on a groan. My eyebrow went sky-high with the challenge. She tilted her head to assess me. I took that moment to slide my hand along her bare thigh and under her loose red shorts. My fingers crept along her seam, and she gasped.

"Don't test me, angel." I pressed my fingers against her damp panties. She moaned and shoved a bite of bacon in her mouth, letting her hair fall in her face. I decided to have mercy on her and pulled away, letting my hand cup and tickle her kneecap instead. She breathed deep. I loved how affected she was by my touch. Excited me to no end.

"So it's settled then. And of course, you guys must come too." Ma directed her pointed gaze at Dean and Oliver.

"A real Southern shindig? Is it like a hoedown? Please tell me it's like a hoedown! I have the perfect outfit," Oliver exclaimed happily. The pip-squeak was a jumble of excitement today. Most of the table laughed enjoying his crazy. Dean shook his head as if he was exasperated.

The day went on and I was in pure heaven. Aspen and I took my brother's boys to ride the horses. She actually had experience riding. Said her parents made her learn as a kid, and damn if she didn't look good up on a horse. Her red cowboy boots, tiny red shorts, and white ruffled top about made my knees buckle. Her pale legs looked impossibly long. She even took Hunter, one of the twins, up on her horse. He took a real liking to her. Holt preferred to be with the men, so I pulled his small body up onto the front of the horse with me and we took off around my land.

We stopped every so often to give the horses a drink of fresh water from the creek and let the boys explore.

The day couldn't have been more perfect. We dropped off the boys and went to get ready for the gathering at Ma's.

Later that evening, my girl came down the stairs looking like a vision. She wasn't wearing one of her men's suits, or tight form-hugging skirts and silk blouses. She was wearing a white sundress. It had little flower shapes with tons of little holes, like a doily you'd find at my Grandma's house. It was held up by two thin straps on each shoulder. On her, the simple look was devastatingly beautiful.

I couldn't tear my eyes away. Her golden hair was pulled back into some type of clip, leaving half her hair to hang down her open back.

"Aren't you going to say anything?" she asked shyly.

"You really are an angel. I love you in white." My throat was dry and scratchy. She smiled a secret smile and then looped her arms around my neck to kiss me. Her mouth slid along mine, softly, just a hint of tongue to whet my palate before she pulled away.

"Shall we, stud?"

I nodded, still unable to say anything.

When we hit Ma's, the party was in full swing. My cousin's band was playing top forty country hits off to the side of the yard; a wooden dance floor finished the section. Old Man Henry was at a huge six foot by four foot grill that boasted everything from chicken, to dogs, burgers, and corn right on the flame. My mouth watered at the sight, not having eaten since breakfast. The entire yard had about twenty tables, checkerboard print spread throughout where people were mingling and carrying on.

My mother and father both greeted Aspen and me. Pops was even so kind as to shake Oliver's hand and clasp Dean on the back with a manly whack. Dean grinned and gave as good as he got, pounding on my pops's back and asking what the score was of the latest baseball game.

Oliver was practically bouncing in front of us, taking in the entire yard. He had on a fitted plaid shirt tucked into a pair of fancy-pants jeans. Poor fella didn't know that cowboys pretty much only wore Levis and Wranglers. Those Calvin Klein numbers he went on and on about were doing nothin' but making him stick out like a sore thumb. Didn't matter. As long as he stuck with me, I'd stare down anyone who tried to throw a harsh word at my little buddy.

"Holy shit, Pen. That's a real motherfuckin' cow!" Oliver squealed with delight and ran over to the guard fence.

Even though Mom and Pops were retired, they still had a heap of cattle on their land. It helped Heath and Jess with overflow when the herds were mating and pushing out calves left and right.

"You've made him so happy." Aspen hugged my side and watched Oliver. Dean just shook his head a huge smile on his face as he watched the man he loved try to pet cattle.

Heath and Jess made their way over with a couple of drinks and handed them to us. A beer for me, spritzer for Aspen.

"What's got your attention?" Heath asked, and I pointed over to Oliver, whose electric blue cowboy boots were dangling out in the air as he tried to balance on a rung and touch the cattle. "Shit for brains! What the hell's he doin'?" We all laughed, but Heath went over to save him. I could see my brother pulling at some hay being used as seats and whistling over the nearest cattle. Oliver was enjoying every second of it.

"Guess he's never seen a cow, eh?" I looked over at Aspen who was watching the scene play out and smiling wide.

"Nope. We're city folk, stud. Cows are not a regular occurrence on the streets of Manhattan."

"Well I'd never believe it with my own eyes if I wasn't seein' it myself! Hank, Hank Jensen, is that you?" I knew that voice. I'd heard that voice more times than I could ever forget. I turned around and spotted her. She certainly had aged over the past decade, but the purdy girl that stole my heart back in the day was still there and standing right in front of me. *Shit!*

Before I could stop her, she barreled over and had her arms around me, squishing her large breasts against my chest. There was a time that it would have had an effect on me. Now was not that time. "Oh my God, Hank. You look... wow. You look *real* good," she said and then hugged me even tighter.

A throat clearing from behind me had me yanking back. "Um, uh, Susie this is, ah…"

"Aspen Reynolds. You are?"

"Susie Shoemaker." The only two women I had ever loved shook hands. My own hands quaked as I downed my beer in one huge gulp. This was going to take some maneuvering. "And how do you know each other?" she asked.

I pulled my arm around Aspen. "We're together," I said proudly. The smile she had on her small lips faded. She pulled a hand up and twiddled with her blond curls. That was a signal she was uncomfortable. Some things didn't change.

"I see. That's great. You've got yourself quite a catch here," Susie said to Aspen.

"That I know," Aspen responded with a hint of sarcasm. She snuggled into my side. "Hank, looks like you need that beer refreshed. Shall we?"

I nodded dumbly. "Catch ya later, Susie," I said stupidly as Aspen practically dragged me away from the surprised eyes of my ex.

"So, you dated her then?" she asked as we walked away.

"I did." I wasn't planning to offer much else in way of conversation.

"How long ago?" She was trying to sound sly, but I could tell she wasn't happy. She had this little tic where she'd rub the ring she had on her right finger over and over when she wasn't happy or was thinking intently. I saw her do it all the time. At this moment, I wondered who gave her the damned ring. I wanted her doing that with a ring I gave her. *Fuck!* Those thoughts could not be pressed right now. I was in a shit storm and I needed to think fast.

"About a decade," I confirmed. She visibly relaxed. Her shoulders sagged and her breath left her lungs in an audible whoosh. "How long were you together?"

"Long time, angel. 'Bout seven years, but that was in the past. She's been married since then," I added, hoping that would help her mood.

Her gaze searched mine, but I looked away. I couldn't handle an inquisition right now. Just seeing Susie brought up some serious shit I had locked away. The last time I saw her she was in a heap of tears, crying, begging me not to leave her. But I couldn't stay, not after what she did.

"Hank." Her hand came up to cup my cheek, a soft thumb skimmed across my cheekbone, and I leaned in to her touch.

"Leave it, darlin'. Let's just enjoy the party, okay?" I grabbed her hand and physically hauled her toward Oliver and the cattle. He'd take her mind, and hopefully mine, off meeting my ex. We reached Oliver, who was happily feeding the few goats that had pushed their way through to get to the food he was dishing out. Aspen started to help and I turned around to take in the group, but my eyes scanned the yard and settled on Susie. Our eyes met from across the span of yard, and I knew that we had unfinished business. I wasn't going to sleep right until I'd closed that door forever.

"Darlin', I'm going to check on Old Man Henry." I kissed her cheek, and she tilted toward me.

This was the kind of woman I wanted. One who crooned for my touch, the one I couldn't do without. I turned her head and clamped my lips over hers. She let out a surprised little yelp, but jumped right in tangling her tongue with mine. The spritzer made her tongue cool and fruity. I ate her up, dipping my tongue in repeatedly for more tastes of heaven. She pulled away, wrenching her lips from mine. Breaking the contact was almost painful.

"Jesus, Hank. Keep it PG. There are kids here for crying out loud." She pecked my lips and then pushed me away. "I've got some goats to feed. This is so cool!" Oh, no. It looked like she was caught by the Oliver bug. The two of them together were a sight. Dean came over and put his arms around Oliver. He leaned back into the large man.

"Having fun, are we?" He kissed the side of Oliver's

temple and tugged on Aspen's hair. He'd watch my angel. Even though he constantly joked that Aspen took him away from Oliver, I knew he loved her. I could tell when a man loved my woman, and he did. The same way I loved my brother's wife, Jess. I'd protect her from harm, make sure that everyone around knew that she wasn't to be crossed. Basically, we were men who would protect our families. I knew that Aspen was as much Dean's family as I was Jess's. He was good people and I trusted him.

"Dean, these are real goats!" Oliver said in wonder. I had to get the little fella to the ranch more often. I made a pact with myself that when I moved to New York, we'd visit half a dozen times a year and we'd bring the little fella with us. He needed some roughin' up.

I turned and headed back toward the main area. I could see Susie waiting for me, standing stalk still in the same spot I'd left her a good fifteen minutes ago. She'd seen me kissing Aspen and I told her we were together. Still, I felt the need to open that wound up, so I could stitch it up fresh and clean, let it heal without the ugly scar I'd been carrying around for a decade. No more avoiding or pussyfooting around. Now was as good a time as any.

"Susie. Can I have a word alone with you?"

"God, Hank, I hoped you would."

Fuck. Her breathy tone was not helping. She was going to get this mixed up into something it wasn't.

"Let's go to the old wagon," I said, not having to explain where I meant. She knew. I'd kissed her more times behind that wagon than I could count. I'd even fucked her there one cold, dark night that changed everything.

CHAPTER SIXTEEN

After about an hour of feeding every farm animal known to man, I decided it was time to get a drink and locate Hank. He'd been gone a long time. I'd expected him back within ten or fifteen minutes. I scanned every table and all the partygoers standing around mingling. No Hank. The little hairs on the back of my neck stood up, but determined to not be a sissy, I squelched the panic stirring within my untrusting brain. I looked around the space trying to find another face...she wasn't there either.

Damn it to hell!

I had a feeling that woman would be trouble. The way she looked at Hank when he introduced us was not just admiration for his physique and handsome face. That, I was used to. No, the look on her face matched my own. A woman in love. She wanted Hank for a lot more than his physical attributes.

After searching the entire area, I still couldn't find him. Finally coming upon his brother, Heath, I tapped him on the shoulder. He turned around with concerned eyes. "What's up, Pen?"

"Have you seen Hank? I can't find him anywhere. Is there somewhere on the property he might go to be alone? Away from the party?"

His mouth pulled together and he tapped his lip with one long index finger. "Well, back when we were kids he used to hang out by the old wagon, watch the stars." He shrugged and cocked his head to the side. He pointed off to the right edge of the house. It was dark, but I could barely see a couple of figures, way out in the distance, about half a city block away.

"Thanks, Heath."

"No problem. You havin' fun, darlin'?" Heath said "darlin'" just like my Hank. I snorted in an unladylike manner. The man was so sweet, and a good mixture of their mother and father with his sandy-blond hair and dark eyes. Hank tended to take after his father. They both had broader chests than the younger Jensen. Hank had the same chiseled muscles, and though Henry's were a great deal softer in his old age, he took care of himself. You could tell he was a lady-killer in his younger years. Now he just looked like a handsome, distinguished cowboy who, in his words, loved his wife somethin' fierce.

"The best. Thanks. I'm going to head on over to the wagon now, in case anyone is looking for me."

He nodded, and I walked off in the distance of the dark wooden structure. The closer I got, the more the feeling of dread seeped its way into my psyche. *He's not with her. He wouldn't.* It was possible he was looking at the stars. Maybe reminiscing about old times. That's all.

Mumbled words and phrases could be heard from the other side of the giant wooden structure. I saw two sets of feet, one definitely female, through the spindles of the large wagon wheels. Hank's cowboy boots were undeniable.

The hushed tones seemed to subside and sway with the wind over to my side of the wagon.

"Hank, you have to believe me. I never would have

done that if I thought—"

"But you did!" I heard Hank's angry reply. "You can't take it back, Susie."

"We were so young, and in love, we had so much ahead of us. I thought…I thought that you'd leave me if I didn't." Her voice trailed off into a sob.

"I left you because of what you did!" His voice was scathing and no longer whispered. I could hear his heavy footfalls pacing in the tall grass about ten feet away from my hiding spot.

"We were good together, Hank. Don't you remember? You and me against the world. We still can be." Susie's small voice got stronger. "You heard about me and JJ, we're over. We're divorced. He was just another big fat mistake!"

"Jesus Christ, Susie. You want me back?" Hank's shocked tone broke. Those words dug a knife deep into my heart. I held my breath, waiting, dreading, but needing to hear her reply.

"Oh, God, Hank. Yes! I've always loved you. JJ was a mistake! I should have tried harder to come after you, made you see that it was you and me. Always you and me since we were kids!" she cried. "But you left me, Hank. You left me that day and it was the worst day of my life!"

"Fuck, Susie. This couldn't possibly have come at a worse time." He cleared his throat and I could tell he was emotional. The woman still had a place in his heart. "I'm with—"

"You're with her. That city girl. Hank, you can't seriously think she's right for you. Look at her. Oh, she's beautiful, I'll give her that. But does she know how to wrangle a horse, feed the cattle, cook a man like you a feast each night after a hard day's work? Take care of the children you want so badly?"

Hank wants children? We'd never discussed it and he'd never brought it up. A niggling thought pierced my subconscious.

It's because he doesn't want them with you!

That had to be why he never broached the subject of children. He was closing in on his mid-thirties. It's probable that a man his age would want to settle down, have a family.

"Don't talk about Aspen. You don't know her!" he said in my defense. A glimmer of hope was thrown out and I hung onto that raft for dear life.

"No, I don't know her. But, Hank, they are a dime a dozen, those city folk. And I was told by your ma that she's got tons of money. What could you—a builder, a cattleman—bring to the table that she doesn't already have or can't get for herself?" Her words confirmed everything I had ever feared. In the back of my mind, I'd always worried that my money and our lifestyle differences would break us. She was waving it in front of his face like a pork chop to a hungry wolf.

"I need a man who can take care of me. One who I can take care of in return, just like we used to. Hank, I'd do anything for you. You know that. What happened back then is history. It was a terrible, terrible mistake. There isn't a day that goes by that I don't wish it were different! I miss you and love you so much!" She practically screamed the last part.

Under the wagon, I could see Hank go to her. She finally broke him. He was holding her in the perfect home, his embrace. I could hear him shushing her and telling her it was going to be okay. The distinct sound of lips on lips was unmistakable.

He was kissing her.

That's when the world stopped; it no longer turned on its axis. It was over. The bubble had finally burst. Deep down, I knew it would. We were too different...worlds apart. I was too enamored with Hank and the goodness he represented to really understand it could never work. And now he'd proved it. He cheated, just like Grant.

Without making my presence known, I darted from the wagon and set out at a full run toward the house. My body was covered with sweat, tears pouring down my face, when I reached my destination. I couldn't breathe. Stars were shooting off in my peripheral vision; I tried in vain to blink them back. I ran to the side door of the house, dodging people left and right. I made it through the double doors and ran right into Ollie and Dean.

One look at my face and Dean's eyes burned into white-hot pokers. Ollie scooped me into a full-body embrace. "Oh, no. Shit, Dean, we gotta go." Oliver gestured to Dean. I did my best to choke back the heaving sobs that were desperately racking my body, escaping through my mouth in agonized groans.

Oliver and Dean dragged me out to the front of the house and into Hank's truck. Dean jumped into the driver's seat as Ollie laid me in the back. Hank must have left the keys in the ignition, because we were off with a squeal of the tires and rocks flying in our wake.

"Fuck, no fucking cell service," Ollie screamed, but the voices were starting to get jumbled. "Princess, what happened?" Ollie asked in the most caring voice. I knew that voice. He used that tone after every breakup, fight with Rio, or a knock-down, drag-out with my mother. Basically, any time he saw me in pain.

"He kissed her. He loves her," I choked out, and covered my face. Misery—deep utter regret and misery—took hold. He didn't see me as enough. I had to get out of his home, out of Texas. I needed to be home. On my turf.

"Hank kissed another woman?" Ollie asked and I nodded. The ability to speak was gone, my throat dry, hot, and scratchy as if I swallowed razor blades. "He loves someone else? But he said you, he loved you! He told us all that!" Ollie started to cry, and Dean shushed him the same way Hank had comforted Susie. Bile rose in my throat, and the sour taste filled my mouth with saliva.

Oliver petted my arm, fat tears ran down his face as he cried with me. He always did. If I was in pain, so was he. It's the way it worked with us. He was the only man I could ever truly love that wouldn't hurt me. God I was stupid.

"H-He's going b-a-a-ack to his ex!" I managed with the last bit of effort I could muster. The agony was just too much. Shards of pain dug deep into my gut, and it took everything I had not to heave and retch what little I had to eat today on the floorboard. It wasn't like this with Grant. The bastard cheated on me twice and I took him back, never so broken so distraught. In fact, I'd never actually felt this type of suffering in all my twenty-eight years. It was overwhelming, all encompassing, it took over my entire being.

The men pulled up to Hank's house, but Ollie suggested I stay in the car. I did what they said, not really caring what happened next.

Visions of Hank smiling, calling me angel, making love to me tortured my thoughts. His laugh, the way his body seemed to glow after he took a shower burned into memory. His silly nicknames for everyone in my life, including me. How he fought with Gustav, and the taste of his skin first thing in the morning...pure bliss. The welcome home kiss at the end of each day that stopped my heart from beating. The way he cupped my cheeks and groaned into my mouth as if there was no place he'd rather be when he'd first press his solid length into me. All gone. Fuck. It was too much.

All too soon, I was being lifted and moved into another car. A taxi. Bags were being tossed into the back hurriedly. The men settled into the cab, Dean in front, Ollie in back holding me close. Dean's phone was ringing off the hook. Ollie was screaming orders into his cell phone.

"You better be at her fucking jet in three hours or you're fired, Captain!" He hung up. Ollie ran his fingers through is hair. It was as unruly as I'd ever seen it. The man was worried about me. Dean's phone started ringing again.

"Oh, God, please just answer the phone," I croaked and leaned my head against the cool windowpane.

"We're leaving." He paused. "Don't even think about it, partner!" He breathed deep through his nose. "Safe, don't worry." Dean's tone held a scary edge to it.

"Yeah, well you should have fucking thought about that before you decided to kiss your ex. Asshole!" Dean hung up and the tears welled again. Just when I thought I had controlled them for a moment, they scuttled down my face. I just let them fall.

★ ★ ★ ★

She sobbed against my chest. I tried the best I could, saying anything, everything that would calm the woman down. Susie was special to me. She *was.* I shushed her, patted her back, held her until her lips trailed up my neck and before I knew what was happening her lips were on mine. The feel of her mouth—wet, warm, and familiar. It wasn't what I wanted, what I craved. My arms flew out and almost shoved the woman from my chest.

"What the fuck are you doing, Susie!"

"Hank, you want it as badly as I do! I can feel it. Don't fight it. We're both free now. We can be together again. Raise that family you want so badly!"

"No, Susie. We can't go back. I can never go back. You took something from me and I'll never forgive you. Never." The anger that boiled in me from ten years past bubbled to the surface and spilled over. "I don't fucking love you. Maybe at one time I did, but that was a long time ago. I have everything I could ever want or need now!"

"She won't be what you need her to be, Hank. She's not capable of it!" Her voice was scathing and jilted. The cry of a desperate woman. It sickened me to see what she'd become.

"Don't you get it? She's what I need. The woman she is. Yes, she's a city girl, and damned if I ever thought I'd fall for a woman that was all kinds of wrong. But you know what, Susie? It's so right. When I'm with her there's nothin' else, and I want to be that man for her. Only her."

"No, Hank. Please, please give us a second chance," she begged. I shook my head and turned on my heel to find my angel. I'd been gone a long time and she must be panicked or drunk by now. The thought of my angel tipsy, laughing those sweet laughs, hanging out with her best buddy and his watchdog of a man tickled me to no end. They were my new family now and that gave me great joy. Gave me hope. That door to the past was shut forever. It couldn't hurt me anymore.

I made my way through the throngs of people, searching for my angel in white, but she was nowhere to be seen. Then I realized that neither were Dean or Oliver. I enlisted my brother and his wife to help me find them. The property was big but they couldn't have gotten far. We checked the house, the yards, the stables, the barn, nothing. Until Old Man Henry finally came up to me.

"Boy, didn't you drive your truck here?"

It dawned on me that when I checked the front I hadn't come across my truck. It was gone along with my girl and her two friends. *What in the hell was going on?*

Aspen had left her phone back at the ranch so I didn't bother calling it. Oliver's line repeatedly went to voice mail, so I called Dean.

Dean answered after several attempts. "Dean, what's going on, where are you? Where's Aspen?"

"We're leaving." His voice was cold, very unlike the smooth-talking fella I was used to.

"What the hell do you mean, you're leavin'? What's going on? Just stay at the ranch, I'll jump in my brother's truck."

"Don't even think about it, partner!" Dean's voice was angry, madder than hell, and I hadn't the slightest idea why.

"Dean, where is she?" I begged.

"Safe, don't worry."

"Don't tell me not to worry about the woman I love,

Dean!" I screamed into the phone.

"Yeah, well you should have fucking thought about that before you decided to kiss your ex. Asshole!" The line went dead, and so did my heart.

I threw the phone down to the grass and looked up at the heavens. "FUCK!" I screamed, and my brother came running over. *Oh God in Heaven, NO!*

"Did you find her?" Heath, Ma, and Jess were at my side in a second.

"She's gone!" I closed my eyes and let the fear swim a circle around my body then rush in waves over every pore.

"What in the dickens do you mean, she's gone?"

"Christ, Ma, I messed up. I messed up bad." My shoulders sagged and she pulled me into her arms.

"Oh, Punky, no Tell me what happened. You know your mama can fix anythin'," she cooed.

"Not this time. I've lost her."

Dean's words screamed through my head like a high-powered locomotive.

"You should have fucking thought about that before you decided to kiss your ex. Asshole!"

She knew. I don't know how or why, I just know that she found out about the conversation Susie and I had. She knew about the kiss. What she needed to know was that it wasn't what she thought. That I loved and wanted her. *Only* her.

"Give me your keys, Heath!"

"No way, Hank. You're in no place to drive," he warned.

"Give me the goddamned KEYS!" I roared at my brother.

"Settle down. I'll drive!" he screamed. "Take care of the

kids and Jess, Ma!" Heath hollered over his shoulder as we ran as fast as our boots would take us, hopping in the truck and heading to my girl. I prayed that I could talk some sense into her. Losing the best thing that had ever happened to me was not in my cards. It just couldn't be. I'd fix it and fix it fast! She'd listen. God willing, she'd listen.

They were nowhere to be found when we arrived, lock stock, and smokin' barrel at the ranch where I was ready to claim my woman. I ran through the house like a horse at full gallop, but there was nothin' for me to find. They'd left. My truck haphazardly parked in the driveway, the back door still wide open. They'd left in a hurry, and with the kind of money and a private jet that my angel owned, there was no luck she'd be waiting at the airport.

Heath gripped my shoulder and patted my back. "What happened, bro? Why'd your girl hightail it outta here?"

I explained the whole story to him over several beers. At least my brother had the decency to see me through it, let me talk it out. I told him everything about Susie and our past, shit he'd never known. When I left Susie all those years ago, they all thought it was because I'd lost interest or she cheated. I'd never told anyone the real reason. The one thing I couldn't forgive her for. The reason why I'd left.

Heath took his hat off and pushed his fingers through his hair, repeatedly shaking his head. Butch pushed through the screen door and sat on my feet then leaned his furry body against my leg. His head provided a welcomed comfort against my thigh. Man's best friend for sure.

"I had no idea, bro. Sayin' sorry doesn't seem quite good enough." He took a long pull from his beer, and I followed suit.

AUDREY CARLAN

"Nope, it doesn't. I still can't believe she pushed to get me back, and because of her, the one fucking woman that'd hurt me the most, I'm losing the best thing I've ever had. She's taking her away from me too, bro."

"Nah, you'll get her back. You just got to talk to her. Tell her about what happened with Susie way back. Then tell her about what you think she already saw, but explain your side." He paused and then looked at me. "Aspen's it for you. I knew the second I saw you huggin' on her. You treat her like there is no other woman in the world. Just like my Jess. She's my only. She's my life. Aspen's yours." I nodded. There was no denying that. He continued, "Even if she is a fancy city girl from NYC. We don't get to choose who makes us right, Hank."

"No, we don't. But I'm going to do it right this time. I'm going all in. She admitted she loved me. Fuck! That was just last night, bro, and I've already screwed it up!" My arms physically ached to hold my angel. I needed to bury my face in the crook of her warm neck, smell her vanilla goodness, and taste her honey lips and body. Only then would everything be right again.

"So what are you gonna do?"

"I'm going back to the job I started. Doc said I could go back to desk work and manning the jobsite as long as I didn't do any of the lifting or physical work."

"Okay, then what?"

"Then I'm going to start putting in for loans to get the capital I need to expand Jensen Construction."

"You could always sell your half of the family ranch That would give you the funding you need," he offered. I loved my brother more in that moment than I ever did before. He'd be willing to have to deal with an outside party owning half his company to help me. To make me happy.

"Not ever gonna happen. That's for Jensens only. No way, no how, would I ever sell my half of our family business. Our kids will be gettin' the ranch one day. You hear me?" He nodded.

"I will tell you, though, that I have some options with Oliver. If he'll talk to me." I sighed. "He had some good ideas, but I'd have to buckle down and be humble to it." I'd gnawed the inside of my cheek to painful proportions thinking this plan through.

"Hank, you do what you have to do to get your girl. And when you do, you never let her go. You hear what I'm sayin'? Never!"

Marriage. I'd known the second I looked into those clear blue eyes that day she'd hovered over me, a pipe ripping through my shoulder, that she was the one. The universe— the heavens, whatever—had seen to giving me an angel in white. Oh, how I loved to see her in white. I'd damn near do anything and everything to see her walk toward me in a perfect white dress, to bind her to me for all eternity. Fate was on my side. I had to believe that above all else.

CHAPTER SEVENTEEN

"Up and at 'em, princess!" Oliver's voice ripped through my sleep, shattering the perfect dream I was having. Hank and I were in a meadow, having a picnic. It was lovely. The comforter was shrewdly yanked from my form curled around the halo of warmth and solace.

"Enough of this!" Oliver sat down and patted my bare hip. "You're killing yourself. Why don't you just talk to him?" It was the same damn question, every damned day.

"You know why, Ollie. Stop asking. I mean it this time." As much as my broken heart didn't want to admit it, Hank and I were over. Finito! The last few weeks had been pure, utter hell, but the end had to be in sight, somewhere.

"Pen, I can't see you do this to yourself anymore. You went from comatose to an evil bitch. Do you realize you've fired three people since the shit hit the fan with Ha—?"

"Don't! Don't even fucking mention his name." I breathed deep, in through my nose, out through my mouth counting to ten.

"I'm worried about you. I've never seen you like this. The front room looks like a fucking memorial with all the flowers Hank has sent. You spent a week in bed, then the last two weeks you've been a tyrant. I don't like who you've become."

"Then why don't you just leave!" My tone scared me. I'd never had so much as a fight with Oliver in our eight-year friendship.

"You don't mean that."

"Maybe I do." Tears welled in my eyes.

"Well, it's a good thing for you that I don't give a shit what you say right now. You're not in your right mind. You're sick. And the only thing that will make you better is tall, tanned, and can ride a horse and you"—he pointed an arrogant finger and dropped it on my nose in a playful stab—"into next week!"

A full-bellied laugh bubbled to the surface, pushing through all the sorrow and heartache. God, I loved Oliver. He knew me sometimes better than I knew myself. If only love were so easy; I'd be rich in more ways than one.

"He cheated, and he's meant to be with his first love." The tears ran down my face. "We're just too different. Our lifestyles can't work. Don't you see that?" I tried to make him see what was so clear to me.

He didn't buy it.

"The only thing I see is a heartbroken woman who I love more than anything. And that woman loves a cowboy from Texas, who loves her in return. Please, just give him a chance. He hasn't given up on you. He's sent flowers and notes every day. He's back at the jobsite and well... I've, uh..." Oh no, this was not good. If quick-talking Ollie was stuttering, he'd done something. Something I wouldn't like.

"Spit it out. What the hell did you do?"

He actually had the self-respect to look openly guilty. "I've talked to him. I, uh, I've talked to him pretty much every day for the last two weeks. But—"

"You traitor! You're Judas!" I screamed and threw myself out of the bed. It was Saturday, but I was going to get ready and get the heck out of here. Maybe I'd go to work. There was always something that needed to be done there.

"Princess, I am not a traitor. That's totally unfair!" Ollie stamped his foot like a five-year-old in trouble. "I admit it. I talked to him, but I gave him a ration of shit so deep his eyes turned espresso, I promise! I just think you need to hear him out. You're miserable and need to—"

"Don't tell me what I need, Ollie! I'm tired of everyone telling me what they think I need. I know exactly what you did. You talked about me behind my back. You let him in. I'm so pissed at you!"

"You're being unreasonable. It's been three weeks. I'm tired of seeing you curled up in bed completely broken, or running a marathon in the gym here until you drop. Or the other fun alternative of working yourself to the bone. It's not healthy, and I won't stand for it anymore!"

"Well, you can just go fuck yourself! Why don't you go spend your weekend with Dean and leave me and my life alone for one goddamned minute?" My voice was shrill. He ricocheted back as if I'd struck him, pain and hurt clearly visible on his pointed wrinkle-free face.

"Fine. I'll go. Enjoy your pity party for one…bitch!" He ran out of my bedroom, and I threw the pillows off the bed onto the floor, ripping at the bed sheets to try and straighten them. It was no use. I couldn't make a bed for shit.

Even my own lack of domesticity proved how wrong I was for Hank. Just like the little Country Cunt said. He needed someone who could take care of him and the house. Cook his meals. I had Gustav. I continued to throw things around the room, muttering to myself.

Why did everyone think they knew what was best for

me? Besides the droves of flowers Hank sent every day, I'd also gotten cards and letters. I didn't open any of them. They sat in a neat little pile on my nightstand. He was trying hard to breach the wall I'd put up, but going to Ollie and securing his vote was beyond reproach. I couldn't believe my best friend had taken his side.

Needing a man, any man—including Ollie—was going the way of the wind. It was time to take charge of my life. Oh, who the hell was I kidding? Without Ollie, without Hank, I was a shriveled-up old hag. There was no joy without them. But was it possible that everything that happened with Hank could be mended? Did I even whisper a hope? No, no way. He'd break my barely glued together heart all over again. I had to be strong. Men, though beautiful and necessary sexually, were not necessary to live my life. It would be okay.

I dialed my sister. London answered on the first ring. "Pen, what's up?"

"Are you with a client?"

"No, no. I was just hanging out with Tripp, actually. Are you okay?"

I considered lying, telling her everything was rainbows and unicorns, but my fight with Ollie broke the seal on my emotions, and I needed her. "No," I whispered, holding back the storm of tears wanting to break free.

"Okay, okay. I'll be over in thirty minutes. The traffic is brutal."

"No, no. I need to get out of the house. Let's meet at The Place downtown. Is that okay? I'll call ahead and get my usual table."

"Sure. We'll see you there."

I took a hot shower and pulled my hair into a ponytail.

It's about the only thing I could muster without Ollie, and I just didn't have the energy to put forth any real effort. I threw on a pair of dark skinny jeans, a tank top with a loose overshirt that hung off the shoulder. The outfit was completed with a pair of silver ballet flats. Jewelry was too much to think about. Bare, low-key Aspen would have to do. Grabbing the biggest pair of Jackie O sunglasses I could find to cover my puffy eyes, I was out the door in twenty minutes.

London and Tripp were already seated when I got there.

"Hey." London jumped up and hugged me tight.

Tripp pulled me into a full-body embrace as well. I loved these people. They were two people I could be myself with. I didn't have to hide the fact that I was hurting with them. They knew just by looking at me.

London's gray-blue eyes scanned my body. "I ordered some comfort food. By the looks of the weight you've lost, you could use it."

My body was on point with my mind. Only when I was about to pass out from hunger did I actually shove down a small bowl of cereal or a handful of almonds. Wine, however, was in great supply and helped to dull the ache I felt when I spent any time thinking about Hank. *Stupid cowboy!*

"How are you?"

"Fighting with Ollie," I said.

"I see. So you've taken out your anger and hurt on the one man that loves you the most in the universe."

Tripp shook his head. My eyes narrowed at him.

"Oh, don't think London's so innocent. We've had some whoppers in our time. Haven't we, Bridge?"

"True. But in the end, we always come back to one

another." Tripp smiled and nodded. "You and Ollie will make up. I guarantee he won't even go a day without making amends with you."

God, I hoped they were right. Fighting with Ollie on top of my breakup was unbearable. I hated that they were consoling me. Technically, I'd instigated the fight and said the harsh words. He was guilty, though. He'd talked to Hank behind my back. That offense deserved a major payback and the silent treatment.

"So what'd he do?" London asked. I explained the entire fight. They both listened and nodded where appropriate, letting me finish my entire side of the story until the food and drinks arrived.

"Are you ready to talk to Hank?" London asked.

Just the mention of his name hit my heart like a sledgehammer. Saying I missed him was like saying a person misses a limb when it's been amputated. Hank was ever there. His presence permeated all the space around me. The wretched tears pooled, and I did my best to hold them back.

"I don't know. Honestly, I figured he'd have moved on by now." I shrugged.

"I spoke with him," London said softly, and my head whipped back to hers so fiercely I worried I'd given myself a crick. Her eyes were downcast. Jesus! Was everyone talking to my ex besides me? "He told me everything that happened. Of course, it was his version. I really think you ought to give him a listen. Might change the way you feel," she hedged.

Tripp's hand came out and held mine. "Bridge wasn't trying to hurt you, Pen. He came to the loft unannounced. Begged to talk to London, and I broke down and let him in. She was pretty pissed at me." London nodded frantically and sucked on her straw, biting the thing to oblivion. It was such a disgusting habit of hers, gnawing on straws until they were unable to function properly.

"Do you want to know what he said?"

I shrugged, trying to pretend nonchalance, though I was burning to hear anything about my beloved cowboy.

"He said he loved you. Said what you saw was a mistake." My eyes darted back to hers. "He also said that the chick was in the past, and she needed to stay there. Said he told her as much."

"Yeah, well that's not the way I saw it. Who are you gonna believe?" I gritted through my teeth.

"Pen, I'm on your side. What the hell!" Her blue eyes were shining so bright it was as if you could see through them. "I'm always on your side. I don't care who's right or wrong. I only know what he told me and how miserable you are." Her tone softened and I knew she meant well. Everyone did.

"So, you think I should talk to him?" Both she and Tripp nodded. "I wouldn't even know what to say," I whispered as I lost the battle with my emotions. Tears scuttled down my cheeks.

London rushed around the table, plopped herself in my lap, and pulled off my glasses. She held my cheeks in her cool hands and wiped the tears away. I held her by the waist as she searched my brokenhearted gaze. Tears ran down her face. She was never able to see someone she loved in tears. She claimed it was her empathic ability. I believed it was her pure heart.

"I love you. Tripp loves you. Ollie loves you. Dean loves you. Mom, Dad, Rio all love you. And more than all of those people put together, *Hank* loves you."

The sobs racked my body, and my sister held me as I cried into her chest. I didn't care that the tables surrounding us were probably watching the train wreck in front of them. Crying, releasing all the ache I had pent up while my sister held me, was cathartic to my bruised soul. After what felt like eternity, I was all cried out. My tears dried, but London still kept me close, humming into my hairline, rocking me lightly.

★ ★ ★ ★

"How the hell am I going to get my girl to listen if she won't talk to me?" I snarled at Mac over a pint.

He'd finally gotten me out of the apartment and to a sports bar. The Cowboys were playing, but I couldn't focus on the game. My thoughts were always on a stubborn, beautiful angel who refused to see or speak to me. I'd sent flowers and cards every day. I'd waited a few different times in the lobby of her building, but she'd somehow escaped me. She was a smart cookie, my girl. At the office, she always had throngs of people willing to thwart my attempts to see her.

"Hmm, I reckon' you're going to have to trick her into seein' ya," Mac offered, and took a long pull from his beer.

"What do you have in mind? I'm takin' any suggestions, because I'm damned near out of ideas."

We spent the next couple hours throwing ideas back and forth. Nothin' stuck, though, until around our fourth beers. We were both feelin' pretty darn good, and the Cowboys were winning the game.

"Well, the job is almost done, right? You've been havin'

some conference calls with the architect."

"Yeah, so? If I don't talk to her, I'm gonna be stuck with no crew and no girl!" The thought of all the changes I'd managed over the past three weeks nearly had me bangin' my head on the bar top.

I'd had meetin' after meetin' with some pretty rich fellas, all to discuss the expansion of Jensen Construction. It had taken Mac and me a full week to prepare all the materials. We even enlisted the help of Jess back home, who was wicked smart with the technology end of things. She built PowerPoints and charts that made Jensen Construction look real good. We ordered glossy print materials and gave presentations in the most lux offices I'd seen in all my years bidding on jobs. After five different meetings, we had three separate offers to invest in the expansion of Jensen Construction. And I owed it all to one man: Aspen's father.

After the trouble back home with Aspen, I contacted Mr. Reynolds himself. I didn't go into details about what happened, but what I did do was humble myself and put all my cards on the table.

Aspen's father was a shrewd businessman with a lot of contacts. He said he was surprised I didn't ask him for money. I'd explained that I didn't want his handouts, that what I'd wanted was a chance to present my business plan to some folks who were interested in my line of work. He agreed because he felt he owed me for saving his daughter's life. I assured him the pleasure was all mine, but I still took his handout of prospective investors.

Between him, Oliver, and Dean's contacts, I had presented within an inch of my life to five separate companies. Then the unthinkable happened: We were offered more money than I ever thought possible. Apparently, my work was worth more in NYC than I'd ever dreamed.

We contracted with those three investors, and I was now the proud owner and operator of Jensen Construction, Incorporated, with a division in Texas and a division in the Big Apple.

I had Oliver to thank for the office space. Beginning next week, my new office was on the twelfth floor of the AIR Bright building. I was certain that Aspen didn't know about it. He'd gone behind her back and made the property manager give me the two-thousand-foot office space free for ninety days, and then at a rate that I knew was more affordable than warranted for the space.

My little buddy was still hopping mad at me for what went down with his princess, as he called her. He knew, though, that all I wanted was to be with her, that everything I was doing was supporting the goal in the long run—Aspen and me and our happily ever after.

I just hoped to hell I could figure out a way to get her to sit down and talk to me. Not being with her every day was like pouring acid over my open, wounded soul. In all my years, it never occurred to me that I'd physically need someone, or that my heart would cease to beat without its mate, but it was true. I needed Aspen like I needed to breathe, needed to eat, needed to sleep. She was my end-all, be-all, and I had to find a way to get her back.

The hot wings and nachos Mac ordered arrived, and he dug in with gusto. I ate a few chips but only tasted sawdust. Nothing seemed right without my girl in my life. Not even food.

Mac swallowed a gigantic chip with cheese that dripped

down his hand. Then he licked it clean.

"That's fucking gross, man." I laughed for the first time in three weeks.

"This shit is amazing! We don't have this gooey cheese back home," he said, his eyes filled with delight.

"That's because it's not really cheese, man. It's some type of processed, plastic cheese goo created by smart-ass scientists who were bored off their asses and thought, 'Cheese! Let's make it last forever!'"

He snorted around his beer and licked each cheese-laden finger. "You know, I don't even care. It's too good to care," he added, and I cringed as I popped in a French fry dipped in ketchup. Mac stopped chewing, swallowed, wiped his mouth, and then looked off into the distance.

"What's up, partner?"

"Well, she won't see you, right?" I nodded. "But she goes to work every day." I nodded again, Oliver had confirmed that much after repeated attempts at begging. "Why not tell them you want a meetin' with the stakeholders. Update 'em on the project and reveal the building personally? She'd have to see you then."

Mac had more to him than brute strength and the country lifestyle. The man was a genius. I clapped him on the back. "Well, I'll be. You keep on surprising me, partner."

"Lisa says that shit all the time." He tipped his Stetson once at the rim and then shoveled in another hunk of chips and plastic cheese.

This idea could actually work. The architect and I were well acquainted now. He bought into Jensen Construction, and even said he'd be promoting my company to his other clients when they had a job. I gathered I could swindle him into coming to a face-to-face meetin' at the AIR building. Oliver could make sure she had the meetin' on her calendar. He didn't have to say that I'd be there.

The idea was getting better and better with every beer I downed. This was it. The time to get my girl back was now, and I was determined to make it happen. I just had a few loose ends to tighten up on the job and with my plan.

I dialed Oliver's number. He answered on the first ring.

"This better be good, cowboy, because I'm already in all kinds of trouble with our girl over your sorry ass."

He sniffed and I could tell something was bothering him. "What do you mean you're in trouble? What happened?"

"Nothing for you to worry about. I just tried to get her to talk to you and she flipped out, called me a traitor, and told me to fuck off." He started to laugh.

"Well, hell, I'm sorry, buddy. Good news is I've got a plan to get my girl back where she belongs. I think it's a good one, too. But I'm going to need some help from you. You in?"

"I thought you'd never ask."

The biggest smile split across my face. Two fresh beers landed in front of me. Mac and I grabbed the coldies and clinked the sides. "To gettin' the girl," I toasted and drank, my plan swirling, fizzing, and breaking into the perfect way to seal my fate and bring me an angel.

CHAPTER EIGHTEEN

Week four of being without Hank had me in a better mood. A little pep to my step, but nothing to write home about. After lunch with London last week, I went straight to Oliver and Dean's house. Dean answered and filleted me for hurting Ollie for trying to help. I apologized to him, and then groveled at the feet of my best friend. He enjoyed every second. He might have even taken a photo for proof of my transgression. We'd been inseparable ever since.

Work was doing better than ever, bringing in more money than I'd thought possible. My stocks were doing well and the building addition was almost complete. The architect had called an evening meeting with the stakeholders and was planning to walk us all through the new building. At least my physical body and mind had moved forward. The blood-red thing beating in my chest however wasn't. I was hollow inside. Keeping pace yet unable to feel anything but longing and misery for what I'd lost.

Oliver had the meeting scheduled for five. I added a few touches to my barely there makeup in the bathroom mirror in my office. There was no mistaking the tired woman looking back at me. I did my best to cover the dark circles under my eyes, the gray pallor of my skin. Even my hair looked dull and drab. Maybe it was the florescent lighting. Lying to myself was a new thing I did lately. It helped me avoid the truth. The truth I hadn't admitted to anyone: I missed Hank so much it hurt.

Ollie entered the bathroom, picked up the brush, and fussed with my hair. He swept the loose pieces into soft curls and spritzed it a few times. He was a magician, capable of turning something ugly into something presentable.

"So we'll meet in the Sky Conference Room after the walkthrough. Alex wants to take us through the new building first. Said it would be the best way to truly enjoy the final product. Then we'll have a chat about the interior design aspects, then discuss the HR firm we're going with to hire the employees of the magazine."

I nodded. "Sounds great. Looks like everything is in order."

Oliver turned me toward him. He cupped the sides of my neck and put his forehead against mine. "You know I love all your pieces, right?" he said softly.

My body stiffened. I tried to pull back to look into his eyes but he held fast. "Ollie, what's wrong?" I slid my hands into his hairline and tickled his scalp. His breath was heavy against my face. Why was he suddenly so sad?

"Nothing's wrong. Just tell me you love me and no matter what happens, you always will." The alarm bells clanged loudly, almost too deafening proportions.

"Of course I love you. All your pieces. You know that. Nothing would ever make me stop loving you. Okay?" I tried my best to make him feel secure, but not knowing what was wrong didn't make it easy.

"Okay." He rubbed his forehead against mine and kissed the tip of my nose. He shook his head, seemingly to clear it. "All righty, then. Let's get to gettin'!"

His smile was fake and plastered on his face all too

quickly. I wanted to sit him down and find out what was bothering him, but we didn't have the time. The stakeholders were waiting, Grant among them. Seeing him again after the case against Hank was settled would add salt to my open wound, but it was unavoidable. The bastard had gotten away with a couple hundred grand of my hard-earned dollars and a personal apology from me for "my boyfriend's" embarrassing outburst at my mother and father's home. He made me sick. Vile human being.

Oliver and I walked through the office buildings, only being stopped a few times to ask this or that, get a quick off-the-cuff decision on something as I passed. It was the norm and gave me the extra confidence I needed to deal with the boys' club. At least Alex Benson, my architect, was leading the tour. I'd seen most of the building already, but only after hours. Didn't want to accidentally run into Hank.

Silently I thanked the heavens above that Alex had called the meeting at five. Hank's crew started their work at six in the morning and typically ended their day no later than four. I'd made sure of it before sneaking onto the premises to check the progress. Seeing something Hank worked on each and every day made me feel closer to him somehow. Everything was always in order, too. Hank ran a tight ship, and his work spoke volumes to ethics. If only his personal ethics were as authentic.

We met the six stakeholders in the lobby of AIR Bright Enterprises along with the architect. Oliver chose a red power suit for me with leather trim down the lapels and down the side of the pant. Tuxedo-style, he called it. I wore a crisp white shirt with a high, perfectly starched collar. Black sky-high stilettos complemented the look, giving me the extra height I needed to look most of the men directly in the eye.

Grant tried to hug me, putting his hand on my bicep and pulling me toward him. In an awkward move, I shimmied away and presented my hand for a cordial businesslike shake. His eyes widened for a moment, and then he slipped into his cool and professional demeanor like an old suit. He was comfortable in his bored, overly professional persona, and hell if it didn't fit him perfectly.

Watching him now interact with the other men made me realize how completely blinded I'd been by him. He was a smooth talker, had a nice build, but he was also dreary, overly snobbish, and gave a new meaning to the self-righteousness of upper-class man. A gentleman he was not, though he'd like to think he was. I knew better; one day he'd get his for the embarrassment he caused me during our relationship and again with the Hank debacle.

Alex led the group through the breezeway to the new section of AIR Bright. We entered into a wide open space with a pristine granite reception built-in that spanned a good fifteen-foot radius. On each side of the reception desk were frosted glass double doors with the new logo imprinted in the see-through cutouts, prominently displaying "Bright Magazine." The etching of the sun coming from behind the upper half of the logo was captivating. Droplights hung down in varying locations throughout the open space.

"Under each light the designer has chosen special seating areas for guests of the magazine." His hand swept the air in a flourish over the open floor plan. It was pretty easy to imagine, and so far, the stakeholders seemed to like what they were seeing.

AUDREY CARLAN

Alex continued the tour through the doors and into a long hallway with individual offices dotting each side. At the end of the hall, it opened to another large space with cubicles surrounding each wall. "In the middle of the room, there will be an extra-large conference table complete with Wi-Fi, a drop-down graphics screen, all of the latest technology built-in," he continued.

I added to Alex's description of the space. "I'd suggested the open plan so that the staff could meet together right in the heart of the magazine. They could share the up-and-coming trends, columns, the pieces they're working on all within earshot of the rest of the staff. This will promote working together, a team environment. It gives all the staff a sense of belonging and that there are no secrets. Gossip should be minimized with this plan, allowing for staff to focus on what's important—*Bright Magazine!*" The concept was a New Age approach; I truly believed it would return excellent results.

We continued through the space where Alex had added indoor-outdoor breezeways that connected different departments. "I wanted to give a person walking through the feeling of being inside a catacomb of light and air. Greenery will be added everywhere, and the space will be naturally warm with organic light brought in from the sun. The canisters you see throughout will only go on if the sun is not providing enough natural light."

"Alex and I agreed upon this concept after a great amount of research had been done on the productivity of workers who have access to natural light and fresh air through windows and plants, versus working in a cubicle farm The statistics on creativity and productivity in the

275

employees that had regular access to nature's gifts were staggering."

The men spoke among themselves, but overall, the staunch, rich businessmen looked pleased with their investments. I couldn't have been more proud. The only thing that would have made it better was if Hank was seeing their excitement in what he and his team built.

Alex spent the next thirty minutes walking the group from room to room, highlighting specific features of the design. His excitement was contagious. I actually looked forward to hitting the books with these men and making some decisions on the HR firm we needed to hire, the business plan, and the design aspects of the offices, cubicles, and conference rooms. Of course, I was hiring London to design the space. Not because she was my sister, but because she was brilliant and could fit her vision into a specific budget. The stakeholders all knew we were hiring my sister to do the work; they agreed after they'd seen her portfolio, but before I'd told them my relation to her. Grant had a few choice words to say about the decision, but in the end, majority ruled.

We made our way back to the Sky Conference room at the top of AIR Bright. It was on the sixtieth floor and almost completely surrounded by glass windows. Everyone found a chair and settled into their preferred locations around the table.

After two hours of discussing the ins and outs of the building, we agreed upon an HR firm and some of the storyboard designs that London had provided detailing the seating and artwork in the reception area. We also confirmed what an average office would look with the desks, file cabinets, and bookcases she chose to suit the space. Her designs were really quite beautiful. We had agreed that we wanted to go contemporary and sleek with the space, but with an organic, rugged edge to pay homage to the old-school magazines and news-style media rooms that had come and gone in the past.

"Does anyone have anything else to add before we conclude the meeting?" I asked, happy but drained physically and emotionally. This excruciating month had definitely taken its toll.

"I actually have a guest I wanted to introduce to the stakeholders, if you all don't mind. This man made the build possible with only one accident to speak of. His company and his crew beat the odds, met all deadlines, and finished the project a week ahead of schedule." *Oh good God, no.* There's only one man that could be behind that door.

He opened it with a flourish. "Hank Jensen, everybody, from Jensen Construction. Now, you remember that name because he's just expanded and opened a new branch of his firm here in New York City," Alex gushed.

My mouth hung up in shock. He'd expanded his business. Oliver slid his hand over mine, his eyes downcast and pleading. He'd known about this, was probably in on it from the get-go. He was a dead man!

Hank shook the hand of each of the stakeholders, even Grant, though you could tell he'd squeezed his hand a great deal harder. *Caveman!* The thought sent a chill down my spine. He clapped Oliver on the back with an affectionate man's man gesture.

"How's she doin', buddy?" he asked Ollie conspiratorially. I just sat there, trying to take everything in—his larger than life presence, his musky citrus scent, the color of his eyes… Oh, God, I could drown in those honey-green depths.

"But how?" I whispered.

★ ★ ★ ★

My angel was stunned stupid. I grabbed her hands and pulled her up straight against my body. She melted into me, confused, as if she'd been dreaming.

"Where there is a will, there is a way, angel. You're my will. And the way, well, there's only one way: the direction that leads to you."

She opened her mouth to speak, but I took the moment to cover her lips with my own. Sliding my hands up her delicate spine, I tunneled my paws into her perfect golden locks, deepening the kiss. She came willingly. It had been too long. My hands, body, and mouth physically ached for her. Her tongue tangled with mine. She tasted of coffee and sweet vanilla. I needed more.

Her hands intertwined behind my neck, pulling and pressing me into her. It was if she couldn't get close enough either. My angel was greedy for my kiss, swallowing me whole. Her lips tugged and bit at my lips then her wet little tongue dipped in for more. I groaned and then pulled away when I heard an annoying man clearing his throat from behind us. Her entire body went stiff as she realized that we'd had an audience. She pulled back, but I wouldn't let her go far.

Her breath came in heavy pants as she took in the shocked faces of the men in the room. Alex smiled like a loon, and Oliver wiped at his face with a hanky, tears leaking out the corner of his eyes.

"Sorry, y'all. Me and my girl haven't seen each other for a month. We have some making up to do." A couple of the men nodded their heads. I could see that most had shiny wedding bands on their left hands. Yeah, they understood.

"Hank, I…we need to take this somewhere private," Aspen said as she tried to pull away.

I shook my head. "Nope, not on your life are you gettin' away from me now. Not when you're in my arms where you should be." I held my girl firm. She squirmed a bit, and then it dawned on her.

"Alex said you expanded Jensen Construction?" She looked confused and uncertain.

"I did. You see, I contacted your pops; he introduced me to some investors. Actually, one of 'em's right there." I pointed to Mr. Jackson. He smiled and nodded. Small world. Looks like we'd both be dealing with Mr. Jackson in our business ventures. He was a good guy; I couldn't complain.

"Jackson? Really?" She shook her pretty head. "What is going on, Hank?"

"Everyone, you done with your meetin' here? I'd like some time alone with my girl, if it all suits." The men each hopped up and made their way out of the room. Several good jobs and a great work were thrown over their shoulders as they left. Grant sat in his chair, waiting for the show to commence. My eyes narrowed at the bastard.

Oliver went over to Grant's chair, pulled it away from the conference table, and pushed with all his might right out the conference room door on its roller wheels. Grant whooped and hollered all the way out. Bet he didn't expect the little fella to get one over on him. Ollie shut the door hard, giving me a thumbs-up over his shoulder.

I turned to Aspen and kissed her once more. Her surprised gasp turned into a moan, and I got caught up in her all over again. The woman had the power to turn a man into a jelly donut with her sharp tongue, her quick wit, that smokin' hot body, and her grace.

I turned her around, lifted her up, and set her on the conference room table. I forced her thighs wide open, and then yanked her legs around my hips. Why the fuck was she wearin' pants? I needed to talk to my little buddy about her wardrobe. She needed to be wearin' more skirts and dresses. Easy access. I pressed my erection hard against her center.

"Oh, God, Hank. We can't do this. Not here. Not now. You haven't even told me what's going on," she whispered against my neck, then proceeded to suck and bite, making me damned near crazy.

"Can't wait, angel. Been too long." I unbuttoned her pants, lifted her with one hand, and tugged the fabric down her thighs. Her pointed stilts fell to the floor with a loud clunk. She leaned back and let me pull her pants down and off her body. She was wearing red lace panties, and I could just see the faint line of her pussy through the damp fabric.

My mouth started to salivate. She quickly pulled them down before I tore them to shreds. Smart cookie. I ripped at my khakis and shoved them and my boxers to the floor. She gripped my dress shirt and undid the buttons as I stared at her heaving chest.

Those blue eyes of her were almost black, laced with need. I sent up a small prayer to the good Lord above that she wasn't pushing me away. She wanted me. Wanted this, right here, right now. If she hadn't I'd have spontaneously combusted on the spot.

When both of our shirts were open, I pulled her to me and kissed her. She held my face, turning my head where she wanted me to go. She could take the lead. As long as her lips were on mine, she could do whatever she wanted. *Christ! She tasted good.* I reached a hand around to cup her ass. The other hand went straight for the promised land. She was soaked. I sank two fingers into her body. She straightened and pressed harder onto my hand, then sealed our chests skin to skin.

It wasn't enough. More. I needed more.

"Hank, I…" she said as I lined up my cock, pulled her ass cheeks, and forced her down hard on my length, impaling her in one hard thrust. "God!" she screamed.

I stilled, holding us both quietly, letting my body calm. It had been starved for her touch for over a month, and I didn't want things to be over before they ever really even got started.

"Angel." I kissed every inch of her face. "It's good to be home." Tears fell down her face and I kissed them away and started to move in and out of her body in measured, slow strokes.

"I've missed you," she whispered against my lips, her eyes closed.

"Open your eyes," I begged on a particularly hard thrust. She gasped and opened her eyes. They were filled with love, pain, and something else…hope. "I love you. You. Aspen Isabel Bright-Reynolds." I punctuated her name with a fierce thrust. "No one else. There will never be anyone else," I promised as I picked up the pace and started pounding into her.

"What about..." she started. I leaned her back to lay on the conference table, completely vulnerable and open to me. I pulled back and shoved my cock so far into her she orgasmed fast and quick.

"Only you. I've fallen for an angel and there will never be anyone else. You're mine from here on out, until the end of time. You hear me?" I roared and then slammed into her over and over. Her body coiled tight in orgasm, but I could tell she was already building into the mother of all releases. If she didn't want to listen to my words, she'd listen to my body. I'd fuck her into believing the truth.

"God, yes, Hank. I love you. I love you so much," she cried. I pulled her up, holding her face-to-face.

"You feel that, angel?" She nodded on a particularly deep thrust and tipped her head back in a moan. "That's me, inside you. Inside the woman I want to spend my life with. Inside the woman I'm going to marry." Her eyes went wide, mouth opened to lick her lips. "That's right. You're going to be stuck with me. You don't have a choice. This is real...this is real love."

I clenched her body tightly against mine and pumped my cock into her, my release shooting deep within her tight channel. The corresponding orgasm pulled and sucked at my length, a dizzying, unbidden pleasure the likes of which I'd never had before and would only have with her. I knew that I would end up worshiping this woman until the end of my days.

She held me to her, our breath coming in heaving gulps of air. "Never again, angel. We'll never be apart again."

She nodded. "Hank, we have a lot to discuss. So much

has happened." She worried her plump pink lip and I swooped in and kissed her worry away, lapping at the tissue, claiming it for my own.

"Yes, I agree."

Silently we both pulled on our clothes. A brief knock rang out on the conference door just before Oliver entered. He took in our rumpled clothing, Aspen pulling on her blazer, me buttoning up my shirt. A wide grin broke across his face. "So, it looks like you two made up. You ready to go home? The limo is waiting."

Aspen looked nervous, but I clasped my hand with hers. "Yes, Oliver, we're ready to go home."

My angel's eyebrows knit together. "But where are you staying?" she asked as we walked toward the elevators.

"At my home away from home. Where my angel lives is where I live."

"You can't be serious. We haven't seen each other in a month." Her rational brain was about to screw up all my well-laid plans.

"Doesn't matter. I'm going home with you. I'm movin' all of my stuff in, too." Oliver snorted. "What?"

"All your stuff." He laughed. "Like what? All three boxes of it?"

"Shut up, pip-squeak. I'm talking to my fiancée." Two stunned faces and gaping mouths stared at me. "What?"

"Your fiancée?" Aspen whispered.

"Oh, yes, you will be my wife. Sooner rather than later. I hate waitin' and we've lost a month as it is." I pulled on her hand and yanked a shocked Oliver into the elevator.

We took the drive back to the penthouse, and I was happier than I ever thought I'd be a month ago. Aspen was quiet—too quiet—but I had time to get her to warm to the idea of being a Jensen. Before that, though, we needed to eat, and I needed to be home with her where I could explain everything that happened and clear the road to our future.

Oliver left us, exiting on the thirtieth floor. I had no idea the little fella lived in the same building. That sure explained how he was always able to get to her so fast. Or intrude on some private moments with such ease. We got out at the penthouse and the doors were open. I had worked with Ollie to plan a private romantic dinner at home where we could reconnect.

Rose petals trailed along the floor of her home leading to the dining room. "Did you do this?" she asked, awe in her voice.

"I did. But my little buddy and Gusto helped. I wanted our first night back together to be special. A homecoming." She nodded and smiled.

A familiar clicking noise could be heard barreling through the rooms. Gusto's thick accent quick on the heels screaming something in Swedish. I braced Aspen's shoulders and stopped cold as Butch came around the corner and slammed into us.

"Hi, Butchey! Did you miss me? I missed you so much, boy, so much!" Aspen petted and hugged my dog. Her watery gaze lifted to mine. "I'm so glad he's here." Butch was happier than a pig in a mud puddle on a hot day. His long tail smacked against me repeatedly as he spun for Aspen's pleasure.

"Yeah, poor fella missed you somethin' awful. You'd left a shirt back at the ranch, and he found it. Kept it on his bed the whole time we'd been apart."

After a few more scratches and hugs for Butch, we made our way to the dining room, where Gusto had outdone himself. The tables were dressed with flowers, lit candles, and golden dinnerware.

"It's beautiful, Hank. Thank you," she said and sat when I pulled out her chair.

Gusto brought our matching dishes of filet mignon, veggies, and couscous. I requested that special since we had it one of our first nights together. She noticed my shy smile when she took a bite.

God, I was a lucky man. She hadn't said she'd marry me, but I didn't really ask properly yet. The biggest step forward was that she hadn't run away. We were here together, and earlier that day I'd made love to her. However impromptu and unplanned it was, our bodies just needed to be united in that moment. It had been too long. Now, I needed to connect with her emotionally. She needed to understand that Susie was my past and that she was my future.

After dinner, I lifted her and carried her into the bedroom. She didn't say a word. I pulled back the covers, laid her down, and then slowly pulled off her suit, piece by piece. She sighed as I caressed each new expanse of bare skin, placing a kiss here and there while disrobing her. She'd lost a good ten pounds, her curves slight and less soft around the edges.

A pang of guilt slithered into my subconscious knowing that she'd lost the weight because of me. Didn't take care of herself properly because I'd hurt her something awful. I planned on fixin' it all no matter how long it took. I removed all my own clothes aside from my boxers, and then got into bed next to her. She immediately laid her head onto my bare chest and sighed.

"It's time to talk, angel. There are some things you need to know about. Just promise me you'll hear me out."

She kissed my bare chest. "Okay, I promise. I'm ready."

CHAPTER NINETEEN

Hank's body was warm against my cheek. His musky citrus scent filled the space around us. I felt at ease for the first time in a month. We hadn't discussed what happened at his parents' back in Texas. The sound of him kissing Susie may never leave the deep recesses of my brain. Even though it needed to be discussed. Hank had said things that were just plain bat-shit crazy. He's moving in? Called me his fiancée, but didn't bother to put a ring on my finger.

Nestled against Hank's solid chest, I ran my fingers through the small tufts of hair along his abdomen heading down into the boxers that held one fine piece of male equipment. My mouth watered thinking about reacquainting myself with Hank's member once more. As my hand started to creep down Hank's tight muscles, one large hand captured me at the wrist, stopping further explorations down south.

"Darlin', you start that and we'll never get to talkin'. Believe me. I need to be balls deep in you something fierce, but I promised you we'd clear the air for good. I want nothin' in the way of us movin' on the right path." He leaned down and kissed me softly, then settled me against his chest once more, lacing his fingers with my wandering hand.

He took a deep breath and spoke. "I was just about to turn twenty-four. Susie was two years younger. She was a smart one—skipped a couple grades in school, so we ended up in high school at the same time. We dated all through high school. With the age difference, we waited to be physical until she was seventeen. Even then I was worried her old man would kill me." I laughed lightly, thinking fondly of what he must have looked like back then.

"After high school, I went on to college a couple hours away, and she stayed back home to help her family out at their farm. Her mama was sick and needed her to take care of her younger siblings. We'd see each other on the weekend, catch up with friends, fuck. It was hard being at college and her being home. So over some time, my visits home started lessening. Our relationship was in trouble, but I still believed I loved her. Was faithful to her."

The comment about being faithful struck a chord with me; my body tensed like a rattlesnake ready to strike. Hank smoothed his hands up and down my bare back, comforting me into submission. My body was a traitor, starved for his touch.

"Then what happened?" I asked. Walking down memory lane was painful. I wanted to cover the wound with a Band-Aid and let it heal.

"I came home one weekend, and she was cryin' something awful. Took me hours to get her to stop long enough to tell me what was wrong. I figured her mama must've died or something the way she was carrying on. Someone did die, but it wasn't her mama." Hank took a deep breath and licked his lips. "She finally admitted that she was pregnant. Well, she had been. She found out she was six weeks pregnant with my child, and then she killed it. She killed my baby. I never even knew I was gonna be a daddy before she took away my rights. She never gave me the chance to talk about it. Make the decision. She made the wrong one. I'd never kill my own flesh and blood."

"Oh my God, Hank. I'm sorry." I looked up, and tears were in his eyes and leaked down the side of his face. I rolled on top of him, straddling his huge body, and kissed away his tears. His boxers and my panties were the only thing separating me from him. He kept talking.

"She'd had an abortion, and said she did it because she thought I wouldn't want to be a daddy. That I would leave her a single mother back home while I lived my fancy college-boy lifestyle in another city. It was my fault. If I had been there for her, nicer maybe, not so selfish, she'd never have done it. My child would be just over ten years old now."

The guilt poured off Hank in waves. The man believed he was to blame for such a monumental decision made by the Country Cunt.

"Hank, no, no." I kissed every crease, every tear, every line on his beautiful face. "Shhhh…it's not your fault. You didn't know. You can't blame yourself when she didn't come to you. She should have come to you. It wasn't a decision she should have made alone."

He sniffed and composed himself, wiping his tears on his forearm. I leaned up and caressed his face. "So you broke it off with her?" He needed to finish this for good.

His voice cracked when he replied, "Yeah, I just couldn't forgive her. I still don't. You see, angel, my feelings for her are rife with pain, guilt, and regret. That night at my folks' ranch, she begged me to take her back. Start over." I tried to slide off his body. "No, you don't. We face this shit together," he said with more conviction than I felt at the moment. He held me fast before I could escape.

"I was there, Hank. I heard what she said. I came looking for you and was on the other side of the wagon." Tears filled my eyes. "You asked her if she wanted you back, she said yes, and then you kissed her! I heard you kissing her, Hank!" My body fell forward onto his, my face hiding in the crook of his neck while I sobbed. "How could you?"

His arms tightened around me. "Now, you're going to listen to me and listen good. I didn't offer to get back together with her. You heard me wrong. I was shocked by the fact that she wanted to get back together. Then before I could stop her, she kissed me. She kissed me! And you obviously didn't hear everything. Did you hear the part about where I told her I loved you, wanted to be with you?"

What is he talking about? That's not what I heard. I shook my head. "I couldn't bear to hear any more after I heard you two kissing. I ran."

His arms banded around me, and he kissed my temples with featherlight presses of soft lips. "You should have stayed for the fireworks, angel. I told her off but good. Explained that you and I were in love, and that she and I were over forever."

I pulled back to search his face. Ready to beg, to plead for the truth. It was all there in his honey-green eyes. The truth that I almost lost. He loved me. Only me. His hands cupped both sides of my face, his thumbs slid across my cheeks to wipe away the last of my tears. This was it. I would shed no more tears about Hank's past.

"Come here, angel." He pulled me atop his wide chest and hugged me tightly. It was the warmest place and had the power to soothe my ravaged mind and heart. "It's only ever gonna be us from here on out. I promise."

"But what about your business, about your ranch? You love your home and you know I can't leave AIR Bright, Hank. Nor would I want to."

"I do love my ranch, and I do love my home, but I love you more. I've worked it out with three investors. You know Jackson—he was in your meeting today. Then one of Dean's rich friends, and the architect Alex Benson has a company; his firm invested in my company, too. And you know that small office you have on the twelfth floor of AIR Bright?"

I grinned. "Oliver pulled some strings to ensure I got the place without having to go through the rigmarole or get on the waiting list. He also gave it to me for ninety days rent free to make sure I'd confirmed that you were in this with me for the long haul." He smiled a full-teeth smile and I melted. When Hank smiled, the whole world smiled back.

"Oh, I'm in it for the long haul, stud," I wiggled my center against his hips.

His hands crept down to my backside and squeezed. I could feel his length hardening through the thin cotton of his boxers.

"Is that so? Does that mean if some strapping young, incredibly good-lookin' cowboy from Texas were to, say, proposition you for the ultimate long haul, you reckon' you might be willing to agree?" His face was smiling, but I could see the nerves.

"Are you asking what I think you're asking, stud?" I sat up, his hardening length a steel rod between my thighs.

He held my bum with one hand and leaned over the edge of the bed and pulled at his jeans. He fingered a navy-blue box. My breath caught, eyes focused on that tiny square of velvet he casually turned around and around in his large hand. A barrage of worry slammed through my thoughts like a wrecking ball.

Did I want to get married?
Was I ready to get married?
What would my parents think?
What would his parents think after I bailed a month ago?

Thought after thought broke into glimmering pieces throughout the vast void surrounding us and my heart started to pound, I clutched at it.

"Breathe, angel. Jesus Christ! It's not what you think!"

My eyes sought his and burned a hole through those sparkling green eyes. "What do you mean it's not what I think?"

"Darlin', I think my intention is clear. There ain't no way you're gettin' rid of the likes of me. Therefore, I brought this to give to you." He opened the velvet box, and it was empty. There was no ring. I pinched the bridge of my nose and grabbed for the box.

"Okay, what's this for?" I turned it over. The blue velvet was dark as night and just as pretty.

He grinned wide. "That's the box you're gonna use when you put a ring in it and ask me to marry you right proper," he said. He cocked his head to the side and used his thumbs to circle the bare skin on each side of my underwear.

"You're gonna catch flies if you keep that mouth open any longer, darlin'."

★ ★ ★ ★

"I cannot believe you, Hank!" She tipped her head back and howled with laughter. Her breasts shook enticingly with her efforts. I leaned up and took one pale pink tip into the warmth of my mouth. She tasted delicious. Her laughter turned into a deep moan as she gripped the back of my head to her breast and pushed against my mouth. I lavished the nipple with long strokes of my tongue, then swirled a figure eight around and around the tight peak. She mewled like a baby kitten as I suckled at her tip.

Gripping her breast's twin, I provided the other breast with the same treatment. She ground her pussy against my aching cock sending a river of lust through my body. I pulled away and looked up at her sexy body and face. She was more than beautiful—she was my dream. My dream come true. "So, I'll move my stuff in tomorrow, then," I confirmed around a mouthful of luscious Aspen flesh.

"Uh-huh. Yeah, that's so good," she groaned. I flicked the tip and bit down. Her legs tightened around my waist and pressed against my dick, gaining the much-desired friction she was after.

I flipped her over on her back, pulled down her tiny red panties, and spread her legs open. The hood of her little nub was pulled back and the tight little knot of heaven peeked out, waiting for my touch. Her puckered little hole winked open and closed as she gyrated her hips in the air, ready for me to take her. I licked my lips and prepared to feast on an angel.

"I just want to be clear. I'm movin' in. We're officially together for good. I've moved my business. We're keeping the ranch as our home away from home, and I get to fuck you every night for the rest of my days."

She panted as I twirled a finger just around the edge of her pleasure center. She squirmed and tilted her hips up trying to get the pressure she needed, but I held it just out of reach. "Deal, angel?"

"Yes, Hank. You, me, everything you said." Her breath came in heaving pants as if she'd run a marathon. I flicked the bud aching to be touched. "God, Hank. Please fuck me!" she begged.

"My pleasure, angel. All my pleasure." I held my girl's legs open wide, then covered her aching clit with my mouth and sucked. The corresponding scream into orgasm ripped through her. She tried to close her legs, but I was ruthless. I wanted it all. Everything she had to give was going to be mine. Everything I was belonged to her now and I'd take no less in return.

In the morning, I woke to the most blessed sight. An angel was sprawled across my chest snoring lightly. Little puffs of air whooshed out of her bowed, full lips in a lulling cadence. It was good to be home. The past month without Aspen was pure torture. Every minute that passed when I didn't know what she was doing, who she was with, if she was happy or not, gutted me. I'd finally gotten my girl back, and I was never letting her go. My arms tightened around her.

"Hey, stud, you squeeze any tighter and I won't be able to breathe," she whispered, her chin rested on my chest. Those gray-blue eyes an open window to the beauty that lay just beyond.

"Sorry. Good mornin', angel. Sleep well?"

She kissed my peck over my scar a few times and grinned. Man, I missed this. When she finished her worship of "her spot," she rested her check on my chest and snuggled in. "God, Hank. I don't want to ever go another night without sleeping next to you."

"It's a good thing you don't have to…unless of course you wait too long to pop the question. You see, darlin', I'm what you call a catch." She bit the thick hunk of muscle just over my nipple. "Ouch, okay, okay! I'm sorry."

"Were you serious last night?" she asked, her hair a tumble of gold over her face. I swept the pieces covering her eyes away to see those blues once more.

"About what part?"

"You're really not going to ask me?"

"Nope. I'm not. I want you today, tomorrow, and every day after that. I've laid it all out there, darlin'. I'm not scared. I know you're it for me. In order for us to work for good, you have to be convinced of that as well."

Her gaze scanned across the room and into space. She nodded, "So then what do you want to do today?"

"You mean aside from holding you hostage while I ravish you?"

She laughed. "Well, yes, after that."

"I want to take you out. I have a surprise planned." My not-so-secret smirk was fully displayed.

After a blessed morning spent reacquainting our bodies with one another, we arrived at the location. I made her wear a blindfold as the limo drove us. I led her out of the car, and the faint sounds of the carousel music could be heard even at the entrance. The smell of cotton candy was sugary sweet as it filled the air while we exited the limo. It reminded me of being at the local fair back home. I pulled off the blindfold and she gasped. "Coney Island? You brought me to Coney Island? Hank, you are such a goof!"

"I may be a goof, but you, darlin', need to learn how to let loose and have fun!"

The first order of business was the Wonder Wheel. "Have you ever been to Coney Island?" I asked her as we boarded the huge contraption. It took us up and away with a perfect view over the beach and ocean.

She smiled and seemed to think back to a time long ago. Her face got this dreamy quality and her smile grew as she pondered the question. "Yeah, back when I was a kid, Dad sneaked us. Mom didn't want us seen at amusement parks. She thought they were low rent." Her lips pinched together into a scowl. "Dad was big on showing us how the other half lived so we appreciated what we had. Mom thought that was ludicrous and a waste of time." She shrugged.

After the Ferris wheel, we moved on to the Cyclone. It was an old-school wooden roller coaster that sped through its curlicues and giant humps as fast as a whip. Aspen screamed and dug her nails into my pant leg at each dip.

We moved onto the games. I was dead set on winning my angel the biggest prize I could muster. I popped balloons with darts, shot water into a clown's mouth, fished with magnets, even knocked over bowling pins with a softball, but still couldn't get the big prize. She had an armful of stuffed animals, including a frog, a chicken, a bear, even a snake. But I was determined to get her the big dog. The mother of all prizes. The stuffed tiger. It would be mine.

Finally, after an endless battle with the strong man I struck gold. The strong man was no match for me. Plus, it added to my desire to prove my strength after the surgery. Of course, I didn't use the wounded shoulder, but overall it had the wanted effect. She was fawning over the giant tiger, kissing me, kissing its stuffed face, and then kissing me some more. I was in hog heaven.

We walked with my right hand tucked in the back pocket of her skinny jeans. Lord only knew why she referred to them as such. She had a slight body with curves in all the right places. Weren't all jeans considered skinny jeans on someone who was her size? Women's clothing just didn't make sense.

"Hank, this has been the best day." She beamed. Before I could respond, she was rushing over to a booth covered in navy-blue curtains with white stars imprinted on them. The sign boasted "Fortune-Teller" in fancy cursive lettering. "Let's do it!" She practically jumped up and down with excitement. I couldn't deny a purdy little thing like her.

"Whatever you wish. And I bet she says that, too!" I added as she tugged me into the dark space. We were ushered through to a woman who sat at a round table with a crystal ball dead center of the space. She had a candy-apple-red scarf around her long black hair and bright lipstick on to match. She had flowing glittery clothes on and long purple nails. She gave me the creeps. She cocked her head to the side.

"You." She pointed a long purple-nail-tipped finger at me. "You're a nonbeliever. You sit over there!" She pointed to a chair off to the side. Apparently I wasn't going to get a reading today. *Better be half price then.*

She ushered Aspen to sit in front of her. She held her hands and petted the inside of her palm with one of those long nails. Made me shiver. It was weird that she didn't ask what service she wanted, nor did she offer payment information up front. She was probably a swindler. She was going to charge us out the ass after the services were rendered and we'd have no choice but to pay. I was about to speak when she pointed one of those fingers at me again.

"Don't speak." I held my tongue only because she was wicked strange and had my girl's hand in hers. Aspen seemed completely taken with the odd woman.

"Angel," she whispered and Aspen gasped. "Your true love will call you that. It's important somehow."

I tried to think back to whether or not I'd addressed her since we entered. I knew I hadn't.

"You have a lot to offer the world. Not only are you smart, you're creative and you do well in business. Better than most I'd say, looking at how long your success line is here." She continued to inspect Aspen's hand. "See this line? It's your life line. You will live a long, happy life."

She started to cluck her tongue. "Ah, but you see your Line of Heart, it has some breaks in it. You will or have had a couple heartbreaks already. But there is one, the one of your true love, it breaks for a short distance here, then comes back and follows you to the end of your days." She smiles. "You must hold out for your true love. You'll know it, angel," she whispered.

Aspen nodded and smiled, risking a quick peek in my direction. Her shy smile was as sweet as the molasses I put on my biscuit in the mornings.

The gypsy fortune-teller continued. Shared some additional, surprisingly accurate information that even had me believing in her psychic ability for half a second. She talked about a man in her life who was destined to walk alongside her but was not her true love or her lover. Just a kindred spirit. She suggested that Aspen never forsake that relationship because it would get her through important milestones throughout her life. The things that her true love was unable to comprehend.

As we were leaving, the woman grabbed Aspen's arm and turned her around. She smiled widely. "Your aura, it's white and sparkling. Congratulations are in order. If not now, then soon." The woman hugged Aspen tight. "Come back, pretty angel, but leave the nonbeliever at home next time." She glared at me.

I handed the woman a couple twenties, and she tucked them into her bra. "Good-bye, Hank," she said and turned on her heel and left.

"How did you know my name?" I called to her, but she continued walking and waved her hand over her shoulder. We were clearly dismissed.

"That was incredible, Hank. You should have had an open mind." Aspen pouted but hugged her giant tiger. Best money spent on that tiger, not the psychic. At least she could cuddle up to it and remember me.

"I don't believe in all that hocus-pocus."

"She called me angel. She knew your name. And she knew some pretty crazy stuff about my life. You know what she told me?"

"I don't know. I kind of spaced out through some of it."

"She told me that big things were about to happen in my love life and to take the bull by its horns. She said that. The bull. You know, like cattle!"

"Oh, don't listen to that hunk of horse manure. She's joshin' ya. She could read you like a Bible on Sunday in church."

ANGEL FALLING

"Not funny, Hank. She really did know some things. And what was up with that congratulations stuff? What do you think she was talking about when she said my aura was sparkling and white?"

"I don't know. Maybe she took too many hits to the head from pissed-off customers or was dropped on her head as a baby. Don't put too much thought into it." I gripped her around the waist and pulled her to me. "'Sides, the only congratulations that are in order will be when we are both sayin' 'I do' in front of God and everybody." She kissed me softly. "So, when you think I'm gonna be able to make an honest woman out of ya?" I asked, nervous about her answer, but I needed to know how long it was gonna take.

Her face fell a bit. "It's not that I don't want you. I love you. I've never loved a man the way I love you. And for the first time in my life, it actually feels like forever." She smiled and her eyes twinkled as they sought mine. "But we just got back together. I don't want to rush it," she admitted.

"We got nothin' but time, angel. It's me and you against all odds."

"I love you, Hank. All your pieces," she said. I'd heard her say that to Oliver and her sister once before.

"What does that mean?"

She smiled and searched my face and then settled those clear-water blues to mine. "It means that no matter what, I love everything about you. Good, bad, and everything in between. All your pieces."

"I love all your pieces, too, angel."

EPILOGUE

It was October, and we were closing in on the holidays fast. Hank and I had spent the last three months really getting to know one another on a level outside of the physical. He had received a clean bill of health from the doctor who performed his surgery. We were warned that he should still take it easy and work up to lifting heavier amounts week by week, building back up to the couple hundred pounds he was bench-pressing prior to the accident. I added more weights to our home gym so that he could build up, and hired us both a personal trainer.

Hank wasn't thrilled with having what he said was a "half-naked" man working out with me, but all it took was letting him bend me over every piece of equipment in the gym for him to get comfortable with the idea. He said it helped him believe I'd be thinking of what we did on that equipment when the trainer was having me use a particular piece. Such a wacko.

Hank's business was booming as well. He said he had more work in New York than he'd ever had back in Texas. Mac was running the Texas branch and enjoying being at home with his family. A few of the single guys chose to stay in New York, preferring the big city life over the country living. Hank offered to pay them quite a bit more per hour to fit the cost of living and average pay for men that did that type of work here in the city. With Ollie's help, Hank hired a receptionist, office administrator, and a few other needed positions, including a dozen new crew members to serve on the jobs out in the field. According to Ollie, he was going to need to double the size of his staff within a year's time due to the jobs he was turning down even after he'd won the bid. We discussed my concerns that he was underselling his work. He felt it appropriate to make good money for a decent day's work, which kept him beating out all the bids. More bids were approved than he was able to handle, but it was a good problem to have in the grand scheme of things.

Bright Magazine was knee-deep in preparations for the January 1 launch. The buzz was big, and I felt confident that the team we'd hired and the first sets of interviews, photo-shoots, and columns would intrigue the public to take a chance on a new magazine. Plus, we had one of the hottest celebrities in the market half-naked on the cover. You couldn't go wrong with a beautiful man to get the average woman's attention, as well as the married and at-home-mom demographics.

My only complaint was that I constantly felt like crap. The last few weeks had been filled with headaches, loss of appetite, then ravenous hunger, exhaustion, crazy bursts of energy, and the feeling that I just wasn't myself. I knew my body. It was freaking out over the Hank proposal issue. The symptoms were on and off and corresponded with Hank's demand that I request his hand in marriage and not the other way around. The problem was I didn't know how or when to do it, or whether or not I wanted to. Don't get me wrong—I loved Hank more than anything else in my life. He was definitely the only man I could ever imagine being in my future, and the only person I'd ever considered marrying.

Then what is your problem? I actually went to the jewelry store a couple times and browsed for rings. Once, Oliver dragged me and demanded I pick one out. Wouldn't leave until I'd done the deed.

The next day I returned the ring. It wasn't that the ring didn't fit Hank. He wouldn't care one iota what the ring looked like, only that making the leap meant I was ready for more, ready for our forever. He'd been incredible about giving me space, too. He seemed perfectly comfortable with living together and enjoying the last three months, but I knew it was on his mind.

When we'd see couples getting married on TV, in a movie, or receive a wedding invite, Hank would get this wistful look in his eyes. It broke my heart to see his desire, knowing that I could so easily give him everything he ever wished for. But would it last?

My parents' marriage was not one built on love, trust, and passion. It was a marriage of convenience, a business negotiation. Last week when I was feeling pretty down and out about my lack of ability to give Hank what he wanted—namely, me—I visited my father and asked about their marriage.

"Darling, your mother and I were from the same world. Our families had been acquainted for years. The mutual appreciation between her family and ours went a long way toward our decision to be together. The situation just fit," he'd said.

"But did you love Mom?"

His eyes searched mine, but held no sparkle, no fond stories about falling madly in love with my mother and sweeping her off her feet so that he would never be without her. "Darling, I learned to love your mother very much. And besides, she gave me the three best things I'd ever created. You, London, and Rio." He smiled and pulled me in for a hug.

"What would you say if I told you that Hank wanted to marry me?"

He grinned. "I'd say I'm surprised he waited this long. The boy is taken with you, darling. You know he already asked for your hand." He said it as if he'd asked me to pass the sugar for the tea.

"He asked you? When?"

"Two or three months ago. Said he was going to win you back, and when he did, he was going to marry you. Wanted to make sure I was okay with his intentions. I told him that I'd be honored to welcome him into the family. Then I gave him some contacts for his business expansion to look into."

I shook my head and thought about all that my dad had expounded. "Why didn't you tell me? That was months ago."

"Well, I had expected that you would come over and announce your engagement, but since you hadn't, I didn't want to pry or ruin the surprise for you. Just a couple weeks ago, though, I got curious and called him to check on his intentions." He laughed deep in his throat. "He told me he'd turned over the reins on that plan to you. Said he wanted you to be certain you were ready to saddle up with him. His words, not mine." He laughed and steepled his fingers under his chin. "What are you waiting for, darling?"

"Honestly, Dad, I don't know. Oliver is beside himself.

Dean will hardly look at me. London practically cries every time we speak, and now I find out you're having secret conversations with my boyfriend behind my back." I grinned, but it turned into a sigh. "And I just haven't been feeling well. I don't know. One moment I'm fine, the next I'm ready to crawl into bed and close out the world. Both Hank and I have had long days in the office." It was the most plausible explanation.

"How's that going? The expansion?"

"Wonderful. Hank is incredibly smart. Turns out he has an architectural and business degree from the University of Texas."

"Proof that you can't judge a book by its cover." He winked at me and sipped his tea. "If you're not ready to become Hank's wife, then don't rush into it. If the man wants you, he'll wait. And if he loves you, he won't push you to do something that's not right for you."

"No, I know, Dad. He really hasn't. He's only brought it up a couple of times over the past three months, hasn't pushed or prodded at me, but I know he's ready. Knowing that you approve of him helps. I love you, Dad." I got up and hugged him.

"He's a good man and he loves you a great deal. Remember that as you consider your options. Oh, and don't tell your mother. Maybe just elope." He laughed. "And can you please visit the doctor and have a checkup? You've complained quite often of not feeling well."

I nodded. "Yeah, I will. Oliver made an appointment for tomorrow, actually."

The evening had flown by and I'd fallen asleep before Hank even made it home from a dinner meeting. The next morning I slipped out of bed and met Ollie in the spare room that I'd had renovated into a closet and vanity area after Hank moved in. Hank's closet was now the one off the master bath.

Over the past couple months, Hank and Ollie had gotten past any insecurity over each other's place in my life, but my cowboy was not compromising on Oliver's intrusive ways. He would not accept the man coming into our room to wake me. He also preferred he not be anywhere near our morning routine of getting ready. Bought me a silk robe for every day of the week, too, so that I wouldn't be traipsing around in front of my best friend naked anymore. I knew he wasn't being controlling. He just had old-fashioned morals and appreciated modesty more than I did.

"You ready to get your shit fixed?" Ollie asked as he handed me a black pantsuit and a silver silk blouse.

"Honestly, Ollie, I know you mean well, but there's nothing wrong with me. I'm just tired. We've all been working ourselves to the bone, and Hank and I often choose to spend the evenings wrapped up in one another instead of getting that much-needed sleep."

He smirked. "Uh-huh. Whatever. I've heard of people like you who have been exhausted all the time, with extreme levels of fatigue, and they had cancer!" He put his hands on his hips.

"What the hell, Ollie? That's a messed-up thing to say. Are you trying to scare me?"

"Hell yes! I'm scared as shit. You have no idea how many diseases WebMD says you have right now!" His tone was serious, but his eyes told another story.

"You're full of it. I'll go to the damn doctor. Stop

diagnosing me, for crying out loud. I don't have cancer; I'm just under the weather. I probably have the flu."

"You could have walking pneumonia and not even know it!"

I rolled my eyes. "Ollie," I warned. "Call the limo around, please."

Ollie meant well, but sometimes he could take the cake with his ridiculous ideas. But there was a modicum of truth to his thoughts. I had felt like death warmed over for the better part of two months now. It had to be stress and fatigue. Could I handle if it was something more serious? Cancer? No, no, no. My best friend just had me freaking out for no reason. Walking pneumonia. Was that a possibility? I had been on a ten-day course of antibiotics for a sinus infection shortly after we went to Coney Island. Maybe I just needed another round.

A couple of hours later, the doctor led me back out into the waiting room to meet up with Ollie. I'd forced him to stay there, even though it took the promise of a night at one of New York's finest restaurants for the four of us to get him to agree. Sometimes my best friend hovered like a helicopter mom. This time I was grateful for his protectiveness. One look at my pale face, and he ushered me out and into the limo.

"Pen, okay. I'm ready. What's wrong?" His eyes were filled with unshed tears. "You're white as a ghost, tell me!" he screamed.

I handed him the piece of paper that sealed my fate.

"Oh. My. Fucking. God!"

★ ★ ★ ★

My angel was quiet—too quiet—as she sat and looked out the window of the limo. We had dinner reservations at a fancy-pants restaurant uptown. I didn't quite hate the city anymore, but I could definitely live without the hustle and bustle of the traffic, people always in a hurry, running into one another, and all the gourmet crap. Every time we ate out at one of the places Aspen chose, I always left hungry. We'd have to stop by Fat Johnny's Hot Dog Stand on the way home. A big man like me didn't fill up on a speck of meat and a few stalks of asparagus. I needed a ten or twelve ounce steak, a ladleful of mashed potatoes, and a heap of corn to fill the gullet. Throw in a couple pints and you had a happy man.

"Darlin', what's the matter?"

"Hmmm?"

"I asked you what's peckin' at your brain."

"I love you, Hank. All your pieces." She smiled, but it was strange and completely out of the blue.

"Tell me, angel. What's the matter? What did the doctor say today? You sick?"

My gut twisted at the thought of my girl being sick. I'd been nervous all day waitin' to find out the results of all the tests she was gonna have. Oliver had me in a fit with all his printouts from some doctor website that claimed she could have a hundred different diseases...many of which ended in early death. Sweat broke out on my forehead; the hairs on my neck stood at attention as I prepared to hear the worst.

She looked out the window as we arrived at the location. "Let's chat inside. I'm hungry," she said as she pulled across me and hopped out.

I took a deep breath and followed the love of my life

inside, hoping to God whatever ailed her could be cured. *Please, God in Heaven, don't take away the angel you sent now that I've got her back.*

We settled into her preferred table. Having tons of money got her into all kinds of special places. I couldn't care less, but she seemed to enjoy it, and I enjoyed her being happy.

I ordered a beer and she bypassed the wine, which added to my theory that my life was about to change. She took her time ordering her dinner, substituting fish for chicken, which was strange. She loved seafood and ordered it on most occasions when we ate out. She looked at everyone but me. Those damned alarm bells were chiming like mad.

Gripping her hand over the table, I tugged it and forced her to look at me. "You're killin' me, angel. Are you sick?"

"Nothing that won't go away after six or seven months," she said.

"Do you need surgery on something?" My mind was scrambling around, trying to connect the dots, figure out what could possibly need that amount of healing. Hell, even my shoulder was healed up after three months for the most part. "I'm not following."

"I'm nervous, stud. Give me a minute." Nervous Aspen was a new thing. This was not a side to her I'd seen often. She was sitting across from me acting shy, and she looked pale and uncertain. Even her eyes didn't hold the same fire. I couldn't imagine what was making her act this way, but I was scared shitless to find out.

A small smile was on her lips and that tiny little quirk of her lips acted like a balm on my own nerves. She took a deep breath and started again. "Since we've been together, you've made it clear that there were a couple things that would make you the happiest man on earth. Do you remember what you said those were?"

I had no idea where she was going with this, but she bit down on her lip and reached into her purse. She pulled out a piece of paper and the coveted blue velvet box I hadn't seen in almost three months. My heart started beating so hard in my chest I thought that it was possible to hear it thumping across the room.

"Angel," I whispered.

"Look inside." She smiled. I grabbed the box and opened it. Inside were two rings. One was a huge square diamond with three circle diamonds hugging the square on each side. I pulled it out and inspected it. It was obviously for her. She smiled when I slipped it on the edge of my pinky finger to examine it. "Pretty nice." I smiled and she nodded.

The other ring was a band with the whitest gold I'd ever seen. Running through the inside was a raised rope of metal, like one we'd use on roping our cattle back home. "So, does this mean you're asking me to marry ya?"

Her smile fell, and she slowly pushed a small piece of paper across the table. Her finger held whatever it was facedown. After what seemed like forever, her gaze lifted to mine and what I saw there broke me. She had huge tears in her eyes, but wasn't letting them fall.

"That depends, Hank. If you still want to marry me after you see what's on the other side of this piece of paper. The deal is you ask me and in turn, I will ask you."

I feared the little square of paper, but whatever it was, it didn't matter. Even if she had a terminal illness and I only had one more day with her, there would have been nothin' I wanted more than to marry my angel. Her hand was chilled as I covered it with my larger one. "Angel, I will marry you no matter what. There is nothing I want more in life than to be with you. Forever."

"Look at it, Hank. Please. " Her lip quivered, a tear fell, and I turned over the piece of paper. It was black and white and showed a white grainy blob in the center of a dark circle. Like someone had tried to erase black ink off a piece of paper and pressed too hard and got a hazy white smudge for their effort. Aspen's name was on the top left hand, her doctor's information on the other side.

I shook my head and shrugged. "What am I lookin' at, darlin'?"

"That's a picture of our baby." My eyes shot to hers. Huge tears poured down the sides of her face. Her lips trembled and she licked them. I wanted to kiss them, hug her, laugh with joy, and scream. I did none of that. The only thing I could do was stare at the perfect little blob in the grainy image. My child. Our baby.

"Angel, I...I don't know what to say."

"Say you want to marry me," she urged, and I could tell that she was scared this news would make me not want her. God only knew what was going on in that head of hers, but nothing could be further from the truth.

"I want to marry you," I said with as much conviction as my emotions would allow. My voice was strained but loud enough for her to hear.

"Say you'll marry me," she asked and clutched my hand with hers.

"I'll marry you."

"Okay," she whispered with a tentative smile.

"Okay, when?" I asked, gripping her lovely hands to mine, waiting for the moment when I could kiss her.

"I don't know?" She was beautiful when she was confused. She was always beautiful.

"Tomorrow?" My smile must have reached my ears because she stood up.

"No. Soon though." She laughed lightly.

"Okay. Can I kiss you now?"

Her smile melted my heart. I stood and pulled her out of her chair. My hands cupped her face. "You've made me happier than I ever dreamed. Thank you."

And I kissed her. I kissed her as if I'd never get the chance again. I kissed her as though the world was ending when it had only truly just begun. Our worlds were colliding in the best possible way. I'd always remember the day that my angel fell into my arms. The day she agreed to become my wife. The day she told me I was going to be a father.

"How pregnant are we?" I asked, cupping my hand over her belly. If I focused really hard, I imagined I could barely feel an outline of a little something growing there. My baby.

"We're about nine weeks. I didn't even realize I'd missed my cycle last month completely. With all the work and..." I put my fingers over her lips.

"Angel, don't. This is the best news of my life." I pulled her hand and slipped on her engagement ring. She grabbed the box and slipped my ring on my left finger. It fit perfectly. "Shouldn't we wait for the ceremony for mine? Isn't that custom?"

"It's customary to have a ring when you propose. I asked you and you agreed. You going to tell me you won't wear my ring?" Her eyebrows pinched together, and her mouth set into a pout.

"Not a chance. I'll wear it proudly. I love you so much," I whispered against her lips and kissed her. Then I dropped down to my knees in the middle of the restaurant and held her stomach to my face. I nuzzled her belly and kissed the entire surface. She swatted my hands away when I tried to lift her shirt to kiss her bare skin. I wanted nothing but my angel's flesh between me and connecting with our baby.

"Hank, you're making a scene." She was right. The entire restaurant was watching us. I couldn't sit here and have dinner. Excitement about getting married, about having our baby, was flooding me and filling my thoughts to the brim.

"Let's go!" I pulled on her and ushered her out and into the street.

We made it home in record time, probably because I was threatening the limo driver every five seconds to hurry up or he was going to get a boot up his ass. He didn't disappoint.

We went straight into the bedroom. Without a word, I stripped her of all her clothes then laid her bare on our bed, I removed all of my clothing and surveyed her entire body. Now that I was paying close attention, there were very subtle changes.

The fullness of her breasts, the soft glow of her skin, her stomach even looked as if it had rounded out just a hair. Though it was probably wishful thinking. I straddled Aspen and planted my face on top of her belly. I spread my hand out over the entire expanse and looked at her in awe.

"You know, pretty soon you won't be able to cover that space with your hands," she said.

"Oh, I can't wait to see you all round and swollen with my child." I slid my hands all over her bare skin. "Hell, darlin', it makes me rock hard just thinking about it."

"A man who's turned on by pregnancy." She laughed but enjoyed my hands on her.

I spent the evening worshiping every inch of my pregnant fiancée. Knowing I was going to do so for the rest of my life only made the world seem that much sweeter.

She slept through the night, and in the wee hours of the mornin', I stared at our baby's picture. It didn't look like a baby yet, but it was still the most beautiful thing I'd seen aside from my girl.

"You still looking at that picture, stud?" she asked, then stretched out and put her head on my chest.

"I just can't believe it. Ma is going to go through the roof. You better get ready for a visit, because once she finds out you're expecting and we're gettin' married, the whole lot of 'em will be coming to New York."

She kissed my chest and tilted her head up. "I thought maybe we could get married at the ranch. The landscape is beautiful. Just invite our families and our good friends. Keep it small. I'll be a pregnant bride unless we want to wait until after the baby is born," she said.

"Oh, hell, no. My baby is not entering the world a bastard. We're getting married, and fast!" There was no budging on this one. The sooner the better in my opinion. If Ma weren't going to be so happy about getting a new grand, she'd be lecturing us until the wedding day about getting pregnant before the wedding.

"Okay."

"So how do you think you got pregnant, anyway?" I

asked. She'd been on birth control, which is why we never used condoms.

"The doctor thinks it was the course of antibiotics I took when I had that sinus infection after we visited Coney Island, remember? I was on them for ten days. Apparently they can minimize the effects of the active agents in the birth control pills." She snuggled back into my side and closed her eyes with a yawn.

It was still early yet, and we'd gone to bed really late. My girl needed her rest, more now than ever before.

"Did I tell you how happy you've made me?" She nodded and rubbed her cheek against my chest, then her breath evened out, and she was sound asleep once more.

Hugging her close, I ran my fingers through her golden hair with one hand and stared at the image of our baby in the other until sleep took me, too. Sweet dreams of flowing white dresses, puffs of pink and blue twinkle lights danced across my subconscious, along with one perfect vision of an angel falling into my arms and me holding onto her for an eternity.

THE END

The Falling Series is continued in...

London Falling

ALSO BY AUDREY CARLAN

The Calendar Girl Series

January (Book 1)   July (Book 7)

February (Book 2)   August (Book 8)

March (Book 3)   September (Book 9)

April (Book 4)   October (Book 10)

May (Book 5)   November (Book 11)

June (Book 6)   December (Book 12)

The Falling Series

Angel Falling

London Falling

Justice Falling

The Trinity Trilogy

Body (Book 1)

Mind (Book 2)

Soul (Book 3)

ACKNOWLEDGEMENTS

How does one truly thank all of the people that made their dream come true? I guess I'll just start at the beginning and work my way through.

To my husband Eric, for allowing me spend so much of my free time writing and reading, encouraging me to go after my dream, and supporting me through it, I will always love you more. Oh and the two boys we have together, Punky and Monster Madness, I should probably thank you for them too.

To my mentor Jess Dee, it all started with a bit of author feedback on your novel Office Affair. From there it turned into a beautiful friendship, one in which I fear I am the taker and you are the giver. Alas, I will always try to give back in the way of feedback, critique, and little bits of heaven sent all the way to Australia for your enjoyment. Besides your words, your advice, your friendship, you had me at the huge box of Tim Tams you sent. I'll never be the same. I dedicated this book to you because you deserve it. Thank you. For those of you who have not had the pleasure of reading any of Ms. Dee's erotic work, please visit her website at www.jessdee.com. I highly recommend Office Affair and Ask Adam.

To my three soul sisters, Dyani Gingerich, Nikki Chiverrell, and Carolyn Beasley. You read every single chapter as I wrote it, sometimes waiting weeks for the next installment, and allowed me to talk endlessly about the characters and the scenes. For that, I am eternally grateful. Having your own cheerleading team is very humbling and I most certainly have the best. Forever I will support you and your endeavors and cheer the loudest at your achievements. Without you I am not the best me.

To my critique partner on this book, MJ Handy. I would have never believed that a male romance writer could change my life but you did. Not only by helping me understand the male POV with Hank's character but also by truly considering my work and giving me genuine feedback. I thank you.

To my editor, Adrienne Crezo—your thoughtful edits, feedback, suggested changes, and plot hole finds helped make this novel something I think turned out pretty great. Thank you.

To my awesome beta readers Sara Pobanz, Carolyn Kendrick, Jeananna Goodall, and Ginelle Blanch I can't thank you enough for your time spent giving this a full read-through and sharing your feedback, excitement, and joy in something very special to me. Each and every one of you made a difference.

To Rhenna Morgan, my sister Denise, and my BFF Diane Erkens, your review and feedback on the beginning chapters greatly contributed to fixing some fantastic errors and plot issues. You rock!

Emily Hemmer—You are one of the funniest chicks on the planet. Your novel The Break-Up Psychic brought us together (well technically Jess Dee blind dated us virtually but anyway) but Plus None had me in stitches. As in, I laughed so hard I needed to get stiches in my sides. Huge rec for Plus None but don't forget to read Just One first peeps, it's the prequel. You have helped guide me through the self-publishing process initially and accepted me as your book sister. I am so blessed to call you my friend. Thank you. (www.emilyhemmer.com)

ABOUT AUDREY CARLAN

Audrey Carlan lives in the sunny California Valley two hours away from the city, the beach, the mountains and the precious…the vineyards. She has been married to the love of her life for over a decade and has two young children that live up to their title of "Monster Madness" on a daily basis. When she's not writing wickedly hot romances, doing yoga, or sipping wine with her "soul sisters," three incredibly different and unique voices in her life, she can be found with her nose stuck in book or her Kindle. A hot, smutty, romantic book to be exact!

Any and all feedback is greatly appreciated and feeds the soul. You can contact Audrey below:

E-mail: carlan.audrey@gmail.com
Facebook: facebook.com/AudreyCarlan
Website: www.audreycarlan.com